*Perils of the S̶o̶u̶...*

# THE ROYAL'S
# FORTUNE

## S. E. JANE

**The Royal's Fortune**
Perils of the Soul and Sea

Copyright © 2020 by Sarah Elizabeth Jane

www.sejane.com

Cover Images
© _IB_ | pexels.com

All scriptures are taken from the Life application study Bible, New International Version Bible, copyright © 1988, 1989, 1990, 1991, 1993, 1996, 2004, 2007 by Tyndale House publishers, Inc..

This is a work of fiction. Names, characters, incidents, and dialogues are products of the author's imagination and are not to be construed as real. Any resemblance to actual events or persons, living or dead, is entirely coincidental.

ISBN: 9781658827065

To Him,
Though I am unworthy,
He bought me and made me Royalty.
My God. My Savior.
My Fortune.

"Mightier than the waves of the sea is his love for you."

Psalm 93:4

# Contents

# *Acknowledgements*

I have been beyond blessed by God's grace. Thank you, Mommy and Daddy, for being so encouraging of me and praying for me. Jack, Grant, and James, thank you for inspiring several of my characters, unbeknownst to you.

Liza Baber: Thank you for being gentle and encouraging with my vulnerability in my first book. I would not have finished without you. Because of you, *The Royal's Fortune* is a very different book than the one I first gave you, thank the good Lord for that!

Alicia O'Neall: you are a gift from God to me. You helped me through my frustrating Dyslexia, and after hours of patience teaching me to read, it seems fitting that you edited my novel. I appreciate it more than you know. Thank you!

Annette Bergsagel: God has blessed me beyond my belief with you. Thank you for editing my novel so thoroughly. You are incredibly gifted. Thank you!

# PART ONE

# Chapter 1

San Juan, Puerto Rico   May 1722

Breathtaking, elegant, doomed, the *Huntress* floated in the San Juan harbor, basking in the glory of another heroic adventure on the horizon. Only God knew it would be her last.

The morning breeze sent a salty spray into the sky. The gulls chattered loudly, and the warm rays of sun gleamed on the water's surface. Even at this early hour, the docks were bustling with activity.

The seasoned *Huntress* had many places where repairs had been made. She was, after all, a pirate hunting ship. Her mast had been replaced more than once, her hull had suffered several cannonballs, and her sails been patched and re-patched. But none of that mattered. As her crew found their places, the necessary supplies safely stored in her hull, she waited for one last person to board, her beloved captain.

Jonathan Williams kissed his wife goodbye. Lila's eyes had tears in them as she held him close, though her protruding belly put them at an awkward distance. He stroked her dark brown hair that fell in waves down her back.

He whispered to her. "Goodbye, my love."

She buried her head deeper into his chest. A goodbye frozen on her.

"Focus on caring for you and the baby. I shan't be gone more than a year, but don't fret if it's later than that." He knew she would worry; her father had left her and her mother when she was eleven. A shameful act, and Jonathan knew it still hurt his young wife more then she would admit. Her greatest fear was losing him. Yes, he had to come back.

She gave a tearful nod. Three times they had been separated like this since they married. It never got easier.

His heart nearly broke to see her so upset, but he was too close to catching that blasted pirate Bartholomew Roberts to give up now.

A boy tugged at his naval coat sleeve. "What about me, Father?" Jonathan scooped up the six-year-old.

"Preston, you protect your mother, alright? Take good care of her."

"Yes, Father. 'Member how I chased 'way the fox from getting to da hen and her chicks? I'm a very good 'tector."

"Well protect your mama. You're the man of the house now. You're old enough to take care of her." He ruffled the boy's blond hair, the same as his own.

"I'll protect Mama! I'm big enough now! See?" He scrambled down from his father's arms and stood as tall as he could. Then gave a mighty salute to his 'ranking officer.'

Jonathan saluted back. "Well done soldier." Just then, the church bell struck five as the sun finally peeked over the beautiful San Juan mountains.

"It's time for me to go now." He kissed his wife one last time, then leaned down and kissed her belly. "Goodbye, baby Briana."

"You're sure it's a girl?"

"Quite sure, you've already had a boy."

"I don't think it works that way," she said smiling.

"I still think it's a girl," he said with a knowing wink.

Lila just smiled as she watched Jonathan walk up the deck to his ship the *Huntress*. He waved to his young, beautiful wife and growing son. How hard it was to let them go…

Two months later

Preston awoke to a gutwrenching scream. He rolled over and put a pillow over his head and pulled his quilt up as far as he could.

After supper, Mama hadn't felt well, so she sent him to get their neighbor and friend Mrs. Cagney. Mrs. Cagney had come quickly with a few other ladies from other houses.

It was not nearly his bedtime when Mrs. Cagney swept him off to his room, and he reluctantly did as he was told.

"Try to sleep, little one," Mrs. Cagney had said. As always, Preston had no trouble sleeping, but that night the screams started. Terrified, Preston had hurried to see what was wrong, only to be sent back to bed before he even got to the door of his mother's room.

Preston rolled over and counted the stars out his window, as his father taught him to do when he could't sleep. Every so often he would drift off, but another scream would jerk him awake.

Finally, the sun began to rise and the terrifing night was chased away by dawn light. But the terrors of the night did not leave with the darkness. To Preston's dismay, the screams only intensified, rising in frequency.

One of the exhausted ladies fixed Preston his breakfast and sent him off to his little school where all the chidren learned to add and subtract, read and write. He was the youngest, but he didn't mind; he could do everything the older kids could do.

When Preston walked into the house that afternoon, there were no more screams, to his relief.

Perhaps everything would go back to normal.

As soon as he stepped in the door, a disheveled woman whisked him into his mother's room. The room smelled of blood and sweat. The small room, with the one window providing most of its light, consisted of an arm chair, a bed, and a night stand. Five women stood around the bed. They looked as though they had been standing there since the evening before. Mrs. Cagney came forward with a bundle in her arms.

"Preston, would you like to hold your baby sister?" She placed the tightly-wrapped, wrinkly child in his arms.

He took her timidly. Her head lulled back.

Mrs. Cagney hurried to correct him. "Hold her head. Like that."

He held her ever so carefully, her rosy face peacefully asleep. "Father wanted to name her Briana," he told Mrs. Cagney.

Mrs. Cagney smiled. "Briana it is then." A rustle from the bed brought a frown to her face and knit her brows together. "Come child, bring the baby."

Preston carried the tiny girl over to the bedside. He barely recognized his mother. Her sickly pale skin and black circles beneath her eyes made her look much older then twenty-seven. Her eyes were glazed over in pain, pain she was much too young to have.

"Preston, my son," she rasped as she slowly slid a shaking, pale hand over to him.

"Yes, Mama?" said he.

"Promise me to take care of your sister, just as you have taken care of me," she managed.

A woman near her bedside said, "Don't speak Lila, save your strength."

"It's too late." Lila whispered. "I've... I've never been a strong one." The despair in her voice sent a pang of fear tearing through Preston.

"What's wrong, Mama? What's going on?" Tears threatened to drop from Preston's eyes. His shakiness prompted Mrs. Cagney to take the baby back.

"Promise me you'll take care of her."

"I promise. But Mama, what about you? I'm gonna to take care of you too. Like Father said."

She smiled. "My son, won't you... sing to me... as you do when I feel sad?"

Trembling, Preston started her favorite song. She had sang it to him since he could remember. As the song progressed Preston watched his mother. Her breath was ragged and barely visible. The light outside seemed to dim as her breath let out and the song ended.

Everyone watched, waiting for the blanket to rise again. But it did not. Her ashen face withered in pain became still and peaceful as the breath left her nostrils. A woman cried out and fell on her knees at the bedside. Some wept, others stared solemnly. Panicked, Preston pulled on his mother's hand.

"Mama!" His fears gathering, he clung to his mother's hand with all his strength. "Mother!"

He didn't understand. Preston crawled up to her in the bed. Someone tried to pull him back. He latched onto her, refusing to let go. She can't just leave. Not while Papa was away! Preston watched her face as his tears wet her lifeless cheeks. The last of the color drained from her blue eyes.

She was gone, and he had failed his father. Somehow that idea managed to snake its way into his mind to burden him for the rest of his life.

But Briana was there. His sister uttered a soft cry. The sound was agonizing, enough to tear at Preston's young heart and pull him away from the mother they had both lost. The infant needed him.

"Don't cry Briana. I'm here. I'm here, and I shall always take care of you. I won't let anything bad ever happen to you, ever." That was his new promise, and this time, he would not fail.

Five years later

"Faster Preston!" Briana exclamed, her dark curls blowing in the wind.

Preston tugged harder on the little wagon, and she squealed with delight. The bread and milk bounced in their sacks as they hurried down the dirt road.

Most streets in San Juan were cobblestone, matching many of the buildings that lined the bustling streets. But this dirt road led him outside the city. The peaceful little city was framed by the countryside in stunning splendor. Its bright green hills dotted with fluffy white sheep surrounded the growing town on three sides.

Further on was a thick forest, which rose into high mountains and steep cliffs beyond. The clear blue ocean that met San Juan's fourth side was the livelihood for many. The port was always busy with incoming and outgoing vessels of all shapes and sizes. Today, the warm sun chased off the morning chill as it rose to take its high place in the sky.

Preston slowed as they came in sight of their destination. The long dirt road had brought them to the very outskirts of the city. The orphanage had been their home for five years, for the great Lieutenant Jonathan William had never returned from sea.

The two of them had just finished their Saturday errands and the day looked promising. After chores, the amiable headmistress always allowed Saturdays to be play days.

Preston lifted his sister out of the wagon and sat her on the ground. She waited for Preston to give her a sack to carry. "May we visit Mr. and Mrs. Cagney today?" she asked.

The Cagneys were their best friends. Preston loved Mr. Cagney's sailor stories. They were bright and humerous but always contained a lesson. Briana would spend her time in the garden with Mrs. Cagney. She had helped plant seeds and lived for watering them. Likewise, Preston would often spend time with Mr. Cagney who taught him to hunt, fish, build, and even the "lost art" of sword play.

Preston gave one bag to his sister and arranged the other three in his arms. Contemplating, Preston weighed the decision. Briana had never been able to walk the whole way. He always had to carry her.

8

"Come on, please?"

"Alright, fine. Don't beg. Come along. Let's put these away quickly then."

It wasn't long before the two children set off. Multiple times, Preston had to check himself to a slower pace for his unusually small sister. She was weak for her age and got sick easily. The mistress said Briana had him wrapped around her finger, but he didn't care. She adored him and that was all the reward he needed.

As they walked, Briana sang. Her sweet voice filled the woods. When her happy child's song was finished, she turned to her brother.

"Why don't you ever sing? Even in church?" she asked.

He cast her a side glance, but kept silent. He didn't think anyone noticed his lack of singing.

Annoyed, she tried again. "Do you even know any songs?"

He hesitated. "One."

"Won't you teach it to me?" When Briana saw he was about to say no, she slid her hand into his. "You don't have to if you don't want to." She blinked up at him.

Preston looked down at her. "Not now."

She would have to settle with that. "When I'm eleven like you."

"Maybe."

"Oh look at the daisies!" She bent down and fingered the little white flowers at the road side.

"How beautiful they are. Well done God!" She turned to Preston. "Didn't He do a good job?"

"Uh, yes."

It wasn't long before the pair came to the little house near the shipyard and knocked on the door, which opened within seconds.

"Ah, how are my two favorite children?" Mr. Cagney bellowed. "I was hoping you would be coming around today."

"Is that Preston and Briana?" Mrs. Cagney poked her head around the hall corner from the kitchen. "Well don't keep them standing there John! Come in children!"

Mr. Cagney stepped out of the way and Briana rushed in.

"Can I water the flowers?" the little girl asked, already tugging Mrs. Cagney out the door.

"Briana," Preston reminded.

"Please?" she added. Both the Cagneys laughed, and Mrs. Cagney took her hand and together they skipped out the door.

"And while they're doing women stuff..." Mr. Cagney called back his attention. "I have something for you, Preston." As he led the way to his little parlor, the once quartermaster on the *Huntress* walked rather awkwardly. A long ago injury prevented Mr. Cagney from ever sailing again, so now, a middle-aged gentleman, kept the port's records.

Mr. Cagney made his way to a dresser where he pulled a little leather pouch from a drawer. "About five years ago, this came into my possession. Sent to me without a name."

"You don't know who it's from?" Preston took the little sack and dumped its contents into his hand. An expertly shaped metal cross attached to a leather string fell into his hand. The string showed several years of age, but the sun still glinted off the cross like new.

"I can take a guess. Now I don't know this with certainty. But I think your father sent it to me."

"My father?" He was enraptured by the masterpiece. Surely it cost a great deal of money. Where had his father gotten such a thing? Preston ran his hand over the piece, but was surprised when he felt a defect. He tried to scratch away at the raised dot of metal, but it held firm.

Mr. Cagney leaned over his shoulder. "Odd, it's barely been out of the sack."

Preston felt the rest of the cross and found six more little raised spots scattered across it. When he flipped it over, however, not one blemish marked it.

"How do you know it was him?" Preston asked.

"I took to the smithy here in San Juan. The man said this particular type of metal doesn't rust or tarnish. It's rare and expensive to make. But your father, I know, came across metal like this when he hid the treasure of Bartholomew Roberts."

"How do you know?"

"Well, because Roberts' stole this metal from the Portuguese. Or that's where the smithy thinks it came from."

"Didn't Roberts kill Father?"

"No. Roberts' first mate killed your father. You see, Jonathan and his partner, a duke from England, found their pirate lair. The two removed the enormous amount of treasure inside and hid it somewhere until they could capture Roberts."

"Then what happened?"

"They planned to ambush them. The duke would attack Robert's ship and your father would attack Roberts' first mate's ship. Your father lost a battle with the enemy's ship. But it wouldn't have mattered anyway. Both ships had blown so many holes in each other they both sank before anyone could rescue them. There the *Huntess* sank."

"So Robert's first mate died?"

Mr. Cagney nodded. "Some of the crew members of both ships were able to be rescued. The duke was abel to capture Roberts and his black galleon. After all was done, the pirates were hanged. Your father's mission accomplished and his death avenged."

Preston was quiet for a few moments. "And the treasure?"

Mr. Cagney brought his eyes to Preston's face and his thoughts back to reality. "Ah, my boy. Now there lies the mystery. Your father and the *Huntress* hid the treasure. Only he knew exactly where it lies in the Atlantic. Even the crewmen who lived could not relocate the island. The duke seached, but to no avail. So now, Roberts' treasure remains, lost forever."

When the sun began to dip low in the sky, its day's course drawing near to completion, Preston and Mr. Cagney came in hot and tired from training with Mr. Cagney's old swords. Plopping down at the kitchen table, Preston felt good. His muscles felt well worked and his mind well tested, but today he felt especially good because of the praise he had received in his training.

"Well done, Preston! Your left handed skill and strength has improved," Mr. Cagney had commented.

The smell of freshly-baked tarts permeated the room, and he could hear his sister's gentle footsteps coming from the kitchen. He stood to greet her as she proudly carried in a tray of his favorite. Reaching over her head, Preston snatched one of the soft, round treats.

Briana gave him an annoyed look, then gave a gracious three tart portion to Mr. Cagney.

Mr. Cagney smiled broadly. "Thank you my dear, why the extra delicacy, sweet thing?"

She smiled up at him, as innocent as the morning. "Good things come to those who wait." She gave Preston a pointed look.

Mr. Cagney bellowed a laugh, watching the interaction of the two siblings. The charming, but shrewd little sister and the bested older brother. "Well put, darlin'."

The twosome waved goodbye to their dear friends and then plodded down the path toward the ophanage. Preston felt anxious, for the pink sky did little to illuminate the forest. The path before them was dark, and Briana stayed close. Keeping a good pace, they came within the last half mile before Briana began to fall behind.

"Wait up!" she called, jogging in order to keep up with his quick pace.

"Come on!" His thoughts were riding waves as he fingered the cross around his neck. There were so many things he wanted to tell his father: How sorry he was that he failed his mother, how he promised to take care of Briana, how he wanted to grow up and be a seaman just like him.

The sun finally dipped out of sight, leaving behind an eerieness with the quietness of the forest. The wind whistled through the treetops and the lapping of the waves seemed to echo through the valley. Crowned by a clouded ring, the moon was swollen and heavy in the sky, scarcely illuminating the path ahead.

"Carry me, Preston!" Briana had fallen even further behind and the shrillness of her voice told Preston she was scared.

Annoyed, Preston jogged a few steps to feel his last bit of freedom before he would give in and carry her.

"Alright fine." He turned around to find that she was much farther back then he had thought. Briana had finally sat down and was pouting. "If you can get to me, I'll give you a piggy back ride the whole way back," Preston hollered.

Stumbling, she got up and continued along the path. The light had finally deserted them and Preston could barely see her; he knew they had to hurry.

"Come on!" he hissed.

A sudden scream sent him sprinting torwards her. Briana was not one to scream for no reason.

When he reached her, he saw she was trying to shake something off her foot. Horror swept over him and he raced to scoop her up high. As he did so the thing let go of her.

That's when Preston identified the attacker, a fer-de-lance snake. Its patterned body curled to end with a dimond shaped head. Its grey eyes and slit-like pupils stared at him.

In panic, Preston took off toward home, fear and adrenaline giving him the strength he needed. When he came to the back door, he pounded on it with what was left of his strength. A maid came quickly and took the crying child from his arms.

"What's going on?" she asked, her face taut and lined from long years of worry.

"She was bit by a snake."

Her face went ashen. "What kind?" She hurried to a chair and gently laid the child down.

"A racer." He already knew. They were deadly.

15

One glance at the girl's swelling ankle sent the woman rushing to ring the bell; she rang it once, the signal for an emergency. "How long has it been?"

"Twenty minutes, maybe more," he replied, still gasping for lost breath. Preston had not been able to run very well in the thick vegetation, but now he wished he had just charged right through it.

The headmistress swept in with the rest of the staff and the maid relayed the information.

"Someone must run for a doctor. Now," one annouced.

"I'll go!" Preston cried, desperate to do something.

"No," the headmistress replied sharply. "He must stay here. Get Ronald," she barked and the staff members jumped to help the suffering child. Ronald was a sixteen-year-old that was charged with the horses. Everyone knew he was the fastest runner on the grounds.

Though several women huddled around Briana, Preston could hear her struggling breaths. Tears had thoroughly drenched his face, and his sniffles were scarcely a concern. Why had he left her behind? Why had he not hoisted her onto his back like he always did? Why had he not been watching for dangers? These thoughts panged through his mind, the guilt eating at him. Preston knew: it was his fault. He had let down his guard and failed to protect her, to take care of her. Just as he had failed to care for his mother. Oh what would father think of him now? Two promises failed on *his* watch. Preston felt the metal cross around his neck. His father protected nations and died saving them from the threat of pirates. And what had he done? He had failed to take care of his mama, and now he had allowed his sister to be hurt. *Yes, hurt.* Preston thought in one desperate attempt to convince himself. *Just like last summer when she skinned her knee. It'll hurt, then she'll get better.*

But this was not the same.

"Preston, darling." The headmistress called to him with an extended hand. He took it and walked forward his agonized sister. As the women made way for him, he saw her curled up on the chair, her body so small she fit perfectly. Someone had laid a blanket over her. Her sweet, innocent face was white, and even the curls of brown hair that fell in tangles around her head looked sad. He could hear soft words between heavy breaths as she spoke to someone holding her hand. When Preston came near, the woman passed him her frail little hand saying: "Here he is, dear one."

Preston took his sister's hand gently before collapsing next to her. "Briana, I am so sorry! I didn't mean for..." He broke down. "Please don't go...I can't lose you," he choked. "Briana, not you too." The room seemed to pause as she began to speak.

"Teach me that song." She whispered so quietly it was hardly audible.

17

Preston's throat closed. *Not now, oh Lord, not now!* He begged. But one look into her blue eyes, the life in them so full and radiant, brought the song back to him in a violent gust. Swallowing, Preston sang in a cracked voice for the light of his life.

"*I love you Lord, and I lift my voice*
*To wor-ship You,*
*Oh my soul, rejoice.*
*Take joy my King, and in what You hear*
*May it be a sweet, swe-et sound in Your ear*"

Preston sang it twice in a shaky, out of practice voice, with tears streaming down his face and his hands quivering. His sweet little sister's breathing had become more and more labored before it finally stopped. Her pain was finished. His pain was only beginning.

Just so, there was another. Another who also neared a beginning. A beginning of a search for the treasure hidden by Lieutenant Williams. After all, he was rightfully the heir to Bartholomew Roberts' treasure.

# Chapter 2

San Juan, Puerto Rico    July 1736

The sky was by no means dark, despite the lateness of the hour. The backdrop of blackness was alight with countless stars and the round moon so bright that the eye could pick out the craters and mountains that made up its face.

Preston Williams scribbled ferociously under the starry blanket. Actually, it was not scribbling at all. He was filling the ledger with tiny numbers in neat columns that would be easy to check later.

Dropping his pen back into the ink, Preston snatched up his sextant and held it up to the sky for the hundredth time that evening. He sat cross-legged atop the roof with parchment scraps and various devices spread haphazardly, yet somehow systematically, around him.

"Eighty-seven and... no... forget that. Eighty-six point eight and forty... unless... wait... oops. That's Hyades. No wonder. Now where is Aldebaran? Why are they so near each other?"

Most would probably think him crazy to hear him now, mumbling so.

S. E. JANE

"Ah, I see you." Preston muttered under his breath. Grinning, he dropped down again to do more figuring. He scratched at his elbow. Finally, setting his pen aside, he sat back on his heels to study his book triumphantly.

After nearly an hour of work, he finally had his prize: the latitude and longitude of his current location. Not that he hadn't done it a dozen times before, but this time he had not used a time piece, as though he were actually out at sea, sailing as Captain Williams.

In his dreams maybe. And only in his dreams.

"Bien joué!" Preston praised himself quietly. He had not expected to produce correctness, he only knew it was done. Gathering up his books and parchment, Preston vaulted over the roof's edge to the ground.

By the time he saw the danger, Preston's tongue was too twisted to shout a warning and he plummeted down onto an unsuspecting pedestrian. With an 'umph' Preston flattened a young urchin.

"Hey!" the boy protested.

"My apologies, young man." Preston regained himself and helped the boy, no more than ten, to his previous upright position.

Still dazed, the child looked up at the sky in confusion. "Did you fall from the sky?"

Preston chuckled, a deep sound that rose in his throat and vibrated his chest. "No, my good man. I jumped down from the roof. Next time, I'll be sure to check the area for unprepared victims." He stooped to pick up his dropped items.

"The baker's roof?" the child asked. The baker was not a very kind soul, nor would he be kind to someone doing calculations on his roof. The thing was, the baker's roof was the highest roof that still had a flat top. Too good an opportunity to pass up.

"Indeed." Preston avoided the fact that he lacked permission for such a stunt.

"What were you doing on the roof?"

"Mathematics." He flashed the lad a smile laced with interminable patience. "See?" He opened the book and held it low.

The boy stared at it, as though trying to comprehend what he saw. "What does it say?"

Preston's heart weighed. *Poor lad. Can't even read.* "Why, these numbers don't speak like words do. But they do say some things. Look here." He flipped one of his scrap pages over and wrote the numbers one through nine. He pointed to the first of the numbers. "This is a one. One represents an amount. For example, we have one, err, what's your name son?"

"Nathaniel." Nathaniel smiled for who was bound to be his new favorite person.

"Well, we have one Nathaniel." Preston pointed to the boy then back at the number one. "My name is Preston. Now, how many Preston's are here?"

The boy pointed to the number one on Preston's parchment.

Preston's dark eyes reflected the sparkle of the stars. "Very good Nat! You are a brilliant boy!"

The boy frowned. "That's not what Papa said."

A knot twisted in his throat and threatened to make Preston wretch. A deep breath cooled his bubbling blood, which would have led to 'Papa' getting a fist to the stomach.

"Nonsense! You are a very intelligent boy! Don't you ever forget that, hear?" Preston knelt down to the young man's level. "Hear?"

The boy nodded solemnly. "Yes sir."

Preston smiled again. "Good lad. Now I must be getting home or my aunt won't be pleased. Best you go on home too. And..." He held the parchment out to the boy. "You can keep this and study it. When I see you again, I'll teach you the rest of the numbers."

Nathaniel smiled and took the paper before bouncing off, back to his broken world. Preston watched the child, not so unlike himself. He only prayed little Nathaniel would not end up like him.

Trotting toward the home of the Cagneys, now his adopted aunt and uncle, Preston pulled his mind back to the troubles of life. Doing calculations on rooftops were his way of escaping, to clear his mind. Earlier that day, Preston made a decision, a decision he had been rolling around in his mind for a while. Now, he faced the problem of announcing it to the two people who had taken him in nine years ago, after his sister's death.

He entered the quiet house just past ten and slipped upstairs to his small room. Tomorrow, at breakfast, he would tell them.

Routinely, Preston ran through his morning chores with the chickens and the cow, pulled up fresh water from the well, and brought in firewood for the stove. His mind wandering, he hardly noticed when the little farm cow mooed in annoyance at his haste to milk her.

How discontent he was!

On his way in for breakfast, Preston met "uncle" John on the porch, after the older man finished his own morning chores at the shipyard.

"Morning, son. I received a telegram from Captain Lank. He wants us to install the swinging bowsprit in his ship."

Preston's brows knit together. "How did he hear about that?"

"I'm not sure. One of the men probably."

"Well for goodness sake it's still in testing! Last time we tested its abilities we nearly ran aground!"

"True. But I thought that was from lack of experience of your men."

"It needs to be easier to handle. I've a more fluid joint but we haven't tested it yet."

"Good. Because Lank is hoping we can get it done by Christmas."

"Christmas!" Preston clenched his jaw. *What if I don't want to publicize it? I meant to prove it works then put it away forever.* Preston swallowed. *What if it fails? What if it fails when it's needed most?* Preston averted his fiery gaze before it got him in trouble. "You can't just 'install' a swinging bowsprit! It's structural! And then the jig sails have to modified! And..."

"Easy. We'll discuss this when it's finished. Needn't you worry, it'll work. I know it will."

Preston's muscles slowly released a tension he did not know he had. He hadn't meant to sound harsh. Oh, why could he not communicate like the rest of the world? What was so wrong with him that he could not make others understand without losing his temper?

He swallowed and nodded. When John motioned him forward, Preston led the way into the house.

Coming into the kitchen, Preston smiled when he saw his "aunt." The little woman clearly had no idea they were there as she hummed a lively tune and stirred her oatmeal. Not the brightest, she had a habit of forgetting things and losing them. Because of this, Preston watched the spoon slide down into the pot and noticed the recipe peeking out from her pocket.

Aunt Marcy turned toward them and jumped into the air. She slapped a hand over her heart. "How could you scare me so?" She straightened her apron as she looked at her husband, trying hard to scold him.

"Aw, come on, Love. We're just hungry," said Uncle John.

"Well, if you don't interrupt me, maybe you'll get to eat before it burns."

Preston grinned, it would not have been the first time he ate a burnt meal.

"Well, then, I apologize for interrupting. We are practically starving!" Uncle John held his rounded belly.

"My, my, in that case, hurry and wash up," Aunt Marcy said in mock pity.

Preston paused before turning toward the wash-basin.

"Now where did my spoon go?" He heard his aunt mumble to herself.

He strode over to her pot. "Here it is." He pulled it out of the pot where it had slid.

"Thank you, dearie. Now what about my...?"

Preston reached over to her apron pocket and pulled out her recipe. "Here it is." He offered her a kind, gentle smile.

Aunt Marcy smiled at her almost son. "I don't know what I'd do without you." Preston saw Uncle John over her shoulder rolling his eyes. Both of them knew that it was usually Uncle John that kept track of her things.

After sitting down at the table, Uncle John led them in prayer. Light conversation followed, including activity at the shipyard, next week's market

25

sale, and a possible visit from a nearly forgotten cousin.

John gulped down a mouthful and turned to Preston. "Preston, when do you think the swinging bowsprit will be finished?"

"Actually, not any time soon."

This was the opportunity for his announcement, especially since it was a perfect way of dodging the current line of conversation. "I've decided to look for a job on a ship."

Silence met him.

Preston winced inside. *That didn't come out right at all!* He hadn't meant it to sound ungrateful. *Now what?*

"Uh, when?" Uncle John took a sip of his water.

"I'd like to look for something at the dock today." Preston winced at his own words.

Unfazed, Uncle John scratched the scruff on his chin. "My dear," he turned to his wife who sat quietly, unmoved by the conversation. "What was it I said when we took this boy in?"

"You said 'Marcy, we'll give him a home for as long as we can keep him on land. And after that, we'll give him our inheritance and call him our son.'"

"And I meant every word of it." He grinned his encouragement. "Now off you go."

Surprised, relieved, moved, Preston smiled at each of them and then was out of his chair and reaching for his hat.

"Preston, dearie," Aunt Marcy called to him. "This house is yours to come home to. You can keep whatever you don't take with you in your room. So don't you go off and forget us now." She pointed her finger at him. "I love cooking for you too much."

Preston laughed, excitement building. "Well then, you have nothing to worry about."

Preston navigated through town to the docks. On his way, he crossed paths with Captain Donny Anderson. The portly, jolly man was swaggering into town from the docks. He was the kind of man that one would always hear before see.

"Mr. Williams!" the captain hailed.

"Greetings, Captain," Preston replied. "Welcome home! How was your voyage? Did the *Maria* suit you well?" Captain Anderson had bought a new ship from Mr. Cagney several months ago.

"Ah, Mr. Williams, she is the finest ship I've ever sailed on! Didn't spring a leak once, she didn't! Not only that, but can she move! Yes sir!" He paused for a breath. "So tell me Mr. Williams, has the sea called your name like it did your father?"

Now would be the time to ask for a job, but Preston didn't dare. This man was so scatterbrained it was a miracle he stayed afloat. Plus, he had another ship in mind. "Only on clear days, sir."

Captain Anderson paused, then roared with laughter. "Indeed Mr. Williams, indeed!" The jolly sea captain then sauntered on.

The San Juan port was large compared to most. It could almost rival Port Royal. Close to thirty ships were docked, busily being loaded or unloaded. Walking over to one he recognized, Preston asked for the captain. When the man came forward, Preston greeted him. After a brief conversation, Preston continued on in disappointment, for the captain regretfully told him that his crew was full.

Repeating this procedure several times, Preston found that securing a job on a ship was not easy.

"You, sir!"

Preston turned to find a medium-sized man striding toward him. The man was older, with greying hair and beard. He was dressed finely, with a dark coat, a three-point hat, and a white sash looped across his chest and large belly. Most remarkable were the talismans hanging round his neck. One was a small vile of an unknown substance, another was a rock with an odd marking on it, and the last was some unidentified object. Rings covered his fingers in various shapes and sizes, representing a variety of things including stones, countries, and cultures. The man looked around a moment as though expecting something.

"Yes, sir?"

"I apologize, for I could not help overhear you be asking for ja job, yes?" The man spoke in an odd accent Preston had never heard before. "I own that beauty over there, the *Raven*. And, well, circumstances have made me one man short. See?" He pointed to a Barque docked next to the *Maria*.

Preston could not help but smile. *Thank you, God!* "Yes sir. I confess though, I've never worked on a ship at sea."

The man looked thoughtful. "I tell you what. I take you on a trial basis. If things go well and I find your work satisfying, I accept you into my crew. See? And if it does not work, I not hesitate to leave you on the next ship. That is agreeable, yes?"

"Indeed," Preston replied.

"It tis settled, then. You green one shall join my crew on the *Raven*. A trial, yea? As for your inexperience, tis no trouble, I just recently picked up ja new crew. They are all still learning. You shan't be far behind. Yea?"

Excitement ran down Preston's spine. He offered his hand to his new captain and they shook. "Absolutely, Captain..?" Preston was amused at this odd seaman.

"Ah, my manners fail me! Captain Bartholomew Henry. Shall we start training here? Whenever I am addressed you shall use 'sir' or 'captain.' Always. Understand, yea? Now, we sail day after tomorrow. 'Tis bad luck to sail out on a Sunday, lad. I'll have you help the men load tomorrow afternoon. Bring your belongings to be stored. Loading delays shalt not be tolerated the day we sail."

"Very well, Captain Henry, I'll be here tomorrow, sir."

"Good lad." Captain Henry turned and strode toward the *Raven*.

A whoop rose in his throat. Preston contained himself and smiled.

The next morning, Preston and the Cagneys walked to church in their Sunday best. When the churchyard came into view, Donny and Dan Longing, from one of the few other English families in San Juan, came running up to meet Preston.

"Mr. Williams! Mr. Williams!" the nine-year-old twins called.

Preston grinned down at them. "Hello boys! You gentleman didn't leave your sister by herself, did you?" he asked when he saw six-year-old Honey running up the hill in an attempt to catch her brothers. The two looked at one another, then looked at Honey.

"Nope, here she comes. We're watchin' her," said Don.

Just then the church bell rang a five-minute warning.

"You boys go ahead to class. But first, I believe it would be quite chivalrous of you two to take Honey back to your ma," Preston taught Sunday school to the boys during the adult service before the congregation gathered for praise and prayer.

As usual, Dan and Donny agreed with Preston. They both hurried to take Honey's hands and lead her to their mother and father, making a gallant effort to win Preston's high approval.

After the service, Preston, as promised earlier, played a game of ball with all the young boys as the adults mingled before dinner.

As the game wound down, one of the younger, more quiet boys, tugged at Preston's sleeve.

Preston squatted to his level. "What is it, Toby?"

"Why don't you sing in church? Ma says I have to cause I'm praisin' God."

Preston's ribs squeezed in on his lungs. "I sing with my heart because my voice is not very good." Preston tapped him under the chin. "You listen to your ma though. You have a very nice voice and you use that to praise God, all right?"

The boy nodded and smiled, then hurried off.

Preston sighed. Oh, to be a child again! A pang of guilt singed his conscience. True he was not completely honest. He really had no idea whether his voice was good or not. But he had never felt like singing. Nor did there seem to be a reason to sing even though his heart rebuked such a thought. Years ago, Preston vowed never to sing again.

Tired after the competitive game, the boys helped lay out the food at Preston's request then

31

gathered around the table. As the young boys ate, Preston walked over to Reverend Morton.

Though pastor of this new congregation when it started last year, Reverend Morton was only a few years older than Preston. Tall and lanky, Morton had dark hair and eyes and a large nose. His smile was his most becoming feature and he had surprisingly straight teeth.

Just such a smile appeared on the reverend's face as Preston approached. "Good morning Preston, you have clearly done wonderfully with the boys this morning." He glanced at the boys talking over Joshua and the battle of Jericho.

Preston smiled back. "Thank you, Reverend. It's always a delight to teach them, and I probably have more fun than I should." He turned to face the reverend directly. "Last week, I asked that you pray for me."

"And I have, every day. That the Lord might guide your footsteps along a path of righteousness. And that He would teach you to pray, 'Your will be done.'"

Preston swallowed and nodded. "How does one know if a path that opens is deemed by God?"

"Every path is opened by God, some to test and tempt. But He never leaves one without help. As I said, pray that His will is done. Pray for His eyes and ears. Learn to seek what He seeks. Consult Him always. I believe He will reveal it to you."

Preston watched the children a minute, and the reverend patiently waited. "I have accepted a sailing job, and I'm leaving tomorrow on a merchant ship. I intend to go. I just hope that's what the Lord wants."

The man nodded slowly. "As long as you always seek Him, I encourage you to go. You were not made to be here. But do remember Preston, just because trouble befalls you does not mean God did not approve. We'll miss you though. The entire congregation will for that matter. You have blessed us all greatly. Although I am not sure who should miss you most, the Cagneys, the boys, or the young ladies."

Preston reddened. He was not oblivious to the looks many of the young woman gave him. Just the same, he did not feel adequate to take care of a wife. Perhaps one day. Besides, he wanted no part of any woman that would make a fool of herself over him.

Reverend Morton turned kindly to his friend. "Don't worry about things here Preston. I will check in on the Cagneys often. When you come back though, I hope you might save some time to tell me about your adventures."

Preston dipped his head with a gentle smile. "That I shall do."

# Chapter 3

London, England

"How I do adore these hunting trips! They're so exciting!" Anastasia gushed from atop her roan mare. Not uncharacteristically, a series of young women's voices echoed their agreement.

"I find the most exciting part to be when the men show their kills to us," Madeline said, edging her horse up beside Anastasia's.

"Or when we all dine afterward," a girl with a cute freckled face said from behind them. Giggles chorused a response.

Cassandra Chandler mindlessly followed at the tail of the group on her little grey dappled gelding, Shadow. Thankfully, Shadow didn't mind being behind the group, as she liked to study the surrounding vegetation and ignore the girlish chatter of the group ahead. The spoiled girls from vastly rich families invited her along on these excursions for one reason, and it was not for her company.

She was a duchess of England. No matter how different she was from them, she could not deter them from extending her an invitation.

*Wonderful.*

Cassidy, as she liked to be called, loved nature, all nature. Including the deer that the hunting party, which they currently trailed, were tracking and killing.

Sighing, Cassidy shifted in her sidesaddle. It had only been two hours and already she was terribly uncomfortable. How she missed when her brother would let her ride in his saddle; she and Shadow would gallop through the meadows without constraint.

But now, Andrew Chandler was hardly around to take her on rides. Her brother was sailing his ship around the world carrying out business for their father, a duke. Great with people, superb at smoothing feathers, spectacular at negation, Andrew was completely worthy of the trust their father had bestowed upon him.

Laughter broke her thoughts.

"I'd bet a pound Ben gets the biggest buck!" Anastasia shouted.

"No way! It'll be George!" rivaled one.

"Ha! You mean Edward!" another said.

Cassidy crinkled her nose at their backs. *Foolish girls.* She watched them, listening to them talk and interact. *Or maybe just stupid girls, poor dears.* Cassidy knew each of them cheered for their sweets. Personally, she thought Daniel was the best at hunting. His quiet, patient temperament and impressive record made the middle-aged man a safe bet. But, of course, he was not as exciting as the other charming young men.

A sudden shot rang though the valley, spooking their mounts. Cassidy startled in the saddle, though her faithful gelding was unmoved. Sweet animal. Her family had bought him for his gentleness. After all, Cassidy had always been frightened of horses. Then again, she was frightened of most things.

"They shot something!" Madeline gasped.

*Just because a shot was fired does not mean it hit its target.* Cassidy rolled her eyes.

Another two shots were fired, then silence. Wincing with each shot, Cassidy imagined the poor buck brought down. So unnecessary.

Throughout the valley, the birds deserted their song, as though afraid they would be the next targets. The unnatural quietness made her stomach uneasy and discomfort snaked down her spine.

The girls ahead shrieked their delight.

"Come on!" Anastasia shouted, urging her horse into a trot. Cassidy held back a snort, which would have been most un-duchess like, at the young woman's lack of training in the saddle. She bounced around making Cassidy wince for the poor mare she rode.

The other horses jogged after the leader, whether told by their riders or instincts only God knew.

Cassidy sighed. "They'll be lucky if they don't get shot themselves," she told her mount. Shadow waited for her instruction, though he clearly wished to join the now cantering herd. "Alright, let us go." She gave him his head and rose in the saddle, nudging him with her leg.

Shadow broke into a smooth canter. She patted him on the neck and slowed him to a trot as they overtook the group. Ahead of them, those in the lead slowed to a walk.

"We must come upon them with dignity, ladies," Anastasia said. Cassidy decided it was to catch her breath and ease her discomfort.

Agreement and approval was readily given by the others to their lovely heroine. Anastasia was beautiful, with hazel eyes and honey-colored hair, but all other virtues were well-hidden.

Soon enough, they came upon the hunting party who had now begun to prepare their meat. As the women rode into the clearing, they were warmly welcomed by the men. Many came hurriedly to help whichever lady they fancied.

At the back of the group, Cassidy expected no assistance and did not hesitate to dismount. Thus, she was caught off guard when a hand tenderly grasped her own mid drop to the ground. In surprise, Cassidy landed less gracefully then she meant and stumbled, gripping the hand for support.

"I'm glad I caught you." She turned at the smooth voice of Benjamin Darrick.

*As though you did not almost cause me to fall.*

Tall and dark-haired, he was one of the most handsome of young men. Due to his high social status and being heir to a fortune and a half, Ben Darrick was considered the most eligible of men in the English society. Cassidy had been made very aware of this fact.

"As am I." *Not!* "Thank you, Mr. Darrick." Cassidy slid her hand out of his and wondered what Anastasia thought of this. No doubt she saw. She always saw.

"Of course, my lady." He bowed deeply.

Cassidy thought up a quick reason to escape his company. "Excuse me please. I would like to see the latest catch."

"Allow me to show you, Lady Chandler." *Must I?* Ben tied a sulking Shadow to a tree. He motioned to the middle of the clearing, prompting her to take the lead.

*Patience please, Lord on High! Patience!*

"Who shot it?" she asked as they walked.

"Well, we came upon two bucks locked in a head battle. Edward saw them first, he shot one, not the one he meant to but he won't tell you that. Daniel had to shoot the other as it ran away."

Cassidy nodded expressionless as she felt Ben's gaze on her. Perhaps this was part of the reason she disliked him, she supposed.

"Lady Chandler!" Edward was suddenly in front of them, sweeping a bow. "May I show you the buck I shot?"

"I was actually going to show her. Thanks though, Ed." Ben's continuous smile having disappeared.

"But I shot it. I think I've earned the right to show her."

For the first time that day, a smile twitched the edge of her lips. While she thought neither of these flirtatious men as suitable partners, being fought over had an interesting effect on the young duchess.

"Why don't we let Lady Chandler decide?" Ben reasoned. Both men turned to her expectantly.

Behind her, another voice interrupted Cassidy's momentary panic. "Before you go choosing, Lady Chandler, I would like to cast in my offer as well." Daniel LaFeit winked at Cassidy as he came to her side, dear man. "But my offer is to show you the one *I* shot, the biggest and most fine of the two."

Before the others could interject, Cassidy spoke up. "I don't see how I could turn down such an offer." With a sweet smile, Cassidy slipped her hand into the gentleman's offered elbow.

As they walked away, Cassidy leaned close to whisper, "You saved my life."

The hunter chuckled. "With that brother of yours off at sea and your father too busy for these excursions, someone has to step up."

"And you would most certainly have their gratitude for it."

He eyed Cassidy. "When are you going to marry, though? I'll be too old for this job soon."

Cassidy laughed. "When I find the right man, I suppose. Any suggestions?" she asked good-naturedly.

He took his time in surveying the group. "I see your point. Heck, I wish my son were a decade older."

Cassidy giggled at the prospect. "If only. Do let me know if you find anyone that meets your approval."

Daniel grinned. "I'll send them calling."

A gentle knock came from the door. "Lady Cassandra, it is time to dress for supper," a voice called from outside Cassidy's door. She sighed and put her book about Christopher Columbus down. Must she always be interrupted so? And right in the good part too.

"Come in Mindy," she called.

Mindy entered and huffed after one glance in Cassidy's direction. No doubt her reaction was because Cassidy's wild curls were no longer in the place she had put them that morning after Cassidy had spent most of the day outside. But Cassidy didn't care. All her time outside was well worth the trouble of re-controlling her hair, though Cassidy knew that Mindy would disagree.

With determined steps, Mindy strode toward the wardrobe and began pulling out various dresses. "What would you like to wear tonight? Ah, never mind. I found the perfect gown." She held out a jade satin gown with short sleeves. "Green is your best color, you know."

Cassidy nodded, hoping to mask the displeasure in her emerald eyes. "Thank you, Mindy. That shall suit me just fine."

Mindy helped her dress before sitting to brush out her tangled, dark brown hair. Once the tangles were free, Mindy piled the long curls onto her head in the latest style.

With Mindy's final fluff to her dress and poke to her hair, Cassidy finally descended the staircase for supper. Cassidy's brown-haired father, a Duke of England was just seating her mother.

"Cassandra, how lovely you look tonight." He leaned close. "I see the lovely Ms. Mindy has controlled your untamed locks."

Cassidy grinned. "She didn't seem to like my adventurous look. Personally, I didn't mind it so."

"Now that I think about it, I don't mind it so either." Charles said with a chuckle before helping her with her chair. "What a lucky man I am, spending the evening in the company of the two most beautiful woman in England!"

Cassidy's mother, Elyse, eyed her husband. "A pleasure for only the most wonderful man in London," she said with the same bright smile she passed to her daughter. Mother and daughter both had the dark ringlets, though Mother managed to make hers do whatever she pleased. Likewise, both women had large green eyes and elegantly high cheek bones. However, Mother had beautiful, unblemished skin that Cassidy had been especially jealous of. Cassidy's own skin still had the shrinking scars of her early teens.

"Ah, my dear, you are too kind to me." Father learned over and kissed his wife on the cheek.

Mother playfully ignored her doting husband and changed the subject. "Charles, did the diplomat settle the situation in Holland? The Dutch always seem to be up in arms about something. Even such small matters of sugar and spice trade! Surely tea is too small a matter to start a war over."

"It is all taken care of, Elyse," he said.

Father blessed the food, and the three began eating. About halfway through the main course Father cleared his throat.

"Cassandra, how would you feel about visiting Aunt Emma in America? England is at peace for the time being, and this is the best time of year to travel. We thought the trip could be your eighteenth birthday present."

Surprise and delight competed on her face as she took a quick intake of breath. "Oh Father! Truly? America?" Excitement tingled down her spine and made her chest tighten. Cassidy had not seen her favorite aunt for several years, since Emma moved to Virginia.

"Yes, my dear. It's settled then?" Father said.

Cassidy nodded in excitement. This was what she had waited for! Some sort of change to draw her out of this boring life.

"Good. You'll be leaving three weeks from now."

More subdued, her thoughts whisked away to her brother and she asked, "Will Andrew be taking me?" She had never been allowed to actually ride on the *Virtue*.

Ah, the lovely *Virtue*. Andrew Chandler had named the ship not wanting it to sound like it belonged to royalty, something they all respected him for. Being related to the King and Queen was not always a pleasant thing. In fact, Cassidy longed to be normal, though several years ago after a heartfelt discussion with God, He brought her to accept her role and to be thankful.

Her mother smiled sympathetically. "No, dearie. Andrew is not expected back for a few months more. Fear not. It is all arranged. The *Queen's Merit* is one of the finest ships England has to offer."

Later that evening, Cassidy sat on her bed thinking of America. Andrew had told her about America. "The sun is almost always shining and the ladies must take fans wherever they go because of the constant heat. Of course, if you go much higher than Virginia, the weather is cooler, like here. Now the Caribbean, on the other hand, is more beautiful and hotter than anything I've ever seen..." Andrew had gone on for hours. "Really though Cassidy," he had told her (Andrew was the one who had given her the nickname), "Of all the places I've seen, and all the countries I've gone, I would love to live in America."

Cassidy knelt at her bedside with her Bible in front of her. Nervousness squeezed at her stomach the more she thought of the unknown. She needed this. Needed some change. Needed to be more than just the duchess stuffed into a social box. Still, Cassidy could not help thinking of what she was leaving. Her family, her home, her friends, all she had ever known.

Cassidy spent a lot of her life being intimidated. As a little girl, she used to hide behind her father at any new place or whenever they were around new people. She had been a skittish girl, until her brother taught her to ride and shoot and love the wildlife. Until then, most had thought her too much of a weakling for such things.

Yet she flourished.

Cassidy loved to think of the time when Andrew took her out to the pasture, a place she loved, and showed her how to ride a horse. First, she had refused. She loved animals, but she had no interest in trusting one enough to sit on him. Then Andrew had knelt down to look into the face of nine-year-old Cassidy and quoted Joshua 1:9: *"Have I not commanded you? Be strong and courageous. Do not be afraid; do not be discouraged, for the Lord your God will be with you wherever you go."*

That day, Cassidy learned to trust and how to overcome fear. Though still she would tend to pull back into her shell, she worked hard to be the woman God wanted her to be. Now, Cassidy smiled at the memory. *"Wherever you go."* The words echoed in her heart. *This is my chance to finally overcome my fear and learn to trust God!*

"Dear Father," she prayed quietly. "I feel as though I am leaving my parents forever. My childhood, moreover. Is it your will Lord? I am eighteen, and yet I still live like a child. Is this my way to become as you want me? To cast aside my childish ways? I long for a change, to be useful to Your will. Surely there is a better use for me than to be the adornment of England. Use me, my God! That I may be in Your kingdom with a single jewel in my crown so that I can cast it at Your feet unashamed. Your will be done, Oh Lord." After her prayer, she crawled into bed with a feeling of peace.

*For the Lord your God will be with you wherever you go.*

# Chapter 4

## San Juan, Puerto Rico

Monday morning Preston was up with the sun as instructed. His bag was loaded on board and he stood at the dock with the Cagneys. He shifted his weight nervously as he stood there facing them, anxious to be getting on board.

"Now don't you get impatient with us, Preston Williams! We stuck with you this long and we at least deserve a decent goodbye!"

Preston frowned at himself. "Sorry, Aunt Marcy."

"Now listen to me, boy." She took his elbows and dragged him closer to her, working hard to hold back tears. "If you die out there I will serve you cold suppers for a month!"

Preston was not entirely sure about her logic. "Yes ma'am, I should be back to visit soon."

"We'll be looking forward to your return. Know that you will always have a home here," Uncle John said. "Do something for me kid. Memorize this: *Then they cried out to the Lord in their trouble, and He brought them out of their distress. He stilled the storm to a whisper; the waves of the sea were hushed.'* That's

Psalm 107:28-29." He paused. "It was one of your father's favorites."

He nodding solemnly. Preston tried not to show the way his stomach had just twisted and lurched inside of him. Oh dear, this was not the way to start a voyage at sea.

Preston quickly gave Aunt Marcy a hug before he strode swiftly up the gangplank.

Shouting one last goodbye, Preston put all other thoughts behind him before he got to work helping the crew cast off. But before they let down the sails all the men stopped and stood in silence. A few even removed their hats. Preston asked one of the nearby men what was going on.

"Cap'in always blesses the voyage 'for we go. Somthin' with 'is religion."

Preston watched as Captain Henry walked to the front of the ship and made a series of hand motions with an undistinguishable object in his hand. Preston didn't like it, though the crew seemed more bored then bothered. When Henry finally finished, the sails were unfurled and they sailed out of port.

The day before, Preston had attempted a friendship with some of the crew, most of which were not much older than he. Though many were rather cold toward this newcomer, he had managed a friendly exchange with one crew member, Corey Davis, who promised to give him the full tour once they left port.

Not quite six foot, Corey had straight brown hair, blue grey eyes, and a kind round face. He was not one to offer information unless it was asked for, but upon Preston's curious investigation, Corey proved to be a willing source of information.

"Those triangular sails there," Corey said pointing to the bow, "are jigs. Or fore and aft sails. They improve the upwind sailing ability of the ship. Or lift of the front end. So those are almost never furled."

By the end of that day Preston could do many things. Preston also received advice from Mr. Bentley, the quartermaster and navigator, who taught him how to measure the ship's STW (Speed Through Water).

"Ya stand at tha bow, thar, with that thar log tied to a rope. Hold on to one end, then ya shout to me and drop tha wood with plenty of slack. I'll stand at tha stern with this here stop watch." He had held it up for Preston to see. "And I'll start tha watch when ya shout. When the log passes me at tha stern, I'll stop the watch and ya'll pull the log back up. We'll calculate how fast we're goin' by comparin' how long it takes for tha log to travel the 99 foot length of the ship. Got it?" Preston nodded; he already loved this job. Measuring and calculating he could do.

That evening, Preston and Corey went down to the forecastle after supper, both off watch.

"Have you been on the *Raven* long?" asked Preston.

"I signed on three weeks ago with most of the crew. Captain hired everyone, all having never sailed before, but Mr. Bentley and the cook, at the same time. They taught us everything we now know about sailing. You seem to be taken to the seas better than the rest of us."

"My foster father taught me a lot about ships. He was the quartermaster to my father who was the captain of the *Huntress*. Though I never learned how to sail one," Preston said as he unpacked his things around his hammock. He took out his Bible and the small portrait of his mother.

Seeing the Bible, Corey's eyes bulged. "Are you a believer?"

"Yes, are you?" Preston nearly dropped his belongings, overjoyed at the possibility of a true friend. *Thank you, Lord for providing for me!*

"Indeed." Corey said. "I haven't known another Christian in the world since my caretaker in the orphanage I grew up in. She taught me about Jesus."

The smile died on Preston's face. "Did you ever know your parents?"

"Never knew my father, nor do I know what happened to him. My mother died of disease when I was seven," he said with a sad smile. "But the Lord took me in and cared for me instead."

Preston nodded. "I'm afraid I can relate."

The weeks drifted by like the waves. Preston flourished at sea, adapting to the lifestyle easily and enjoying it immensely. He loved to rise with the sun to read his Bible, and experience the adventure in sailing.

Whenever the sky was clear, Preston would work with Mr. Bentley with navigation. It delighted Preston to surprise Mr. Bentley with his experience, who was equally delighted that Preston could take over the majority of his duties as quartermaster.

The work was hard. The elements forced the men to gain strength and callouses very quickly. The sun burned and tanned them, and the rain left welts on their skin. But the worst of it came one clear day, while they were on their way to Bermuda. Preston, after the morning routine, climbed up the rigging to take his turn as lookout.

Here, in the crow's nest, he was free of all people and sound. It was just he and God. Preston would relax in the wind, talking to his heavenly Father while scanning the ocean. His eyes had learned to adjust to the glare on the water and detect something as small as a dolphin nearly a mile away.

As he whittled at an old piece of a board he had found, he caught sight of a growing cloud to their six. The breeze rustled Preston's blond hair. *We could be in for rain.* He looked down at the face of his carving and added details to the face and hair. Preston held the little woodman back to examine. He laughed.

Was it a pig or a dog?

Preston put the carving down and brought his eyes to the sky once more. To his surprise, the little grey cloud had grown to be a long, black mass. *That can't be good.*

"Six, ho!" Preston hollered.

Below, men turned and gasped in surprise. The captain clambered up from his cabin with his spyglass. After a good, long look, he performed a few odd motions with his hands and rubbed one of his talismans.

Preston could hardly see his captain, but he knew what he was doing. He rolled his eyes, his patience running thin with this nonsense.

Finally, Captain Henry took charge. "All hands on deck! Tie down anything loose! Lock all the hatches! Let all the sails loose! Outrun it!" he thundered. "Come down Williams!" – using 'Mr.' was becoming difficult above the wind – "I have no desire to lose a crew man if it can be helped!"

Within the hour, the ominous clouds turned into a tempest, and although the wind was with them, it was not as strong as that which pushed the storm.

"Douse the sails! Secure the belaying pens!" Captain Henry yelled at the end of the hour. This was no normal storm. "Until this storm passes, I want half the crew up here at every moment. By night I want two, six-hour shifts and by day I want four shifts of three hours. Mr. Bentley take a half of the crew, and Mr. Williams, you are to lead the other half. Choose your men!"

Preston eyebrows rose at this sudden promotion, though he had no time to dwell on it. He chose the men he knew would work hard for him, first Corey.

Another hour went by. The storm horrifically engulfed them. Soon, there was no telling if it was night or day. Terrifying, black minutes became hours. Hours became days of wet, cold, darkness. The nightmare seemed unending.

Preston drove the crew hard day and night. Constantly dumping out water, catching and retying ropes, repairing sails, fixing boards, and trying to keep from washing out to sea was a full-time job.

Staying alive was a full-time job.

"Preston!" He heard someone yell as he worked under the blanket of pounding rain. He turned to look for his partner, who looked around in the dimness just as unsure. Then Preston heard it. A terrible roar almost above them.

"Hold on!" he screamed to the man beside him and he shoved the man over to the main mast.

The two were able to wrap their arms around the mast as a wave crashed over them. Preston felt his body being drug ferociously toward the sea. Tightening his hold, the two waited out the water's terrible grasp until it slid back into the ocean.

From then on Preston made sure each person that went out on deck was tied to a partner in a more durable location. This was tricky business.

Exhausted, cold, hungry, wet. The *Raven* was going nowhere, or rather everywhere. The ship was tossed every which way by the waves that rose well above the main mast. The only light was the occasional lightning strike. Even below deck, without dry kerosene there was no way to have light.

Living in darkness was new to Preston. It was as though they were no longer in the world, but somewhere that held nothing but misery and terror. The horror of the engulfing darkness stung his heart and tormented his soul.

*Jesus? Where are you?* he managed to pray. *Where are you? Where are we? Will we ever see day again? What was the sun like? Was it really so hot that it would dry up the water on the road after a rain?* Preston could not help but ask such misery filled questions. Man was not meant to live in darkness, this he was sure of. It hurt their heads and scrambled their minds until they were numb. He was regretting ever coming to sea, as was every other man aboard.

For two days, Preston struggled to stay in control. The crewmen were panicking, and Preston fought to keep them from utter terror. Several times he had to pull a man aside and talk sense into him.

For one poor man, Preston had to tie his ankle to the main mast to keep him from leaping over the edge. Twice the man tried to drag his partner with him into the black sea. Never had Preston witnessed anything so horrifying. With Corey's humor, the two were able to stay bright, but after that day neither felt like joking around.

On day three of this monster, a new struggle showed itself. Preston found the crew with less panic and more numbness. They ran out of the survival adrenaline that kept them working hard.

"Men! We're alive, aren't we?" He scanned the group. "Aren't we? This storm can't last forever! Although we can't see it, there's a world out there! A home where you all belong! Now listen here! Think of those who want you home! Now tie down the yards! Put another nail in that cracking board!"

This motivated the men enough that they would struggle to their tired feet, but it did not last. By the fifth day, their leader had lost his hope as well. Something boiled in Preston's blood that never had before. Survival. But no, survival was the fur on the animal. A raging sense of injustice – yes, injustice, that's what it was – brought fire rather than the numbness that the others experienced.

Aunt Marcy had warned Preston of his fire. *"When used right, it will be warm and comforting. When let out of control, it will damage and burn that which is close."*

Preston could no longer hold in the anguish. Anger swelled in his heart, deprived of the light that he had depended on. Was that what his faith was based on? Did he have to see to believe? Would he believe only when things were easy?

Preston climbed up the rigging, by feel more than sight, and into the crow's nest with natural athleticism. Falling on his knees in the midst of the tempest, Preston finally allowed conviction to bubble up from its buried place.

"Lord, why? Why did you lead me here to die? Do you not care?" he screamed into the wind. He let the water cool his burning face.

Without warning a verse came to his mind, *Then they cried out to the Lord in their trouble, and He brought them out of their distress. He stilled the storm to a whisper; the waves of the sea were hushed.* He didn't memorize this verse Uncle John had given him, yet here it came as clear as the day.

He had been praying for the storm to stop. Had he not? Actually, Preston had spent very little time in prayer. Between the constant distractions and his own spite against God, he not said much to his King.

"Lord Jesus," Preston whispered to the wind, unable to find it in himself to shout. "I am of little faith. I am weak and unwise. Forgive me for questioning you, Lord. I am not worthy of your rescue, but please, give us relief, please."

Preston continued to beg and repent for a few minutes more. The burden on his heart was lifting, replaced with peace, and the relief he already felt was remarkable. It was not his job to get them through the storm. Preston knew that God might not save them.

*That is up to Him,* Preston told himself, *my responsibility is to encourage and be faithful.* "Thank you for showing me Your light, please do the same for the others."

He drew his eyes up and there, half a mile away, was a pillar of light. The surrounding storm was tinted grey with its arrival. Preston flew down the rigging to alert the men.

"Look!" he yelled. Men scrambled to see what Preston pointed to. What it was, he didn't know. But the storm pushed closer and closer toward it.

Within a quarter hour, the *Raven* floated into the column of light. Although the waves still rose, there was no wind. Preston had never seen anything like this. A quarter mile in every direction was the storm, unable to circle any tighter.

"It's the eye of this monster," said one crewman finally. The entire crew basked in the sun as life was restored on the ship. Then Mr. Bentley spoke up.

"It's tha eye alright, which means we're in for tha other half of that storm. And judgin' by our condition..." He looked around at the damaged ship. "There ain't a chance we'll last."

Preston looked around at the crestfallen faces.

*Oh Lord my God, save me.*

# Chapter 5

London, England

"Stockings, stockings. Why do I even need stockings?" Cassidy muttered to herself as she sorted through her dresser.

She was nearly packed for her leave tomorrow, her things divided into two trunks. Now, she gathered the little things, and taking her time at it. There was to be a ball for the nobility, and much to Cassidy's dismay, she was *still* a duchess and *still* had to attend. Dressed in a lavender gown with white lace, she was ready.

Mindy had packed her things already. Now Cassidy was going over the items and adding a few things even though Mindy, indeed, had done her job well.

Cassidy sighed, knowing there was nothing more that should keep her, and it really wasn't fair of her to make her parents late. So, she brushed the lint from her gown and came out of her room to meet her parents in the hall.

She could hear her father playing their grand piano and her mother's sweet voice before she entered the room. Smiling, Cassidy joined in. Her rich voice accompanied her mother's sweet tone and the notes of the piano beautifully. The happy family played and sang a few more songs before Jacob interrupted with the news of the waiting stagecoach.

Father swung his wife around the room before exclaiming, "Your voice has never been so lovely, my dear." He tucked her hand into his right arm. Jacob extended his arm to Cassidy, and they strolled outside.

Jacob helped her in before closing the doors and climbing into the driver's seat. Cassidy leaned her head back, closed her eyes and silently prayed for energy and patience. Parties and socializing were not her idea of a nice evening.

When she opened her eyes, he addressed her. "I'm sorry, dearest, that you have to go to this. We don't plan to stay longer then we have to, we want you well rested for your departure tomorrow."

"It's all right. Besides, this way I can say goodbye to everyone before I leave." Cassidy said.

A while later, the coach arrived at the Buckingham House. The Duke of Buckingham had built it about a decade ago, and loved to host balls there. Its expansive halls and grand ballrooms made it an ideal place for the nobility's dances. Cassidy did enjoy this place. She had seen many beautiful mansions, though none were quite like this.

As Jacob helped her out the steps of the coach, she marveled at the huge estate.

With a delighted grin, Father escorted both the ladies into the ballroom. Cassidy much preferred this arrangement. If she walked in by herself, the young men would jump at the chance to take her in.

The evening went by smoothly for Cassidy; she busied herself with the most talkative people, the ones that only required smiling and nodding. This approach served her well until one unfortunate encounter with Sir Wealthtop. One way or another, Cassidy found herself in the presence of the stiff faced man. Dreadful anticipation bubbled up from its forced position, and Cassidy knew all too well that it would be rude not to at least attempt a conversation with the intimidating old miser.

"Sir Wealthtop, you look well this evening," she said in a gentle, non-threatening way. When the man only nodded, she went on, gathering her courage. "A friend of mine, a young lady in my Bible reading class, has the name Margaret Wealthtop, is she related to you?"

*Well, maybe not the best thing to say.*

Sir Wealthtop looked at the girl curiously. "Yes, Lady Chandler, I believe you know my niece, my brother's daughter." He let out an exasperated sigh. "That pretty head of hers is always in the clouds. She ought to see the world as it is."

Cassidy tilted her head slightly, the way she did in thought. "This is a grave world we live in, sir." She knew he would agree with that statement, as he had seen much of the world. *Perhaps that is why he is so hard.* "I believe that if one can live in their own perfect world for a time, so be it."

Sir Wealthtop furrowed his brow. "If one did that, she would experience a rude awakening when finally experiencing the world as it is. I am simply trying to save her that trouble."

"Yes, but a pure heart can touch many lives. Hurting or not. A hardened heart can do no such good."

The elderly man pondered this a moment. "Indeed, my lady," he said simply.

Seeing there was no further conversation to be had, and that Sir Wealthtop was not going to walk away, being a gentleman, Cassidy spared him further. "Good day," she said with a slight curtsy, then went off to find her parents, not at all sure if the conversation went well.

Weaving through the crowd at the edge of the ballroom floor, she met the gaze of a young man coming toward her. *Who is that?* Cassidy started to look for shelter, but then realized that it would be too obvious to do so. Besides, she had promised herself, her parents, and God that she would try not be so timid, and perhaps this was a chance to make a new friend.

"Good evening, Lady Chandler." The young man bowed low. "I am Quinn Harris. Would you join me for a dance?" Quinn was not one that a person would find delight in his appearance, nor was he one to attract any sort of attention. In fact, Cassidy had noticed several young ladies avoiding him earlier in the evening. He was rather awkward and short, but his kind smile told Cassidy that he was genuine.

Filled with sympathy, she gently took his arm. "It would be my delight," she said, and watched a joyful smile spread over his face. Friendliness was all he asked, and she gave him that easily. It was something many of the other men she had danced with had forgotten about.

The following morning, Cassidy was up before dawn. She dressed in a simple traveling gown before wandering to the garden with her Bible. She took a quick side trip to the kitchen where the aroma of breakfast made her mouth water. As usual, a few lumps of sugar were waiting for her. She noticed a few extra, the cook's way of telling her farewell.

A few minutes later, she sat in her stunning garden just as the sun's rays peeked over the trees. With the sun came larks and jays, swallows and chickadees, swans and cranes, all making their morning remarks. There was also the resident peacock that strolled about as he sang his peahen attracting song.

Cassidy began a long prayer before breaking into song.

"The earth is the Lord's, and everything in it,
the world, and all who live in it;
for he founded it on the seas
and established it on the water." ~Psalm 24:1-2

The strong notes came from deep within her, as though her heart flooded out in beautiful harmony with the sound of her voice. But this morning God had a special gift for her, as the antlered head of a great stag appeared behind the bushes. She watched him in awe as he stepped out into the open. His antlered head moved with majestic grace. His finely-toned body was statuesque, reminding her of a mythological Roman god she had once seen. Though he did not come any closer, he seemed to watch her, like a guardian of the forest.

For several minutes Cassidy believed she was in Heaven, the guardian stag protecting her in a paradise garden. Then the breakfast bell rang the great creature bounded back into the wood.

Breakfast was Cassidy's favorite. Toast, eggs, sausage, and beans. The entire household went out of their way to properly see her off. Mindy had brought in some daisies, her favorite flowers, for the table; Jacob brought out Lucky and Chance, her favorite of the draft horses, to take them to the dock; and Mrs. Ann, the hat maker, knocked at the door with a new sun hat for her as a surprise.

"You shall need it, dearie. I hear the American sun is always shining! And a lady with your complexion ought to be well prepared," said Mrs. Ann.

At the port, Cassidy met the captain of the *Queens Merit*. Captain Finley was a jolly gentleman with a large belly and a smile that was a friend to all. With his mischievous, child-like manner, she hardly believed that a man like Finley could really be captain of a sea vessel.

As the men loaded Cassidy's things, Captain Finley took the trio on a tour of the ship. She was a huge, elegant Ship of the Line initially designed for war. Now, she was used as a merchant ship, one that few would dare try an attack on. With this fact, her parents were satisfied that Cassidy was in good hands.

Mother embraced her tightly. "Wherever you go, God is with you."

Cassidy nodded, her head buried in her mother's shoulder.

"And tell Aunt Emily hello from us. Oh, and invite her to visit for Christmas."

"Perhaps she can come back with me," Cassidy said. She next tuned to her father.

He cleared his throat. "Captain Finley should be there to take you back just before Thanksgiving. He has some business in the Caribbean before returning to England. If for some reason his plans change, I have arranged for him to send a ship he trusts to fetch you. Good? I want my girl home by Christmas. So not too much dilly dallying."

Cassidy nodded. "Yes, Father. Home before Christmas."

As the ship pulled out of the dock, Cassidy could hardly contain her excitement. She watched the crew work for several hours from a crate in the corner where she was out of the way. Other than a polite nod or smile, they ignored her, which was fine with her. Seeing her curiosity as to the activities on the ship, Captain Finley made an occasional stop to tell her what they were doing.

"Leaving and entering port is often when a ship makes the most turns. To help make these turns we use a sail called the a-back sail." He pointed to a sail that two crewmembers were attending to. "This way we have more control of the ship while in smaller acreage." Finley went on about many other topics including navigation and flag code. Cassidy drank it in.

Although Cassidy enjoyed the sea life, she did not fall into it as easily as did Preston. It took nearly a week for her to stomach food. On the rough sea days she could barely stand, much less work, as the others did.

Apart from the occasional talk with the Captain or perhaps the quartermaster, Cassidy found herself rather lonely. Thus, she spent a great deal of time talking with God. She saw her time on the sea as a time spent with God, where she could be who she was. She never needed to worry about social problems or lady-likeness. Walking on the railing, climbing the rigging, and eating without proper manners, were some such freedoms she enjoyed in life at sea.

Knowing such moments were inevitable, Elyse had even allowed her to take a few pairs of Andrew's outgrown sailing outfits for her to wear around the ship, hemmed and taken in by Cassidy herself. Cassidy loved the freedom in these clothes.

The boys were certainly the lucky ones when it came to clothing, she was sure.

# *Chapter 6*

The *Royal Fortune*

The night was eerily still. The sea calm, as it gently rocked the black ship. The wind howled, spraying water into the faces of the men aboard. Clouds blocked the stars from view, but the ominous moon hung low and haunting in the sky.

A tall man stood impatient at the helm. He was not one to be kept waiting. He watched his men with sharp grey eyes as they moved about in tense silence. Anxious, he swung his gaze back out to sea. *Where is that fool?* His patience was running thin – not that it was very thick to begin with. He had a schedule to keep, and he wanted to turn this ship around just to spite his tardy contact.

But now was not the time for rash actions.

Things were finally falling into place, if the report brought good news. In truth, he needed that information, and if he must wait, he would wait.

At last, a shout came from the crow's nest and it was not long before a handsome naval ship halted beside the *Royal Fortune*. The captain came down from the helm to the main deck and stood waiting for that lazy man to come to him. He would demand some respect.

A man in his prime strode across the lowered gangplank with more swag then necessary. His short brown hair, cutting blue eyes, and impressive stature turned heads.

"Good evening, Captain Cade. My most sincere apologies for our delay." The young man gave a low bow with a sweep of his cap. A muscle in Mayson Cade's jaw jerked at his tone, which dripped with sarcasm.

"I'm sure," Cade replied.

The man made a face, but before he could retort, Cade's patience met its end. "Is everything in line, Collins?"

Roy Collins smiled cunningly. "Indeed, sir. At this rate, you'll finally be captured and we shall all be rid of you. Or better yet, you'll be sent to Davy Jones's locker."

Cade knew Collins' games and took no offense. "Well? Spit it out!"

"Words are expensive, Cade."

*The audacity...* Cade's knuckles itched to hit something, particularly his face. Instead, he presented the large sack, jangling heavily. "Now, out with it!"

The good thing about Collins was that he knew when not to push. And the bad thing about Collins, was that he knew exactly how far he could push. It gave him another dose of dangerousness that all seafarers – including Cade – ought to be aware of.

"Our young lord has more firearms than we thought, and he has added to his one ship charade.

The young Chandler just bought an oversized Barque with equal firepower." Collins ran two fingers over the ship's railing. "The *Fortune* is impressive, of course, but she can't take on two ships. You'll be dead, if you pull this stunt of yours."

"The ransom note specifically said not to bring another ship. He wouldn't risk it." His contact's foolishness annoyed Cade, but alas! None can truly outwit Roy Collins!

"He would not risk being unprepared if you decide to attack. Believe me, this kid will bring his other ship and hide it, just in case. Besides, his ship alone would not leave the *Fortune* unscathed."

Cade grimaced. Collins was right, which only further annoyed him. This master plan of his had too many holes, but Cade was in too deep now. It was fight or lose everything.

A smirk appeared on Collins' face, not that it had ever truly vanished.

Cade was not accustomed to being out done. He could feel his pride slipping, and with it possibly his tongue. But Cade had learned better than to pass on Collins' shrewdness, however much grief that meant to himself. Even now, he could see the wheels turning in the young man's mind. "And I suppose ya have a suggestion?"

"Of course, sir. It's like that child's game we used to play."

Wincing, Cade thought of chess, his favorite game. He had taught it to Collins when he was but a boy. They played it often, till Collins decided it too easy after his countless wins. Cade would never admit to it, but Collins was the shrewdest man he had ever met, which was the only reason why Cade took his advice. Besides, the navy had already discovered and made the most of Collins' incredible ability with strategies. If they could gain his loyalty they would have true treasure in their hands.

For now, Roy Collins was split, and no doubt still coming out on top. Cade needed to use Collins while he still could, for who knew where the man would stand in time?

"What has this to do with the noble game, boy?" Cade had had enough.

"As planned, first we need bait – already a well-rolling piece I might add." He paused for effect. "Then we need time. A diversion. We shall make our opponent decide which precious piece to keep. Of course, they will have neither piece until time is on our side."

"What'd ya have in mind?"

Collins smiled widely, a dangerous, cunning smile. "That is a conversation only for the payer." He motioned to the captain's cabin. "Shall we?"

The two started toward the Captain's quarters. Collins studied the crew as they walked, then frowned.

"Where is piece number three, Mayson?" Dark displeasure and perhaps concern spiked his voice, returning to Cade a little bit of his pride.

"I have that completely under control. Williams is the least of our worries."

## The *Raven*

Preston's stomach growled at him, making him dare to slip another cracker into his mouth. It had been nearly two weeks since they entered this hurricane, and although the short passage through the eye brought relief, it did not last. The extreme waves would barely allow for the men to stand, much less hold food. Even the heartiest of men could not hold down more than a few crackers.

Preston looked up from his hammock and surveyed his men. The grey hue in the air proved it was daytime, but those with poor eyesight could not tell the difference.

Some of the men slept, others, like Preston, were eating slowly. A few attempted a game of checkers, and the rest sat or stood with a blank expression. Those who could read did not dare, knowing that it would add to the sickness.

The conditions were almost unbearable. Damp, cold, dark, and stinky beyond imagination. Human waste, mildew, vomit, and the occasional rotting remains of a rat made it almost unbearable. The sensitive noses got rags shoved up their nostrils. The rest eventually got used to it.

Of course, they could go up on deck, but there they fought for their life every minute. So, the exhausted men went on without seeing because of the constant darkness, without hearing because of the deafening roar of the waves, without feeling because of the constant cold. Without life.

Preston fought this most of all. Without life and hope the men were nothing but empty shells. He had told many of them about Jesus, and encouraged each of them at every opportunity. "The storm cannot last forever!" he would say. Or, "There is hope yet!" and "we're not dead yet!" Now, Preston prayed unceasingly, yet not as he used to.

As the hours went by his plea for God's help became a one-word cry: "Jesus!" His weary brain could not think of anything else to say. For the first time in his life, he met utter exhaustion.

*How could God do this? Where is He? How long will He allow this to go on?* Preston did not have the energy to be angry, but his faith was weakening with the rest of him.

Preston looked up from his closing eyes to the door as one of the crewmembers from the other shift walked in. Time was up. Preston could not help but sigh, a sigh so heavy that it carried the weight of the world. He gathered his remaining strength and courage.

"Alright, Corey, Donny, and Michael, your turn at the wheel." He gave out several more instructions as the men picked themselves up.

*It's the thirteenth day. We reached the center of the storm on the fifth. So then why did we not reach the end three days ago?* Preston worried, heading up the stairs to the deck. Doing math brought him comfort. It was something he was good at. In his mind he pictured the swirling circle of the storm, the eye in the middle, and a straight line going through it as the ship's course.

*Straight!*

Horror collided against Preston's rib cage and brought him to a sudden halt. Corey bumped into him.

"You okay, Pres?" Corey asked. Preston didn't hear him.

*We haven't been going in a straight line!*

Yet the wheel was tied down with ropes to keep that from happening, and three men still had to hold it to keep it steady. Surely they would notice if it was no longer attached to the rudder.

*Or would they?*

Preston took off up to the deck taking two stairs at a time, Corey right on his heels and with him the rest of the crew, curious about this sudden behavior.

Bursting on deck, they alarmed Mr. Bentley, who was preparing to go below. "What on earth?" he muttered.

Preston was at the wheel in an instant. His heart seemed to still, but the tempest had only intensified.

"Let go!" he bellowed.

The three crew members looked at him, bewildered, but knew better then to stand in the way of Preston William's wrath. They released the wheel.

When Preston did not grab it to stop the ship from veering off course, Corey lunged for it, but his friend pushed him back.

"Are you daft?" Corey screamed. Mr. Bentley yelled much the same thing, though no one could hear him.

Everyone watched as the wheel teetered with the ship.

In one quick motion of desperation, Preston whipped out his knife and sliced through all three ropes that held the wheel in place.

The wheel was unaffected.

It rolled with the boat, moved by nothing more than the wind and the rocking of its base.

Now everyone stood in astonishment. They knew exactly what that meant: they had no control of where the ship was headed.

Worse, Preston figured it had been broken for at least three days, probably more. It was impossible to tell which way they were currently headed without being able to see the sky.

Preston spun on his heels, more abrupt then he meant. Corey would certainly have noticed if the wheel did not tug like usual. "Corey, when was the last time you had a shift at the helm?" His tone was sharp.

Corey did not meet the gaze of those fiery eyes, so dark and mystifying.

"Six days ago, sir," he replied.

Preston's anger was completely on himself. Between now and six days ago, the rudder broke, and there was no way of fixing it until they could get to shore. They could still use the a-back sails, but not in this storm. Hence, there was no way out of this tempest until it let them go.

Preston wanted to sit down and cry. Tears threatened his eyes and his knees shook. "Jesus!" he managed, a desperate cry to his final Hope.

# Chapter 7

The *Raven*

"Jesus! Please, I surrender!" Preston managed, a desperate cry to his final Hope.

The men around him looked just as shaken, except one. He was moving forward in the crowd of crewmen, making his way to the helm.

> *"You answer us with awesome and*
> *righteous deeds, God our Savior…"*

Preston looked up in surprise at the man, a stranger. A stranger that looked like them, but not just in clothing. He looked tired, as though he had just fought a war. Preston could feel the power of these gentle words. He knew them – yes, they were scripture. A Psalm perhaps. The man went on:

> *"…the hope of all the ends of the earth*
> *and of the farthest seas, who formed*
> *the mountains by your power,*
> *having armed yourself with strength,*
> *who stilled the roaring of the seas,*
> *and the roaring of their waves."*

To Preston these words were a promise, yet also a command, a reminder that God is perfect and his plan is good. *Jesus, Jesus, Jesus…* he said his Lord's name over and over in his mind.

The wind slowed, the waves toppled over themselves until they became tired and lazy. The clouds seemed to lighten into shades of gray. Preston looked around in confusion. The propellant of the hurricane seemed to have stopped. The thunder no longer sounded, and the lightning no longer cracked.

"Thank you." Preston breathed as the world slid from his shoulders. His heart squeezed in awe and wonder. God seemed to have kept them in that storm until Preston shook off his pride and submitted to God.

Trust had come at the cost of his pride.

But now, Preston found it a cost worth paying when he saw something that would stay with him the rest of his life. He took a step toward the starboard side.

Light. A glorious strip of light off the starboard rail.

The crew followed his gaze and yelled to one another. Then, that beautiful clear voice rang out again, finishing the verse.

*"The whole earth is filled with awe at your wonders; where morning dawns,*
*where evening fades, you call*
*forth songs of joy."*

When the stranger finished, Preston went over to him. "Thank you," he whispered, tears pushing at his eyes. The man shook his head and pointed up. Preston followed his gaze, but saw nothing. When he looked back, the stranger was gone.

Corey ran up behind him and slapped Preston on the back. "We are going to be okay!"

Preston turned to look at him. "Did you see that?"

"See what? Willow the Wisp?" Corey paused. "Actually, you kind of look like you've just seen ghost."

"Not a ghost, an angel!" Preston exclaimed, wondering how it could be more obvious.

"An angel? A real one? Like, God's angel?"

"Yes! Well, I mean, he was dressed like us, but he was an angel." Preston stamped his foot trying to make his friend understand. "The one that was singing."

Corey blinked.

Soon the sliver of light became a ribbon, the waves raised no higher than the main deck, and the wind no longer attempted to pull out their hair.

With the light came a purveyance of the damage. The main mast looked to be in sailing condition. There was no more railing, but they did not need that anyway. There were no longer barrels or crates on deck, not even the ones that had been tied down. Many boards were missing from the hull, but the most shocking discovery was the gaping hole at sea level in the side of the ship. Water flowed in and out of it freely. With this discovery came the realization that they were five feet lower in the water than they were supposed to be. Miraculously, they still floated.

Captain Henry emerged for the first time in a few days looking pale. He also looked over the damage and whistled at the hole in the hull. "Obviously, we need to make port as soon as possible. The *Raven* is in no condition to be sailing at all. Mr. Bentley, tonight I want our location."

Two hours later the *Raven* broke free of the storm. The sun shone so brightly that the crew's skin burned instantaneously. A strong breeze proved it was a perfect day on the sea. The Union Jack was raised again and the sails were unfurled, or what was left of the sails.

Once on their way, any spare crewmember set about drying out the ship and doing what they could in repairs. Some wrapped rope around broken wood, other mended sails. Even the cook set out to fill each stomach.

The *Raven* moved sluggishly, unable to gain speed with the sizeable hole, which insisted on holding water.

On deck, the stars were countless. Thousands upon millions of lights twinkled at them, decorating the sky in glory that sent chills down Preston's spine.

Preston helped Mr. Bentley with navigation. As they charted and measured and worked arithmetic, Preston prayed. Finally, when they were finished, he breathed a sigh of relief. The captain waited impatiently until Mr. Bentley approached him.

"Sir, it's a miracle! We'll be at Bermuda by dawn."

Bermuda intrigued Preston, not because of the island itself, which looked about like every other island he had visited, but because of the people. They spoke English, Spanish, French, Portuguese, Irish, and other native languages, according to Corey. Preston could hardly hold back his curiosity to hear what these other languages sounded like. He got his chance the day they docked.

"Mr. Williams, what languages do you speak?" Captain Henry bellowed at him from the helm as they floated into port.

"English, French, and Spanish, sir," Preston replied. He noticed the excitement they were causing on shore. *A half sunken boat must be an unusual sight around here.*

"Good, I want you to help me arrange for repairs. Get your things and follow me as soon as we are docked." The captain ordered.

Preston's eyebrows rose. "All my things, sir?"

A cold glare answered him.

"Aye, sir." Preston nodded, but did not back down, allowing his gaze on the captain to intensify. He could not help the distrust that tingled through his body.

*Why would I need any of my things to walk through town?* Preston locked his jaw and finally headed to the forecastle. Corey met him there.

"Leaving us already?" Corey came to stand behind him.

Preston looked up from his packing. "No,

Captain wants me to go ashore with him, I think he needs some interpreting. I suspect that we plan to stay the night at an inn." He felt better saying that, perhaps there was nothing unusual about the situation after all.

Corey nodded. "Right, 'cause Bermuda is a *great* place to spend the night." He said sardonically. "Stay out of trouble." Corey called after him as Preston strode out the door.

With his bag slung around his shoulder, Preston checked his sword and pistol before they headed back up on deck.

Captain Henry waited for Preston long enough to see him coming then walked across the deck and down the gangplank, (more like up the gangplank due to their lowered height). Preston's long strides easily caught up with those of the older, shorter man.

Over the next few hours, Preston and Captain Henry made arrangements for wood and workers. Preston used his other tongues and even picked up some Portuguese, which turned out to be very similar to Spanish. Everything was going quite well and Preston had nearly forgotten about his ill ease, until Captain Henry led him into downtown.

The place was clearly not on the "up and up," as Aunt Marcy would have said.

When the captain stepped into a tavern, Preston almost called out, "I'll wait out here!" but then he thought better of it and stepped into the most terrible smelling room he had ever been in. That is, if alcohol and cigars smell worse than the decay and vomit of the *Raven*'s forecastle. Then again, perhaps it was not so much the smell that repulsed Preston. It was the evil and carnal worship that tried to push him back outside.

Preston followed his captain to a corner table where several men were. One, clearly in charge, sat sipping a large mug while the others stood waiting. They wore dirty sailing clothes and had dirty, less than pleasant faces. The captain, on the other hand, was dressed finely, with a three-pointed hat and gold charms braided into his long hair and beard.

"Captain! I'm sorry for me tardiness. Got held up in a tempest, we did," said Captain Henry, and to Preston's shock, in English no better than that of a pirate.

"Well Henry, I was just about to give up waiting for ya. A whole fifteen minutes late." The man stood, and Preston was surprised again when he smiled a perfect smile. He had wonderfully straight teeth, which were very white considering the rum he drank.

"Good evening, Mr. Williams." He extended a hand and looked Preston up and down like livestock at auction.

Stunned, Preston managed a "Good evening, sir." He did not like the way this man sized him up. "Have we met before?"

"Please sit." He motioned to some chairs. They sat. Preston sat stiffly in his chair. "Not to fret, Mr.

Williams. I'm not avoiding yer question. I'm Mayson Cade, and no, we haven't met, I heard about ya
on a previous meeting. Captain Henry works for
me."

*Well that would have been nice to know.* It occurred
to him that not only did he work for Henry, but for
this man. Preston decided there was nothing trustworthy about Mayson Cade.

"Don't be so concerned. This isn't nothin' but a
routine stop for payment." Cade said. Preston did
not like how Cade read him so well. "Now tell me,
what is your position on the *Raven*?"

Preston licked his lips. "Second mate, sir. Although I do navigation occasionally."

Cade turned to Captain Henry. "Ya allow the boy
such a position?"

Captain Henry seemed pleased as he fingered
one of his charms. "Not just any boy. I'd trust Mr.
Williams with me life an' tha lives of me crew. In
that storm, 'e had a whole shift under 'is command.
'E also discovered tha rudder was broken when half
me crew missed it. Not to mention 'e's twice as
smart as old Bentley. Yes sir! Yer just gotta earn 'is
respect, then 'e'll work as hard as a horse for ya."
Preston felt as though his best qualities were being
displayed for potential buyers.

*What have I gotten into?*

"You don't say." Cade looked at Preston. When
Preston only reddened, Cade seemed amused.

Henry went on, "Indeed, sir. And he never com-
plains or…"

"I get the point," Cade interrupted, to Preston's relief. "Well, Mr. Williams, I'm in need of a crewmember. A second mate, in fact. I pride myself on having a top-notch crew and pay them twice the going rate. What do yer say?" One of the men behind Cade shifted.

Preston resisted the urge to say, "Absolutely not."

Mayson Cade was clearly cunning and much savvier than Captain Henry. When two of the men behind Cade moved to his side threateningly, a shiver raced down Preston's spine. Cade laughed. Preston ignored him. *This is not good.* He already had his things. They had been planning this for a while.

"If I say no, do you plan to force me?" Preston glanced to the two men at his elbows. His left hand eased to his sheath.

Captain Cade raised an eyebrow at him. "That won't be a problem as long as yer say yes, now would it?"

Preston had long anticipated a response from the men. When one put a hand on his shoulder, he was ready. In one movement, Preston had the man at the end of his sword and a pistol aimed at Cade's head.

The other men had swords and pistols drawn and pointed at Preston while Henry sat unmoved. The entire crowd in the bar quieted, waiting for action.

"There's no need for that." Cade hardly looked at the gun. He motioned for the men to lower their weapons. Preston until the other guns and knives were put away before lowering his.

"Mr. Williams, I don't see ya to be a trouble-causing man. I haven't any ill will. Ya have reason, don't ya? Reason this, there is no reason to say no," said Cade.

Preston was not so sure that made sense. *There is only one way to get out of this.*

"I will sail for you under one condition..." Cade leaned back in his chair. "...that I am on a trial basis. After four weeks, if I do not find the situation fitting, I am a free man to walk away unharmed."

"Fine. Yer follow my commands until four weeks is up. After that, you choose to stay or leave."

The two shook hands, and wrote down the agreement, upon Preston's insistence.

"When should I be at your ship, Captain?" Preston looked down at the papers to find the name of the ship. "When does the *Royal Fortune* leave next?" Now that name did strike a chord in his head. The question was, which chord?

Cade handed a large pouch of jangling coins to a very pleased Captain Henry. "Now. We sail tomorrow morning."

# Chapter 8

## Bermuda

Stepping on the deck of the biggest galleon he had ever seen, Preston met a crew that was dirty and without manners. Most had missing teeth and matted hair. They reminded Preston of pirates. The ship was not in top condition either. For one, she appeared as though painted black. When Preston got close he realized that it was not paint, but rather a dark mahogany wood. The rare and expensive wood possessed the ultimate combination of both beauty and strength.

*Incredible.* Though she was a beautiful ship, she had not been cleaned. Ever. Barnacles and salt stain covered her sides and broken boards which were everywhere. Crates, barrels, and rope littered the deck. Preston seriously disliked the thought of the forecastle. Also, Preston noticed that they did not fly the colors of England. In fact, they flew no flag at all.

"Don't you fly the colors of the port you enter?" The crewmembers within earshot laughed at him, though Preston thought it a relevant question.

"I can't fly what I haven't sworn to," Cade retorted

89

"And what then have you sworn to, sir?" Preston felt a twinge of trouble about these men.

"You'll see, Mr. Williams. You'll see."

Throughout the rest of that evening, every attempt at a friendship had failed. Most ignored him, but a few already hated him. The quartermaster and the recently demoted second mate eyed him disdainfully.

As dusk darkened into night, Preston walked out of the captain's cabin after learning that this large galleon had a third cabin for the second mate. Preston thanked God over and over for the haven, knowing that he would be free to read his Bible and pray without teasing.

Preston navigated his way to his cabin and found it locked securely. Voices came from just round the corner. He had no intention to eavesdrop. Yet he found it difficult to do otherwise as he struggled to unlock his door.

"The cap'in says he's gonna be tha second mate, don't that mean he'll be overseeing our shift?" one said.

"Yep, and da cap'in said if da chap does well, he'll make 'im quartermaster!" a second remarked.

Then a quieter man spoke up. "If what yer saying be true, then we ought to get on his good side, or e'll have the power to off us and get somebody else!"

This brought silence to the crew.

"'He has a point."

"Ya right, we've a gotta make 'im like us."
Agreement echoed through the ground. Preston was not sure if this was good or bad.

When morning came, Preston indeed found that his part of the crew, at least half of the men, were trying to "get on his good side." This came in many varieties. Offering him a seat at supper, showing him around the ship, and offering to help as he learned to handle a ship the size of the *Royal Fortune*.

When they were out in open water and moving steadily in the breeze, Captain Cade came on deck. "Fly the colors!"

Preston was doing figures at the moment, so he did not hear this command. Nor did he see, as you might expect, the Jolly Roger and the red flag of no mercy climb the main mast and take its rightful place over the *Royal Fortune*. Only when Preston was climbing up to the crow's nest for his turn as lookout did he take notice.

Preston first saw a hint of red fabric. *Ah, so he finally proclaims his allegiance. Spanish perhaps?* He tried to get a better look through the sails. So off he went climbing higher and higher. *Is it plain red? No, that means no mercy. Black? What flag is red and black?* Preston was almost as high as he could go. *Two flags!*

He looked down at the deck far below. It could not have been more obvious. Preston scolded himself. Then turned to prayer, pleading with God to let it not be so. He climbed higher; perhaps he was mistaken. When he caught hold of the red flag he spread it wide. Solid red. Then the black one. Sure enough, the skull and cross bones looked back at him tauntingly.

Down the mast he went, his fury mounting. His boots hit the deck and he set off to the captain's cabin. Leaving everyone wondering what had become of him. Anger burned in his brain and radiated through his body. He had been tricked, a new sensation that he had never experienced before. Not about to knock, Preston exploded inside.

"Pirates! You're all pirates! How could you...?" His voice stumbled over the roaring ocean inside of him.

Captain Cade calmly looked up from his desk. "About time, I was beginning to think yer blind as old Johnny. Rest in peace." He crossed himself in mock reverence.

"I am leaving as soon as we make port," Preston declared, and turned on his heels.

The click of a trigger froze Preston in place.

"Are ya, Mr. Williams? 'Cause this here says somthin' 'bout yer bein' a pirate for four more weeks."

As the horror of this sunk in, Preston eyed the gun's barrel aimed at his head. He didn't move.

With the gun still aimed in one hand, Cade began to shuffle through papers while Preston stood. He was smart enough to know this game. For five whole minuets, Cade sorted and stacked and wrote.

Never letting the gun drop.

*How is his arm not tired yet?*

This was indeed a humbling thing for Preston. Waiting had never been his strong suit. His anger sizzled inside him, but he held his peace. Seeming satisfied, Cade finally looked up.

"I knew old Henry would teach ya well, even if 'e never put ya in yer place. That's why I hired 'im." Cade finally stood and casually walked up to Preston.

Preston's muscles tensed. He scowled and bore holes into Cade with his dark, fierce gaze.

Stepping too close for comfort, Cade chuckled. "You can't intimidate me, boy. I rule this here ship and you should learn to fear me. As agreed, yer to obey me orders, or you'll not be sleepin' in peace." His voice never raised, yet his even threat seemed to hit Preston harder than Henry ever could. "Now the next time you barge through my door and yell at me, I will have you keelhauled. And if you ever don't use 'sir' or 'cap'in' again when speakin' to me, you'll be tied to the main mast for three days." His voice was a whisper. "Ask anyone of me men if I follow through with me threats." Cade swung back to his desk.

"Yer dismissed. Oh, and one more thing. Welcome to piracy Williams!"

Preston cringed and left the cabin.

*A pirate indeed!* His mind churned. *Cade hired Henry to train me? Back at the tavern Cade said he is part of his fleet. No, wait… he said Henry works for him.* Preston hurried the last few steps to the deck. "Mr. Dingy, is this Captain Cade's only ship?" Mr. 'Dingy,' as everyone called him, was the quartermaster. Preston did not know whether or not that was his real name or not, but that's what everyone called him. He wasn't a bad looking man either if he would clean up a bit.

"'Course it is," he responded shortly. His eyes trained on the sea with the wheel in one hand and a compass in the other.

"Oh, thanks." Preston was thoroughly confused now.

"Well, don't just stand there, set course for Virginia! Cap'in's orders! What do ya think we're runnin' here?" Mr. Dingy's evident dislike of Preston had clearly not changed with that of of the other crew members.

Preston set his jaw, biting back a smart remark "Virginia. Right on it, sir."

Nearly a week later, the *Royal Fortune* reached Virginia waters. However, they had to be stealthy in their headings. Although this galleon could take on one or two British ships, the 'Brits' often traveled in fleets.

At first, Preston refused to take any part in helping them, his anger still boiled and the thought of working for these evil men made him sick. But Cade threated not to feed him and after two days without food, not even his anger could keep his boyish stomach from growling. So Preston did his job. He did no more and no less than he did on the *Raven* and he made it clear he would not help them any further.

Even with this reluctance, the captain seemed pleased with Preston's work, for the rough man began to teach Preston the tricks he had learned over the years, such as how to maneuver the huge *Royal Fortune*, and how to get the best out of the crew.

At first, Preston was careful and lacked trust for Cade. Yet the man's knowledge of the sea, his genius methods of maneuvering the ship, and that cunning and sly way of bucking the system, led Preston to respect him in a "you're good at what you do" kind of way.

Throughout the week, Preston learned more than he ever had on the *Raven*. Although he kept his wits about him, he could not help but enjoy his time on the *Royal Fortune*.

When Preston brought word that Virginia was on the dawn, the captain seemed quite pleased. "Excellent timing. Another day it would have been too late, and a day earlier we would have been at much higher chance of running into trouble. Gather the crew on deck, I have orders."

"Yes, sir." Unease settled over Preston, fearing whatever was about to happen. In a few minutes, Preston had every crew member that could be spared gathered and waiting.

"Mr. Dingy, set a course for Cade Cove," the captain ordered

*Cade Cove?*

95

The men around Preston grinned eagerly, almost greedily.

"The ship we're gonna ambush is the *Queen's Merit*, she's carryin' great valuables. As usual, Mr. Dingy and me'll lead a company. Mr. Williams, yer to keep five men on board. Everyone else is boarding that ship. Now... Let's give this English blood a warm welcome!"

*Oh Lord Jesus, help us!*

*Remarkable,* Preston could not help but admit that Cade Cove, as his captain had named it, was an excellent place for ambushing passing ships. This island was just big enough to hide a large ship, but not much else. Its wall-like cliffs sheltered them incredibly. At the entrance, a rock was just high enough for a lookout to have a good view, and yet he could leap into the outgoing ship as it passed by.

Preston's head swarmed with prayers, for the captain to change his mind, for no one to be hurt, and for Jesus to come through the clouds to take him home. He even attempted to talk the captain out of it, though to no avail. The man had only said, "Ah, son, this is when yer shall see how wonderful the life of a pirate is. No rules, no laws, no one to confine you. Don't yer want that lad? Of course yer do! That's what every man wants."

Preston gritted his teeth.

So when the trap was set, and the lookout called, "Sail ho!" he could only dread what was coming and pray that the *Queen's Merit* could outrun the

*Royal Fortune.*

At the first sight of the battleship, Preston's spirit soared. Surely, she could protect herself. The captain, however, did not hesitate. Only then did Preston realize that only one ship would sail away from this.

*Better they live than us.* Preston thought of the innocent on board. The prey was moving as it sat low in the water under much weight, the predator, although close to the same size, would easily catch them. *What if this warship is no longer a warship? She carries no guns!* Preston looked through the spyglass in dismay. Perhaps a few cannons remained on board, but nothing compared to the artillery of the *Royal Fortune.*

As they emerged from the rocks and caught wind, the chase began. Immediately, the *Queen's Merit* saw her attacker, sails were let down to gain speed. A few minutes later, however, it became obvious, they would surrender or be shot down.

As if to make sure her business was clear, the *Royal Fortune* fired warning shots close to the other ship. The other ship did not seem to look back, but rather sailed on. Dread filled Preston as her cannons ceased fire.

Cade wanted to board. The Royal Fortune slid into place next to her victim. Nothing remained for Preston to do but pray. As guns began to fire, Preston vaulted down the stairs, down to the hull where extra supplies were stored. There he knelt. Sweat dripped down his face and dampened his shirt.

Rocking back and forth on his heels, he prayed aloud. Soon he could hear nothing but his own pleading.

# PART TWO

# *Chapter 9*

## The *Queen's Merit*

Cassidy heard the cannon fire. She heard the panic on deck. She felt the ship catch wind. The truth penetrated her brain like a crashing wave.

The *Queen's Merit* was being attacked.

She sat alone in her cabin reading a book. They had been sailing almost eight weeks and were close to their destination. Cassidy's heart raced as she hurried on deck. Climbing the stairs to the helm, she spotted their attacker with a gasp. A huge black galleon was gaining ground behind them with incredible speed. The Jolly Roger and the red flag of no mercy flew over her. Cassidy's knees felt weak and her heart hurt. Fear had occupied much of her life, but this was not like her past, mundane fear. This fear gripped her heart, tensing her muscles and exhausting her mind.

"Lady Cassandra! There is no place for you here. Please, go back to your cabin." Captain Finley said.

His effort to be calm failed to cover his tenseness, and she knew he was right. She glanced down at the dress she wore, and she hurried back to her cabin. She knew as well as the captain did that they were about to be boarded. Cassidy found the gun that her father insisted she bring. After clumsily changing into her comfortable boys' clothes, she strapped the gun to her waist. Finally, she slid a knife into her boot and secured another to her waist – just in case.

*Now what?*

She sat for a moment, attempting to still her racing heart. A forced breath filled her lungs, then she exhaled. *It's okay. We're alright. Alright. Oh dear God, we are all going to die!* She bit down hard on her lip. Maybe it was a nightmare.

She tasted blood. *Darn.*

A boom echoed in the air as a cannon ball dropped into the sea beside them. *Oh God, Oh Father, what do I do?* Her vision blurred. Her head felt light. She steadied herself, pushing on her temples.

As her sight cleared, a plan formulated in her mind. A secret among the Chandler family was that Cassidy had excellent aim. Her eye was sharp, and she had had many practice games with a small gun. Andrew had hated being beaten in their games, yet Cassidy was crowned the reigning champion. Why could she not use the skills she had to protect the ship?

Cassidy stood determined. Every step she took was weak as she shook to her core.

Once on deck, she climbed the rigging, thankful for the practice she'd had. She knew from her days with her brother that she could do more damage without being seen. As high as she dared, Cassidy positioned herself atop the main sail, but still out of sight behind the jig. One, two, three... the minutes ticked by as the imposing pirate ship drew closer.

Calming her racing heart, Cassidy focused. *Lord, spare us. Do not let anyone be hurt. Help the captain to know what to do and how to get us out of here.*

It was a prayer similar to the one her brother in Christ, not so far away, prayed now.

War broke out on deck as the two ships sailed alongside one another. Fearsome-looking pirates swung across to the *Queen's Merit*. They tumbled on deck before leaping to their feet and charging, weapons drawn.

*Deep breath, deep breath.*

Time slowed as she aimed at the rope of one pirate as he swung. She fired. He splashed into the water between the two ships.

Pirates poured on deck. Adrenaline on high, Cassidy fired several more rounds, and the men dropped into the water like flies.

Soon there were no more ropes long enough to swing across, so they lowered a gangplank. The pirates quickly overcame English ship.

Desperation threatened to consume her. As her father had taught her long ago, she turned her attention to the crew in their fight. Repositioning herself, Cassidy found a clear view of the fighting on the main deck, still well hidden from the view of the prowling pirates. Or so she hoped. Firing on one after the other, she brought down several of the crude men.

But Cassidy saw that it was no use. Pirates were overrunning the deck. What could she do? With only a few rounds left, there was no way she could take them all one-by-one. She needed to do something. Her brain spun, her head was light, her chest still throbbed.

"Help, Jesus!" she cried out, louder than she meant to.

Then, to her horror, one of the pirates heard her. He started up the rigging. He hung directly beneath her and she could not get a good view of him to send him back down to the main deck.

Minutes later, she caught sight of him again. He was close. Too close.

Cassidy stuck her gun in her belt and began to climb. She lost sight of him again and stopped at the skysail, huffing from the exertion. She sat for a moment, searching for her pursuer. He grabbed her ankle suddenly, she screamed in terror.

The man laughed cruelly. "Hello, your Highness!"

*They're here for me!* Panic seized her. She fell backwards. The heel of her boot caught the man in the chin with enough force to make him let go of her. Cassidy's hand caught a rope as she fell; she slid down the rope, the deck coming fast.

Pain exploded through her hand and up her arm as the rope took all skin off her hand. She screamed and released the rope, falling the rest of the way to the deck. Cassidy landed on her back. Breath was taken from her as she lay there without feeling or seeing.

All at once she gasped. Excruciating pain shot through her middle and sent her in and out of consciousness. *Don't faint. Don't faint!* Unsure how long she lay there, Cassidy felt someone pick her up, none-too-gently. She moaned in pain, vaguely aware that there was no more gunfire. Blackness finally stole her away.

Perhaps it could be considered unfortunate that consciousness returned not long after it left. She heard what sounded like a cell door being closed and locked. No longer was she in the safety of the *Queen's Merit*.

She pried her eyes open. Cassidy found herself in a dark room, alone. A storeroom, perhaps? It had two barred cells across from one another and separated by an isle. The dark room was wet and smelled of mildew and decay. She hoped it was a decaying rat rather than a human, though the darkness provided no way of knowing.

Cassidy pushed herself to the back of her cell. She trembled, tears clouded her eyes. *Oh Father, I'm alone. Jesus, help me! Please, I can't do this by myself.*

"*Will I ever leave you?*" came a voice in her mind.

Her brother had said those words once. He had taken her into the forest with him. At her skittishness he reminded her, "Will I ever leave you?" The words had given her assurance then. Except now the Lord brought them to forefront of her mind to remind her of His promise.

Several torturous minutes later, the smell of smoke permeated the room. Tears came to Cassidy's eyes as the meaning of the smoke resonated in her brain. Propping herself up against the back of the cell, as painlessly as possible, she prayed fervently for her friends.

The sound of boots brought her out of prayer. Cassidy huddled further back in the cell. She wanted to believe that she could hide there, as if she was a young child again. Oh, what she would give to be at home with her family!

When she finally looked up, she found a man coming toward her cell. His rough appearance made her swallow. He had a prominent and unshaved jaw, no doubt making him look older than he was. A thatch of blond hair fell over his ears and down his forehead, a red handkerchief tied around his head must have held back the strays at one point.

Her eyes found his. His were dark and full of depth, as though they could look into her soul. With a quick intake of breath, she looked away. Heart pounding, she tried to deny the pulsing fear through her body.

Seeming to sense her discomfort, the pirate spoke in polished English. "My apologies, madam." He gave a respectful bow. "I didn't mean to startle you."

She frowned. This was not the voice she

expected to hear from such a gruff man. Apparently, this pirate had mistaken her confusion for misunderstanding. He spoke again, repeating his apology in French. Of course, Cassidy could understand both. She had no idea how this pirate spoke perfect English and even better French. The young man tried again, this time in Spanish.

Although Cassidy was not fluent in Spanish, she recognized the words enough to know he was still trying to apologize. She could not help but find his efforts amusing.

With a natural smile, he assumed she understood, and he rattled off something else, which she did not understand.

She waved her hand to stop him, but the rope burn made her wince. He frowned.

*What should I do?* Cassidy was confused, and in pain, and hardly in a friendly mood. Especially to a pirate. Not to mention that her hands still shook with fright. He said something else before she finally was able to stop him.

"I don't understand Spanish." It came out ruder then she meant.

The man was obviously embarrassed. "Oh, of course, I only thought…"

"I mislead you." Cassidy fought to still her galloping heart. "Where am I?"

"This is the *Royal Fortune*, captained by Mayson Cade. I am Preston Williams. Welcome aboard." His smile was almost charming.

He finally moved his gaze away from her and

eyed the bars between them. "What is that crazy pirate doing now?" he mumbled more to himself than her.

Cassidy slid her eyes back to his face. She studied him briefly. *Who is this man? What is he trying to do?*

"Where are you hurt?" He stepped to the bars. "Never mind. Wait here. I'll go speak to the captain. There has been a misunderstanding."

Confused by this Mr. Williams, concerned for her friends, and in excruciating pain, Cassidy once again slipped from consciousness.

# Chapter 10

The *Royal Fortune*

Heading up the stairs, anger put purpose in his step at he reached the deck, in search for the captain. The thought of the poor girl quaking with fear in that cell make him want to scream. She could be his little sister, probably no older than eighteen. Her thick, curly dark-brown hair was just like Briana's, except this girl had brilliant green eyes. His sister had eyes like his own, dark-brown. It roused his blood to think that these wicked men would take a frightened girl, for who knows what?

As he came up on deck, the sight brought him to a dead halt. What was left of the *Queen's Merit* was in flames.

*No!* Regret and shame swept over him. He had hidden, rather than fought for the lives of the innocent. *Oh Lord Jesus, I am so sorry! I failed. This is my fault! I should have done something, anything, to stop them. Jesus, I...*

"It's quite a sight isn't it, Mr. Williams. Very gratifying," drawled Captain Cade as he came up behind him.

A million responses flooded Preston's mind, any of which would probably have gotten him keelhauled. "Sir, there is a girl in one of our cells. One of the men must have taken her. She is hurt and ought to be given proper treatment."

"Ah, Mr. Williams, you've met the reason we attacked that pretty ship. Tell me, during yer little chat did yer find out who she is?"

Preston clenched his jaw at the captain's sardonic tone. "No, sir." She probably would not have told him her name anyway. Her distrust was only too clear.

"'Er name is Cassandra Chandler, a respected and adored duchess of England."

Preston flinched.

Cade already knew her name. Of course he did. It greatly bothered him how much this man seemed to know about everything. How long had they been planning to attack her? He could not be sure.

Preston pictured her sitting in the corner of the cell in utter terror. Not at all the picture of royalty. Then again, he had noticed her beauty, not something he usually noted – but the sea seemed to do that to a man.

"What do you plan to do to her, Captain?" he said through clenched teeth.

Cade smiled slyly. "Now don't ya go get attached to 'er. We'll be fetchen' a ransom, then lettin' 'er go."

Preston was relieved. "Well then, we should probably hand her back in as good a care as she came, or we'll have the entire British navy on our trail, sir."

"Yer right, Mr. Williams. I'm glad yer lernin' how to do this stuff. 'Tis important to know when yer commandin' a pirate ship. Well, yer probably as qualified as any to tend 'er wounds. Use what you must. Since yer brought it up, she can use yer cabin, or she can stay in that cell, but I don't want to hear another word about it, hear?"

"Aye sir." Preston once again thanked the Lord that he had a cabin. Of course, he would have to stay in the forecastle, but that didn't seem to matter now.

After collecting all the medical supplies they had, which was a sorry amount, Preston made a quick stop at his cabin before heading back down to the cell.

He found her asleep. It took several clearings of the throat for her eyes to flutter open. She tried to sit up, but he saw her jaw tighten with pain.

"Please, don't move," he said gently. "I have supplies to help. May I come in?"

Her eyes widened. "You're a pirate. Why do you care?"

Ah yes, she reminded him of his little sister, honest as the dawn and not afraid to speak her mind. Preston smiled. She was seeing him as he dressed, a pirate, and a dirty pirate at that. "Believe it or not"– he pulled off his handkerchief – "I never intended to be a pirate. I was tricked into signing onto this ship, unaware it was a pirate ship. I'm only a pirate for three more weeks. Then I'm free. Or I hope I'm free. I'm not sure if I must turn

myself in for piracy, just for being on a pirate ship."
Lady Chandler tilted her head in thought. "England does not hang for being on a pirate ship, only for doing what pirates do, though unless you have proof you did not steal or kill you will be on the run for the rest of your life."

Preston shook his head and sighed. "I'll not run from justice. Now, may I come in? I'll fetch a third party if that makes you more comfortable." Not that he had anyone decent to fetch.

She hesitated, but finally she nodded slowly. "Alright."

Weary of her hesitation and fear, Preston moved as carefully as possible. He was determined to earn her trust. After unlocking the cell door, Preston made sure to leave it wide open. "There is a cabin prepared for you upstairs. Though I would rather make you comfortable before we walk up the stairs." He knew he could carry her without trouble, though he also knew better than to offer. This woman was of high standing and no doubt highly protected. Risking making her feel violated was unwise for both their sakes.

She nodded again, this time with a tiny smile. "Thank you, Mr. Williams."

"Preston, please, madam. And the captain wants you in one piece when the ransom comes." He offered a friendly smile as he knelt down and sorted through the supplies for a poultice. He considered using her name, but then decided that if she wanted him to know, she would tell him herself.

"I'm Cassandra Chandler." She slowly extended her hand to him for him to bandage.

Surprised, he took it gently. He heard a quick intake of breath as she did her best not to cry out when he had to pry her hand flat.

Involuntary pain tingled through him as he worked, he knew the pain of rope burns. "I'm sorry. I know that isn't pleasant." This reminded him too much of the time he poulticed Briana's leg when she had fallen on a stone. She had been so brave for him.

Lady Chandler bit her lip. "It could be worse." He looked into her face, hoping she would look back. Instead, she seemed to look toward the pile of supplies. "Unfortunately, I don't think anything in that pile will help my back."

Preston could tell that it hurt every time breath filled her lungs. She could have broken a few ribs. But she was right – there was nothing he could do.

As he tended her hand, she seemed to relax more and more. He guessed that the fight to stay so guarded was finally too much to handle.

*Poor girl.* He studied her a bit, as she was preoccupied. She was even prettier up close. She had high set cheekbones that gave her a royal look. Her huge green eyes were stunning. Pieces of dark hair fell out of her braid in disarray, plastered to her neck and face by the dampness. By the way the dark hair fell, he guessed it was naturally wavy, or maybe curly.

Preston tried not to stare. He wondered what

Briana would have looked like at this age. Would she have been this beautiful? Preston's heart hurt at the thought of his long-dead sister.

Soon, Lady Chandler had a bandage on her right hand, and she allowed Preston to help her up. Her jaw locked in a grimace. At the door of the cell, she stopped, and Preston worried she could not continue. He watched as she seemed to debate with herself.

Finally, she asked, "I must know, Preston, what became of the *Queen's Merit?*" She chanced a quick look at him and then turned her head away.

Preston frowned. "I'm sorry. Captain Cade lit her on fire and left her. He didn't even stop for a few of his wounded men who could not get off the ship."

She gave a slight nod and turned back toward the stairs.

He let her think for a moment, then attempted a change in conversation. "Where do you call home?"

Lady Chandler hesitated. Preston wanted to kick himself for such an intrusive question.

"You don't have to answer that. It was rather prying of me to ask."

She looked at him. He focused on the steps ahead so that she could look at him, and maybe see he would not harm her. "I live in London. In the countryside."

"I've never been to London."

Lady Chandler glanced at him again. "Where are

you from?"

Preston was both delighted and surprised she would ask. He told her about his home with the Cagneys, his time on the *Raven*, and his ending up on the *Royal Fortune*. Although Preston had better manners than to do all the talking, he saw the pain in her eyes when she spoke. Besides, she was clearly quite content listening, and he was happy to talk. Preston used every opportunity to make her smile, something that brought him much joy. By the time the story was finished, he could feel her begin to relax with him.

Once the lady was comfortable in his room, Preston knew he must take his leave. He had refused to go any further into his cabin, her cabin, than the tiny dining table, and he had also left the door open. Still, it would not look well to stay past his time of business.

"I would like to leave you the key." He laid it on the table. He watched her eyes trace a line from the key to his face.

"But?" she prompted, tilting her head at him. Her eyes twinkled in amusement, making Preston smile in spite of himself.

"But I hate to make you get up when I bring your supper."

She thought for a moment, her head still tilted adorably. "Yes, I don't feel like getting up now that I'm finally here. Keep the key, I... I trust you."

S. E. JANE

Throughout his next watch, Preston could not keep his mind from wandering to the girl in his cabin. Something about her intrigued him, and a few minutes with her did not satisfy his curiosity. Preston badly wanted to know her better, but he knew that his first mission should be to get her home. *Focus, Preston. You haven't time to make friends. Besides, you just hid in the closet while she struggled for her life. She deserves your utmost help. It's practically your fault she's here anyway.* This served to put his mind in place, but his heart still tugged in an unfamiliar way.

The supper bell rang for Preston's crew's break and they all filed through the galley and into the dining room. Almost always last in line due to his climb down the mast or settling things at the helm, Preston asked the cook for Lady Chandler's meal.

"The prisoner? Ah yes, I got it right here." He turned on his peg leg and limped to the other side of the galley. He pulled out a plate and gave it to Preston.

It looked disgusting. What might have been some sort of soup and perhaps a piece of hard bread were slapped onto the plate without care. Perhaps this was prisoner food, but this was not what Lady Chandler would eat.

"There's been a mistake. The captain has put me in charge of her, and I plan to have her in good shape when she is returned. I'm sure the captain would appreciate something more substantial."

The old man looked at Preston in boredom. "Sorry Mr. Williams, but that there is what I made for 'er. If she don't wanna eat it, then she don't have to eat, 'cause that's all she's gettin' from me."

The cook was the most stubborn man Preston had ever dealt with. Even Captain Cade seemed to have given up on the old sailor.

Preston bit back his frustration. He knew arguing would go nowhere, and he was not about to bother the captain with it. "Very well, may I have my plate as well?"

"Aye." He handed Preston another plate with much more appealing food. It was even warm, fresh from the cook stove, a rare thing since most of the plates had already sat out long enough to cool before the men got to them.

Preston slipped out the dining room and into the hall. He stopped, contemplating. He was sorely tempted by the warm food in his right hand. It was much more appealing than the food in his left.

Finally, he sighed and shook away the debate in his head. Starting down the hall, Preston sat aside the plate of unappetizing food.

Arriving at his cabin door, he knocked. "Lady Chandler? It's Preston. I have your supper."

"Come in," said a light voice inside. Smiling, Preston unlocked the door and stepped into the cabin. Instantly, he knew he had made the right decision. Lady Chandler sat in the reading chair in the corner. She still looked weak, though much better than she had that morning. She seemed to have washed her face and brushed out her hair. Her dark locks now fell in lush, dark ringlets around her shoulders and down to her elbows. Her emerald eyes were bright and clear. Preston then realized that she had found his Bible.

His heart paused.

"Do you know who this belongs to?" she asked.

A wide grin spread across his face, even though she avoided his eyes. Oh well, he would settle for her ease of mind for now.

"That's mine, though you are welcome to it anytime," he replied, then chuckled. "And my book of navigation for that matter. Though it is not as valuable." The only other book he owned besides his Bible sat on the little stool next to her.

Lady Chandler smiled. He felt warm. "Thank you, and thank you for graciously lending me your cabin."

At that moment, Preston realized the appearance of the situation. His face felt hot and he stammered, "I... I'm sorry, I should have told you before bringing you here so that you may have the option. I couldn't have slept knowing a lady was spending the night in a dingy cell when I could be just as comfortable in a hammock." Worried he had destroyed any trust she might have developed, he went on. "I do hope that –"

"Preston," she interrupted gently. "I trust you. I told you that I trust you. Thank you very much for your generosity. I will indeed sleep better tonight, and I shall pray you do too."

Relief flooded Preston's mind. She really trusted him! This did not sound like the frightened girl he had found hours ago. She was calm and dignified, while still humble and gentle. He gave a slight bow. "Thank you, Lady Chandler."

"Cassidy," she whispered. "Please call me Cassidy. My brother gave me it as a nickname. It only seems right for you to use it likewise."

Preston thought he might fly. "Cassidy." He could not help but like the feeling of her name on his lips, not only her name, but her nickname.

He set the warm food on the table. "I'll be back with breakfast in the morning." Offering one last smile, he backed out of the room.

# Chapter 11

The *Royal Fortune*

Cassidy awoke in a comfortable bed and almost forgot where she was. Looking around, yesterday's events came flooding back. The peaceful morning on the *Queen's Merit*, the horrific battle with pirates, the pain of falling from the main mast, being kidnapped, the loss of her friends, and meeting Preston Williams.

It was a lot for one day, Cassidy slept well despite her broken ribs and very bruised back. Now that she had found a way to minimize her pain in order to move around, she managed to wash her face and clothes the best she could and attempted to finger-brush her very tangled hair. Usually she would have done a braid, but, as she found yesterday, a braid was uncomfortable resting on her bruises. So she left her hair free, even though she knew she looked like a lion.

Gingerly, she sat down at the desk with Preston's Bible and rested her head in her hands. How odd to be rescued from danger, yet still kidnapped by pirates. She was not here by her own choice, but then, she would rather be here than at the bottom of the sea. Tomorrow morning, the *Queen's Merit* was set to dock in Virginia, and Cassidy had many times envisioned her aunt greeting her with open arms. Now, Cassidy wondered if she, like the *Queen's Merit*, would not reach her determined destination.

*The actions of these pirates are strange to me. If they were after valuables and money, why would they sink such a grand ship as the* Queen's Merit *when they could get quite a profit selling her? Would it not be worthwhile to keep the fine ship and sell her later? Why would only I be kidnapped for a ransom, unless they already knew who I am? Is it possible they discovered that a duchess, a relative to the queen, was traveling to America? They would have had to dig deep for that information. Even for a large ransom, this seems rather extravagant. No, I must meet this Mayson Cade and find out if there is more to his plan. Ask him why I know the name of his ship but not of him. Oh, if only I could remember where I heard of the* Royal Fortune.

With a sigh, Cassidy relaxed back into the desk chair. She was tempted to share her suspicions with Preston, yet a part of her still thought of him as a pirate. She shook her head. What had she just told him the night before?

*"Preston, I trust you. I told you I trust you."*

*But why?*

Deep inside her was a sureness that Preston was, in fact, worthy of trust.

She remembered his gentleness and sacrifice for her. The look on his face when she asked if it was his cabin she stayed in. *If I hadn't asked, he was never going to tell me.* No matter what situation she was in, God always provided. Now, He had provided a friend. Certainly, this showed His unfailing, never-ending, unrivaled, perfect love. *Thank you, Oh Lord, for this new friend to help me through another time of trouble.* A knock brought her back to the present, though the smile lingered.

"Cassidy, it's Preston, with breakfast."

Rising stiffly, she went to unlock the door for him. They had decided at supper the day before that Cassidy was well enough to move around. So, Preston had left her the key to the room. Her mind had come to block out the constant stab of pain she felt. There were moments when the pain became almost unbearable, like a knife twisting behind her bruised lungs. This very thing happened when she stepped back, opening the door.

"Good morning," she said. In the next instant, whatever motion she made brought all pain reeling through her body. Stifling a cry, she let out some sort of squeak as she faded from consciousness.

Falling, perhaps, as the light flickered before her eyes. Somewhere far off there was a crash. Then a strong arm lifted her into the air like a light bird. When she was gently lain on her bed, she managed to open her eyes. A moan escaped her lips. Cassidy found she was staring into concerned chocolate eyes.

"Cassidy? Cassidy, are you alright?" Preston bent over her. When she tried to move, he put a hand on her shoulder. He was gentle, though his hand was strong and calloused from work. "Don't move. You need not be moving so much yet. I wish there was a doctor on board. We must get you real medical attention."

"It's fine. I'm alright," Cassidy whispered. The pain slowly began to subside.

Preston looked skeptical. His face made her want to laugh. Instead, she managed a weak smile. He grinned back. "What are you smiling about?"

Cassidy shook her head slightly, as a giggle rose in her throat. "You just seem to have that effect on people."

Preston's face turned serious for a moment, and Cassidy wondered what bothered him. As though nothing had happened, he left her side and strode across the room to the door and picked up something off the floor. A biscuit, in fact, and an old plate that had miraculously not broken. He wiped the biscuit off and put it back on the plate. "Well, it's been on the floor but it's better than…" His voice trailed off.

Curious, Cassidy asked, "Better than what?"

"Nothing. Better than nothing." He finished in a way that made Cassidy question whether he had something more specific in mind. Instead, she simply nodded. He sat the plate on her nightstand and Cassidy thanked him.

"I suppose you can have the key back." She fished in her pants pocket, relishing having pockets in the first place. "I must have dropped it." Cassidy said when her hand came out empty.

"I see it." Preston crawled on his hands and knees under the table.

Cassidy watched, amused. Although he had broad shoulders from strong work, he still had the lanky frame of a boy. After bumping his head twice, he scrambled out and held up the key victoriously. "I'm not sure how it got under there."

"How old are you, Mr. Williams?" Cassidy asked, trying not to laugh.

"Twenty. And how old are you, Lady Chandler?"

"Well, that depends on the day. It is September seventeenth, correct?"

Preston counted on his fingers boyishly. "Why yes. Yes it is."

"Then I'm eighteen, as of last week."

Preston seemed thoroughly delighted. He straightened his shirt in mock importance. "Well, as your elder, I ask that you get some rest. I should be back with dinner."

Throughout the morning, Cassidy read when her head allowed and spent time in thought. She was finding the navigational book interesting and had a few questions for Preston. He was long in coming, though, and as the hours passed, Cassidy became bored. Unable to move much or sing, she found nothing to do. Cassidy played with her bandaged hand; surely there was something she could do. If she did not have this rope burn she could sew. Then again, if it were looser around her fingers she could move them enough to hold a needle.

Stretching the tight bandaging, she was able to gain motion for her pointer finger and thumb. When Preston brought the next meal, she could ask for a needle, thread, and some clothes to patch. As a duchess, she had never needed to sew. The maids were all very handy with a needle. All she needed to do was say the word and the hole in her stocking would be darned to perfection within the hour, but her parents made sure that their children were not handicapped by their wealth.

Both children could do anything the common man and woman could, as well as everything the royals could. Although Andrew was sent to the academy for privileged boys, they both were raised knowing hard work and the life of the people they served. Born in them was the love to learn and work. Andrew was natural with people. He talked easily to anyone from the poor to the wealthy. Because of this, Andrew became one of the most respected and able captains at sea.

Cassidy smiled as thoughts of her brother floated through her mind. They had always been close; the two of them had learned to dance together and to put up with the endless mannerisms they each had to commit to memory. He would teach her to use a sword and she helped him to perfect his aim. Despite the four-year age gap, the young Chandlers were best of friends. Andrew stood up for her and protected her, no matter the consequences.

This led her to thoughts of Preston, the young man who was protecting her from the pirates. *Oh, how much they would like one another!* She could picture the two of them locked in a dual like old friends. One with dark brown hair and green eyes, much like herself, and the other with wavy blonde hair and deep brown eyes.

Cassidy sighed at this thought. The first time she had looked into those gentle eyes, something stirred in her, and a fear knotted in her stomach. *What is it about him? He doesn't mean to harm me... It's just... Why am I so afraid, God? What is it about him?* Cassidy put her head in her hands. His eyes were so honest, so genuine, so gentle. *So real.*

The sound of a bell startled Cassidy. Preston would likely be at her door in ten minutes. She leaned back and waited, forcing all of her unsettling thoughts to the back of her mind. Sure enough, ten minutes later a knock came from the door.

"My Lady, it's Preston with dinner." She could hear the smile in his voice.

"Come in."

Preston opened the door, exhibiting the same pirate look he had when they first met. He must have noticed her eyes linger on his handkerchief, for he quickly slipped it off his head in embarrassment.

"Sorry, I forgot to take it off before coming in."

"No, no. I like your pirate look." She realized the truth in that statement.

He smiled and pulled it back on his head. Changing the subject, he brought over her plate. "How are you feeling? I wanted to change the bandage on your hand but we are out of supplies. A lot of the crew have gunshot wounds."

Cassidy raised her eyebrows, wondering if any of it was her damage. She suddenly felt shameful about hurting anyone. She recounted those she shot at. Ten at least. Not to mention those she dropped into the water.

Preston looked up from setting the tray at her bedside. "What is it?"

"I hope it's nothing serious," she said quietly.

"Nah, they should all live." She could feel him studying her. Her cheeks grew warm.

Preston quickly dropped his gaze and changed the topic like a gentleman.

"I talked with Captain earlier. Apparently, he sent the ransom demand back at Barbados. We are headed to the meeting place now. I'm not sure where that is, but I shall inform you when we've arrived and the ship is sighted. It will probably be another week or so."

*The ransom has already been sent?* "How long do you think he has been planning this?"

Preston must have already thought about that. "Well, he was planning to recruit me for at least a month before he actually tricked me into working for him. There's no telling how long this has been planned. Or how he knew that you were sailing."

Cassidy thought this over. *A funny thing to do so much and then not even come to look at your prize. He obviously has no interest in me. Surely he has more in mind. Unless he's just that idiotic.*

Preston must have thought the same thing. "It's strange. Captain Cade is very savvy and very sharp. But who knows what he is capable of?" Suddenly, a sorry expression came over his face. "My apologies, I should not be troubling you with such thoughts."

Coming from most people, she would not have liked being treated as feeble-minded, but compassion for her friend outweighed any offense. "Don't fret, Preston. Believe me, I have seen and heard of much evil in this world. This does not scare me. The Lord holds me fast, as I hold Him." Preston's eyes rose to hers but she moved away quickly.

"Indeed." She could feel him watching her. "Do you remember me telling you about the hurricane we got caught in?"

"Yes."

"Well, our ship passed right through the center of that storm. Yet in the center, even with all the clouds swirling around us, we were safe. We were in a column of light, where it was peaceful. We could hear the thunder and watch the lightning, but we were relieved of the heavy weight that goes with the storm." He paused in thought. "It seems to me that when one is in the eye of a storm, God relieves them of all their burdens and keeps them in the light."

# Chapter 12

The *Royal Fortune*

Shifting his weight, Preston knocked on the captain's door and waited with as much patience as he could muster. His head swarmed with questions for which he wanted answers, and he did not plan to leave without them. He simply needed to get them in a calm and well-mannered fashion, or he knew he would not get them at all.

"Come in."

Preston did not hesitate. Opening the door wide, he stepped inside the cabin. "Sir, I was hoping we could talk about the plan for Lady Chandler."

Captain Cade did not even look up from his log. "Ah Mr. Williams, yer a curious lad."

When he offered no further information, Preston shifted his weight from one foot to another. "When are we meeting the ransom ship, Captain?"

"Oh, I'm expectin' we'll be comin' to the meetin' spot by the end of the week, though we've to make one stop along the way," Cade murmured and continued scribbling. Preston didn't know that pirates kept such intricate logs.

"Where're we headed, sir? Tonight is a good night for a lunar. I haven't checked our latitude in a while."

"I'm confident I know where we be. As for where we're headed, it's an island that shouldn't be far from 'ere. Then we're off to meet the ransom ship between Barbados and Kingston. It's all working out very well indeed." Cade rubbed his temples and said, barely audible, "So far."

"Have you any more to your plan, Captain?" Preston asked.

Cade looked up then with sharp gray eyes. "Aye. You, however, Mr. Williams, are on a need-to-know basis. I suggest you keep further question to yerself before harm befalls you. Or someone else."

A muscle in Preston's jaw jerked and his stomach felt uneasy. *What if I end up being the reason harm comes to Cassidy?* The idea hit him like a hurricane. His ribs felt like they closed around his lungs. *Oh Lord Jesus!* He cried inside, hoping to steady his rolling mind.

"Well?"

"Yes, Captain. Of course."

"Good. Yer dismissed."

Five days later, Preston was on watch with his half of the crew when the lookout called "Land ho!" Preston grabbed a spy glass and hurried to the railing.

Not more than a dozen acres, a typical Caribbean island with white beaches and a thick forest loomed several miles to their port. It looked rather peaceful, especially to Preston's unsettled mind. Although it might be a pleasant sight, Preston could tell that it would not be a good place to stay long. No coconuts were on the trees this time of year, and water would certainly be scarce. Not even a bird would take refuge there long.

Beckoned by the lookout's call, Captain Cade marched up on deck. He took out his spy glass and studied the island.

"Good timing," Preston heard him mutter. The captain raised his voice with orders. "Get us within swimmin' range then lower the anchor!"

There were a series of "Aye ayes." Preston furrowed his brow. What an odd request. *Swimming range? Oh mercy...*

"Mr. Williams! Take me to see the Lady Chandler. It's 'bout time I meet our guest," Cade bellowed.

*No, Jesus, please!* He looked around desperately. *No!* Not again would he allow harm come to someone he vowed to protect. Not now or ever.

"But sir..."

"Take me to 'er, boy!" the captain thundered back.

Jaw locked, Preston lead the way down the hall, followed by Cade and two of his men. His brain spun. Was there no way out of this? Could he take her place?

When they came to the duchess' door, Preston knew she must have heard them by all the noise they made, but he knocked extra formally, just in case.

"Lady Chandler, it's Preston Williams and Captain Mayson Cade," Preston called, shifting nervously.

"Oh just get on with it. We ain't tha polished Brit nobility," one of the men grumbled. Preston waited to see if Cade would respond. Instead the man waited in silence, his face unreadable.

"Well mind you that she *is* part of the English nobility, so you *will* be a gentleman in her presence," Preston told the man sharply, having switched into his commanding tone.

"Aye, sir, sorry," the man replied to his commander.

"Merci, mon ami. Entrez," came Cassidy's voice from the room. Preston held back a smile. Yes, he was rather fond of her.

"What did she say?" the other crewman demanded as Preston unlocked the door.

Preston did not respond. He opened the door and held it back for the captain as he worked to rein in his wild heart. Adrenaline pulsed through his blood, and his hand itched instinctively to go to his hip where a sword would usually hang. Calling on Jesus, he calmed himself silently.

Cassidy stood, her hand resting softly on the back of a chair. Her hair was worked into a braid that hung down her shoulder. Uncontrollable curls fell out of her braid and framed her face. Her bright green eyes were alert, but Preston caught her hand quivering as she slid it into her pocket.

Preston took his place off to the side but close enough as not to be forgotten. He watched as the captain approached her. One more step and he would have been too close.

Captain Cade bowed his head to her sardonically. "Lady Chandler, Captain Mayson Cade at yer service. If I had known yer were so lovely, I might have stopped by for an earlier visit."

Preston's jaw clenched, every muscle in his body tense. Now more than ever he wished for his sword or pistol.

"Captain Cade, for what dreadful reason do I owe this inconvenience for you?" she matched Cade's tone.

Cade scowled. Preston stifled a grin. "Let's understand one another a little more. Yer always to address me with 'sir,' or cap'in."

"Very well, Cap'in." Her thick English accent was only more evident in her attempt to imitate him. "If you would address me with 'lady.'"

"How dare you talk back to me?" In one quick movement, Cade backhanded her across the cheek.

Preston lunged at Cade, but in the next moment Cade's men were on top of him, wrestling him back from their captain. With arms pinned behind him, Preston fought the men until one delivered a sharp knee to his gut. Doubled over, Preston let out a short gasp as the blow stole his breath. His hair hung in his eyes. He chanced a look up at Cassidy.

Her eyes were wide as she looked at him, her cheek glowing from the abuse. Preston could feel her fear as she turned back to Cade. He strained against his captors. *Jesus!*

"Why Mr. Williams, I expected some resistance from you. But not somethin' so idiotic." Cade mocked. "You ought to be keelhauled."

He turned back to Cassidy and raised an eyebrow at her as she looked back at him in fear. Cade glanced back to Preston.

"Take note, Mr. Williams. This fine young woman fears me after only one punishment. You, however, seem less inclined." Cade sighed for effect. "If only I could teach you through yer own pain, but clearly yer not that kind of man." Cade watched in glee as the young man's eyes widened in fear. In the next moment, Cade delivered a powerful blow to Cassidy's opposite cheek, sending her shrinking to the ground.

Preston's chest heaved. "Enough, Captain! Can you not see she is already injured?" It was all he was able to say before another blow to the gut sent him to his knees.

Cade watched his captive on the floor, her head hung. She did not even attempt to stand. Bending down to her, Cade lifted her chin. "Sorry, little pawn, yer but a piece of a much bigger game and my need for you is complete." Cade rose abruptly and spun toward the door. "Bring 'em both!"

Opposite Cade, Preston could see Cassidy's strained face. His heart ripped to see her so. Every ounce of him wanted to comfort her.

On the trek up the stairs, Cassidy chanced a worried look back at Preston. He forced himself to be strong, praying harder every moment. He mouthed the words "Are you okay?"

She nodded with a failed smile. Glancing at Cade, Cassidy clearly wanted to say something, but decided against it, which Preston thought wise.

When they all reached the main deck, much of the crew had gathered with greedy smiles, apparently well aware of the next step in this terrible game. Some gave Preston concerned looks, seeing him restrained, but said nothing.

"My lady," Cade mocked. "How good are ya at swimmin'?"

Preston saw her swallow as she caught sight of the island. "Good enough."

"Swell." Cade motioned to the men, who shoved her roughly toward an outreaching plank. "Please demonstrate, or die. Because it is of no matter to me. I be simply doin' this as a courtesy."

Preston fought control of his anger. "Captain, do you think that's a good idea? We meet the ransom tomorrow. They would never give you the money without her. There's no point to this!"

"You know nothing, Williams!" Cade snapped.

Desperate, Preston tried again. "Won't you at least allow me to go with her? If she does not survive, you'll have the entire British navy on your back."

Cade snorted. "They're already comin,' boy. This'll just keep 'em busy and there is no way yer goin' with 'er."

"My brother'll find me." Cassidy tugged against her captors.

"I highly doubt that," Cade countered. The man gave Cassidy one last push and she stumbled onto the extended plank.

Regaining her balance, Cassidy turned back to him. "What do you mean?" Her voice was high pitched and filled with fear.

*This isn't fair, Lord! Save her! She doesn't deserve this! Expose Cade's plan, please! Jesus, please, what do I do?* He felt so helpless.

"Go, before I decide to kill you instead!" Cade said.

Preston watched as Cassidy's jaw locked. She looked close to tears. Her curls stuck to her cheek in the humid air, and the bruising on her face had begun to show.

In one brief moment he caught her gaze. Those green eyes collided with his own and looked right into his soul.

Cassidy quickly moved her eyes away, though Preston willed her to look up once more. Instead, Cassidy turned back to Cade.

"If you hurt my brother –" she managed before Cade kicked the board, making it wobble unsteadily, and sent Cassidy into the sea with a cry.

Preston fought his way over to the edge. He saw her come up as she easily stroked through the waves. She was indeed a strong swimmer.

Preston was suddenly yanked away from the edge.

"What 'bout Williams?" Mr. Dingy, the quartermaster, held onto him by the collar. Preston knew that this man would feel no pity at whatever his punishment might be. After two weeks he still did not like Preston, heir to his coveted position as quartermaster.

Preston did not give him the satisfaction of a glance. He looked straight ahead, praying for help.

"'E knows the rules! A day at the mast!" Cade bellowed.

Preston was shoved hard toward the main mast. Back against the wood, Preston allowed his hands to be drug above his head and tied there. In this awkward position, he had to be patient. Preston shifted in attempt to get himself where he could lean against the mast without pulling on his arms, which he knew he would not be able to feel in an hour. Thankfully, his securer did not notice his shift and tied his hands as he was.

Slowly, the sun moved across the sky as the minutes rolled into hours. Most of the crew ignored him, a few gave him pitied looks, and some mocked him.

"Williams, wha'd ya pull on da Capin' to make 'im tie ya up here? Must have been somethin' real bad to get that perfect one in trouble," one taunted.

Preston forced down his rising temper and only hung his head, thinking of how Jesus felt being mocked. He shuddered.

This was bad enough, but to be flogged and hung on a cross with nails through your hands and feet? Preston could hardly bear the thought.

Strong emotion swept over him. Nothing had gone as planned. He wondered if that's how Jesus felt. *No, that was planned for.* Then it hit him. *This was also planned for.*

As his mind went over that scene at the cross when his Savior and King, had hung like a criminal, Preston felt the weight of his Lord's burden. The burden that had been his to bear.

His mind continued to race, unchecked. It was *his* fault that Cassidy got hurt, as it had been with Briana. Everything seemed to be his fault. Depressed, hurt, helpless, and feeling very guilty, Preston barely noticed a tear running down his cheek.

A shadow passed in front of Preston's face. "Yer cryin,' Williams?"

Flushed, Preston lost any control that he had left. Preston balanced himself back on the main mast and clenched his fists. With a sudden swiftness none saw coming, Preston pulled himself up and delivered two boots into the abdomen of the taunting crewman. The man sprawled on the deck gasping for breath, for Preston had not spared much effort.

A man in his fifties under Preston's shift came up next to him. "That rascal Jones finally got what 'e deserved!"

Preston did not even glance in the man's direction. His heart screamed at him, his muscles tense and breathing labored. How could he do that? What was he thinking? That was it. He wasn't thinking.

Cade stomped down from the quarterdeck, having seen everything. *I've really done it now. I'll be lucky if I don't get flogged, or worse.* Something tingled down Preston's arms and through his body at the thought of Cade's prior threat to keelhaul him. *Oh Lord, I am so sorry! Punish me at Your will, but please, is death not a little rash?*

# Chapter 13

## An Island in the Caribbean

Exhausted, Cassidy finally dragged her tired body on shore. The salt burned the tender flesh on her hand and her bruised back was sore from the effort, but she was alive, and away from the pirates.

Sitting up, she looked back out to sea. The grand *Royal Fortune* was sailing away in all her ominous glory.

She pushed herself up and shook herself off the best she could. Her hair clung to her face and neck in a matted, salty mess. Her shirt and breeches stuck to her and were covered in sand. She chuckled to herself. She was a disaster. *Perhaps it was best that Cade didn't let Preston come after all.* Not that it really mattered to her. Still, she would not mind the company. Cassidy scanned the horizon, just in case.

"First things first, let's get a fire going," Cassidy took a deep breath. She swallowed and headed into the little jungle for firewood. After some exploring, tugging, and breaking attempts, she realized that without any sort of blade she could not get anything to keep a fire going. Frowning, Cassidy wandered along the edge of the trees looking for fallen branches. It would be getting dark in a few hours and she needed a fire and shelter, *and maybe some water?* Her mouth was dry; maybe there were coconuts somewhere that she could crack open.

Scanning the high branches for the nut-like seed, she tripped and fell with an "umph." Cassidy could imagine her brother laughing at her and saying "careful, your *grace.*" Pushing herself up again, she chuckled when she saw what she had fallen over. A piece of driftwood.

"Take that, Andrew!" He would have really laughed at that one.

She gathered the wood into her arms and walked a little further. Another piece of driftwood lay stranded on the beach. And another. It wasn't long before she had all she could carry, which was not very much.

Immensely glad Andrew had taught her how to start a fire, Cassidy was able to get a welcome warm flame with minimal struggle. With the fire going at the forest's edge, Cassidy set up camp. She gathered soft fallen leaves and moss to make a bed on the squishy sand.

"It'll be even better than a real bed," she told herself with more hope than confidence.

The blue sky had already melted into dazzling pinks, oranges, yellows, and purples. The young duchess had never seen a Caribbean sunset, and she stared in awe and wonder at its brilliance. God seemed to be making a masterpiece, right there in front of her. The grandeur and beauty of it could not be comprehended. She felt so small, so insignificant.

"Oh Lord, thank you for reminding me 'I am but a handbreadth.'"

Her stomach rumbled. She scanned the trees once again for any sign of a coconut. Her eyes caught on an unusual tree with yellow, crescent-shaped objects growing on it. The tree had three large bushels of the stuff. One was rather green but the other two were bright yellow. She hurried to where the pods, or whatever they were, hung just out of her reach. Jumping did not give her enough vertical, but perhaps she could climb the trunk like she had the rigging.

This proved to be much more difficult than climbing the rigging.

Shimmying up the tree, Cassidy scraped herself in more than one place. Finally, by reaching as far as she could, Cassidy latched onto the stem of one of the yellow bushels. Cassidy pulled, but the bushel refused to come loose from its tree. Pulling, wiggling, twisting, nothing happened except that she slid further down the tree. In one last effort, Cassidy grabbed one of the yellow fruits and pulled. With a snap, the yellow fruit let go of the bushel.

Taking it back to her little camp, Cassidy found a somewhat sharp piece of shell on the ground and filed away at the skin. What was under the tough skin, she couldn't tell, but it was rather squishy. After a lot of sawing and a bit of hacking, Cassidy was finally able to peel back the outside and discover… mush. It certainly didn't look appealing. She must have mashed it into soup. Pulling back the skin further she found a soft, white inside that smelled delectable. Could she eat it? It could be poisonous. But what choice did she have? Starve, or eat it. She might as well try.

Cassidy took a bite of the white part. It tasted… well, not bad. Not like anything else she had ever tasted. Cassidy ate all of it, even the mushy soup. The sun was gone now and the moon was bright and almost full. The stars, thousands of tiny lights, danced a worshipful, choreographed routine.

*Breathtaking.*

The wind rustled the trees. Shadows hunted from behind trees and beneath leaves. Cassidy hugged herself tighter. She closed her eyes tightly, wishing Andrew was there.

Or Preston.

Cassidy stifled a smile. For whatever reason, Preston's presence reminded her of her brother. It brought a safe, comfortable feeling. Usually, she would have bristled at anyone trying to protect her. She would have said he was overstepping and that she could take care of herself. But Preston was different. Perhaps because he did not just assume the role of protector, but took it on sensitively, even when it was by no means convenient for him.

A question sprung to her mind: *Why would he protect me like that?*

Why should he be so devoted to her? She had never done anything for him. *It's because he's a good man,* she decided.

She sighed. Now Preston was facing the consequences for attempting to protect her. It was her fault that he was in trouble. All she had done aboard the *Royal Fortune* was cause him hardship.

Her eyes brimmed with tears at the thought. Was she a burden? How much she valued his friendship! But it would have been better for him if they had never met.

Never mind, it didn't matter. Cassidy would never see him again. She would never see any of her family again. They would never know what happened to her. Andrew would search. Could he find her before she died? *Oh, if only!* Tears slid down her face. *My Lord Father, comfort them. Soften their pain, please. And… if possible…please do not have me suffer.*

Praying fervently, Cassidy finally drifted off to sleep.

Cassidy awoke with a start. *Where am I?*

Her mind first thought she was in her bed back in London, then her bed on the *Queen's Merit*, then her bed on the *Royal Fortune.* Slowly, memory of the previous day came flooding back to her.

She looked around her little island. The hot sun, not fully risen, had already chased away the night chill and the ocean was at low tide. Stretching, Cassidy's tongue felt dry and stuck to the roof of her mouth; she had to find water and soon. *Lord Jesus, please, bring me water. You gave me a fire. You gave me food. Jesus, please sustain me.* She licked her lips and looked out to sea. This was completely in God's hands, and He could allow her to die out here. An overwhelming sense of helplessness came over her as she realized the truth. With a sigh, Cassidy bowed her head.

"Jesus," she murmured. "You have already rescued my soul. You are already my Savior. Whether You rescue my body now is up to you. Even if You don't, O'Lord, I put my trust in You." With that, Cassidy rose to her feet. Her body was sore and stiff, but it worked.

Without water, she knew that she had about forty-eight hours, and she wanted to spend it thanking or praising Jesus. So, Cassidy sang her favorite Psalms as she walked down the beach to collect driftwood.

The waves lapped at the island and the clouds floated by in an array of shapes and sizes. By noon, Cassidy had collected enough wood, gathered a large collection of the yellow fruits, and licked all remaining dew off what seemed to be every leaf on the island. After everything was situated for the day, Cassidy washed off in the ocean, letting the cool water flow over her hot skin, which was now a vivid shade of pink. Ringing her clothes out, Cassidy pulled her tired body under the shade of a palm tree. She leaned back and closed her eyes. The Caribbean sun seemed to extract her energy as quickly as if she had been fighting the great ocean currents.

*If someone does find me, would I go back to England? Or carry on to Virginia? I would first have to send my parents a telegram. Then I suppose I've come all this way; why not spend at least a few weeks with Aunt Emma?* Cassidy's bonfire was more like a campfire, and the trail of smoke in the sky was a sad representation of a signal. As she imagined her rescue, Cassidy's thoughts came to rest on her brother and Cade's words about him. *Oh dear Jesus, keep Andrew safe. Keep him far away from those pirates.* Her thoughts then turned to Preston, still in terrible danger of Cade's menace. *Father please, keep him safe too. Rescue him from such a terrible situation.* Cassidy paused, considering her next sentence. She sighed; God already knew what she was about to pray. *And Lord, please give me a chance to thank him for all he's done for me. Amen.*

# Chapter 14

The *Virtue*

Andrew Chandler stood at the bow of his handsome, naval Barque. Her sails were tied as they sat in the water and waited. The tenseness he felt the past few weeks had all built to this moment. The sun still rose, chasing off the morning chill; yet still, sweat made his shirt stick to him. Thankfully his waistcoat made it unnoticeable. He must not look stressed or out of control.

Andrew held up his spyglass again, eyeing the dark pirate ship that approached them leisurely. His jaw clenched. They had his sister, and he was all business.

"Tanner," Andrew called to his quartermaster and friend.

"Captain?" The man was there in an instant, not that he had truly left his captain's side. Tanner Ross knew the stress his best friend was under, as his usual light and social manner turned to a reserved restlessness after his sister's capture.

"Have the men by the guns, should things go wrong. Be sure they understand that Cassidy's safety is of upmost importance, but once she's safe on board..." he lowered the spyglass and looked at Tanner. "Send them to the depths."

Andrew wished his other ship, the *Blood Moon*, was not on her way to India. He needed back up, even if the ship needed to be hidden. Never mind though, the *Virtue* was sufficient.

"Aye, sir." Tanner hurried to carry out orders.

Andrew took a deep breath to calm his racing heart. If anything happened to her he could not forgive himself. He had to play this right.

*My God, my God, do not forsake me!* Andrew fought for control of his emotions. So many memories of her flashed through his mind. How timid she was in everything. How she always looked to him for protection. How she smiled with all the love and admiration in the world for him.

He sighed, wondering how she was holding up. She was always such a fearful girl. All he wanted was that she was safe, unharmed, and the same sister he had always had. *Has being a pirate prisoner changed her? What if those heartless pirates mistreated her?* Andrew dared not grant freedom to his wild imagination.

Not more than fifteen minutes later, the large galleon sailed up beside the *Virtue*. As soon as the gangplank was in place, Andrew strode across with Tanner at his side. Bearing as much power and intimidation as he could muster, he scanned the deck for any sign of his sister. Nothing. His gaze caught on a young man tied to the main mast. His hands above his head and his head hung slightly, flaxen hair covering his eyes from Andrew's view. Still, Andrew could feel the man's gaze.

"Ah, Lord Chandler." Mayson Cade met him on the main deck. "How good of you to come. It would be a shame for such a pretty girl to be lost at sea."

"Where is she?" His eyes were trained on Cade as he stormed up to him. "If you harmed her –"

"She was not harmed, last I checked," he interrupted, a little half-grin appearing on his face when a few of the men snorted. "Well, mostly."

It was all Andrew could do not to run his sword through the man. "Where is she?"

Cade waved off his threatening air. "If you must know," he spread his arms out. "The Lady Chandler is not here."

Andrew narrowed his eyes on the man and waited for an explanation. It didn't come. "Then you will not be seeing any of the ransom money."

Cade gave a cruel laugh. "Yer have mistaken me, Lord Chandler, for a pirate of simple mind and low thinking. I'm not interested in money." He paused as he often did for dramatic effect. "I want you."

Andrew stood still. He could feel Tanner shift nearby.

"Yer sister is currently on a deserted island, not more than a few clicks from here. And she'll die there if she's not rescued in the next twenty-four hours. So I suggest yer men sail for 'er immediately."

"What are you asking for in return, snake?" Andrew worked to maintain his fragile control.

"I already told you! I want you, Andrew Chandler." He took a step closer, lowering his voice. "I shall tell yer men the location of the island if you join me crew." Cade raised his voice now for all to hear, looking directly at Andrew. "So what'll be, Chandler? Yer life? Or hers?"

Tanner stepped in loyally, but in vain. "Andrew..." he warned. "It needn't be this way."

But what choice did they have?

"It does if 'e wants 'is innocent, beautiful, li'le sister back," Cade said.

Every muscle in Andrew's body constricted. He struggled to breathe. *How has it come to this?* "How do I know I can trust you?"

Cade rolled his eyes. "I need yer men out of the way, boy! And takin' care of yer sister will take time, that's how!"

Andrew ground his teeth together. He knew what the rotten pirate meant. If Andrew's men were off looking for his duchess sister, then they would not be a problem for this Captain Cade. "Fine." He turned to Tanner and said loud enough for Cade to hear, "If you don't find her immediately, sound the alarm. Let her Majesty's navy know that there's a bounty on Mayson Cade's head and every man who works for him!" He tried to think of anything else he could throw in to sweeten the capture of Cade.

"Then I hope you have a decent navigator, English!" Cade hissed at him.

Andrew smirked and strode over to Cade's men. "Now tell him where she is," he ordered, nodding toward Tanner as men grabbed at Andrew.

Cade surveyed the situation, looking for any more advantages he could take. "Take the duke down to a cell. And Williams while yer at it!"

Fire ignited in Andrew's eyes. "Find her, Tanner! Take her to my aunt!"

"Yes, Captain," Tanner said.

The men quickly shoved Andrew down the stairs, followed more slowly by the crewmen with the man just released from the main mast.

Andrew barely heard Cade give Tanner the location of the island. He prayed Tanner would waste no time in setting sail.

Andrew hit the back of the cell hard. He waited to hear the door shut and lock before turning around. The crewmen snickered at him and the other prisoner, or whomever he was, that they dropped in a cell across from him before exiting toward the main deck. Andrew studied the man in curiosity. Only then, as the fellow lay face down, did Andrew see the three long rips in his shirt soaked with blood.

*Poor man.* A three lash beating was not bad. It was merciful, actually, considering punishment of thirty lashings was not uncommon.

The man slowly pushed himself up and to the back of the cell where he propped himself up against the back wall. He let out a sigh and glanced toward Andrew. He was younger than Andrew thought. The black circles under deep brown eyes made him look older. Andrew wondered what the man had done to deserve being down here; after all, pirates did not see stealing and murder as a crime.

"I'm Preston Williams." He bowed his head slightly.

"Andrew Chandler." Andrew replied with a nod. "A pleasure." Not necessarily true, but the words slipped out on habit.

Mr. Williams nodded knowingly. "Your sister spoke of you."

Andrew narrowed his eyes on the man. "What do you know of my sister?"

"Not much, she was on board for a week. But I was her caretaker, bringing her meals and such."

"How was she?" He moved closer to the bars.

"When the *Queen's Merit* was under attack she fell from a great height. Possibly broke a few ribs. She had a rope burn on her hand too." He grimaced. "I tended to her hand, but not much could be done for her ribs."

Andrew ran his tongue over his teeth.

"Cassidy was in fairly good spirits most of the time. She quaked like a leaf at first, but then she settled into her cabin. No one bothered her, thank the Lord."

Andrew scowled at the boy's use of her nickname, the name *he* gave her. "And just how well did you come to know her, Mr. Williams?"

Mr. Williams squared his shoulders and looked him straight in the eyes. "Lord Chandler, rest assured I only cared for her basic needs while she was on the *Royal Fortune*. My intentions were simple and honorable."

Andrew scrutinized him. "How did you end up tied to the mast and whipped?"

Williams did not break their icy stare as he told Andrew about Cade threatening Cassidy and hitting her before marooning her on the island.

"You should be glad to know, the coordinates Cade gave your men for the island are correct. Your men should reach her in plenty of time. We left her yesterday morning," Williams continued.

Though more trusting, this statement sent Andrew's mind in another direction. The man knew navigation? Interesting.

"What is, or was, your position on this ship, Mr. Williams?"

"Second mate. Though I haven't been here long." He went on to explain how he came to Cade's ship. "I never intended to be a pirate, nor do I plan to stay one. I just pray I will not be held accountable for my obliviousness and naivety in signing onto a pirate's crew."

Andrew sat silent. It was unfortunate, but he rather liked this man. With time to kill, Andrew asked for more of Williams story and before long he was talking of his own. Andrew was very glad to find it was a Christian that protected his sister, and after over an hour of talking all mistrust melted from his mind.

"Tell me, why did Cassidy have you call her by the nickname I gave her?" Andrew asked.

Preston shrugged, though winced in doing so. "Can't say, though she did mention I reminded her of you."

Andrew snorted playfully. "Sisters! You and I are nothing alike."

Preston imitated the sound Andrew made. "Not at all."

The two shared a weak chuckle that died into a somber silence.

Andrew's stomach hurt and his chest felt hollow. *Cassidy...*

"At least you have a sister." Preston broke in, sadness laced his dark eyes. Andrew raised an eyebrow at him, urging him to go on. Preston sighed. "I had a sister. She was five years younger than I. My father was a general in the navy. He left a few months before my sister was born and never returned. My mother died in childbirth." A light smile came to his face. "For five years I protected her. It was always her and I at the orphanage, but one day she was bitten by a snake because I neglected to watch her." Preston's jaw clenched tightly, sealed off to fester in his guilt.

"I'm sorry." Andrew could hardly imagine losing his three family members like that. What if he lost his sister now? His head felt light. *Dear God, keep my heart beating.* He changed the subject. "Did you ever find out what happened to your father?"

Preston pulled his attention back to Andrew. "I was once told he went down with his ship trying to capture the pirate Bartholomew Roberts. I don't know any details really."

A funny expression came to Andrew's face.

"What is it?" Preston asked, intrigued.

"When was this?" Andrew's green eyes were alight as he sat in thought.

Preston counted back. "Late 1722, maybe early 1723. Why?"

Andrew slapped his hand to his forehead. "Williams? Like Jonathan Williams! My father was on that mission!"

Preston's eyes widened. "The duke from England!"

Quietness hung as the boys considered this. How could such a meeting be a coincidence?

The duke looked around. "Preston, this ship... this is the *Royal Fortune.*"

Preston stared at him. "Yes, I know."

"Bartholomew Robert's ship."

Eyebrows arched, Preston looked around. "But... how?"

The pieces fell into place in the young duke's mind. "The second mate was never captured... the ship was sold off..." Andrew blew out a long breath. "And the treasure never found."

"Wait, what?" Preston's face was blanketed in overwhelming confusion. Just then, hard footsteps sounded down the steps.

"What's going on, Andrew?"

"I'll explain later."

Several burly men appeared and unlocked the cell doors. Andrew stood, as did Preston, though more sluggishly.

The men escorted the two prisoners up the stairs to the captain's cabin. Inside the surprisingly spacious room, Cade sat behind his desk. "Gentleman, how good of ya to join me in discussin' our next escapade."

"I know what you're doing," Andrew said spitefully.

"Do ya? And do ya know how I plan to do it?"

"If you're planning to have us assist you, give up now. We know nothing about the treasure," Andrew retorted.

"Is that so?" Cade studied them, then shrugged. "That may be so, but perhaps this will help yer memory," Cade reached into his desk and pulled out a letter. Two letters, actually. "It came across me desk on its way to John Cagney."

Andrew heard Preston's quick intake of breath.

Cade handed the letter to Preston. "Though ultimately for you."

Preston started to reach for it, but hesitated. "What if we decide it is not in our best interest to help you?"

Cade raised an eyebrow. "Then neither of you are of any use to me, but before it comes to that, Lord Chandler conveniently told his men to take the lovely Lady Chandler to his aunt's home." Cade shot a triumphant look at Andrew. "Which I know is in Virginia."

Andrew quivered to the very core in anger. A quick glance at Preston told him he was not alone.

"Fine. But we will go free after we get you the treasure." Preston shot back.

"Yer, Mr. Williams, shall be free after yer four weeks are up. Lord Chandler–"

"Captain." Andrew interrupted. He did hate being called "Lord."

Cade glared at him. "*Captain* Chandler may go free after the treasure is found. That is, if 'e doesn't get himself killed first." The two exchanged icy glares.

"Well then, if I may." Preston extended his hand for the letters.

Andrew watched as Preston pulled out two pieces of parchment. The first he read quickly before handing it to Andrew.

"He took me in," Preston explained, his voice rough, before eagerly turning to the letter in his own hand. Andrew read:

*Dear John,*
*I do hope this letter finds you in good health.*
*Our team has been successful in tracing Roberts to his lair. Unfortunately, Roberts, his quarter-*

master, and their crew were able to escape on their two ships. While we shall continue our search, which is narrowing down as we speak, more and more dangers have come to light, making me only too aware that I may never again see my family. Being the one who hid the vast wealth of this infamous pirate, I am, no doubt, on all pirate watch lists. Thus, requiring precautions. Hopefully, you have already received a small package. In it is a gift for Preston when he is old enough, which is explained in a brief note inside the package. I fear that I shall not live to give it to him or recollect the treasure. So, I have arranged for this small item to be both the key to the treasure and my final parting gift. In this letter you will find I have another letter, which is for Preston, please give it to him when you bestow upon him the gift. I implore you to keep it safe, for this is a key to a great treasure. However, most of all, I ask you to keep my greatest treasure safe: My family.

Give them my love.
Sincerely,
General Jonathan Williams

Andrew refolded the letter before glancing at Preston. His friend's eyes were moist. When Preston finished the letter, he held it out to Andrew.

"You don't have to..." Andrew started, knowing it was personal.

Preston shook his head, and pushed it toward him. Andrew took it solemnly, casting a glance toward Cade, who stood still and serious, without a trace of his usual mockery on his face. Maybe the pirate did have a bit of a conscience. Andrew refocused his attention on the paper in his hand.

*My dear son, Preston,*
*I pray you never read this. I pray I give you this gift and explain to you its significance. But if you are reading this due to my death, know that I am in Heaven where I will see you one day. But now, as a man, I want to tell you how much I love you and how proud of you I am. You and your little sibling are more precious to me than any gold. I have prayed for you since you were born and promise to until I die. Trust in the Lord, dear son, and He shall guide you and not forsake you.*
*As for your gift: I give this to you to remember me and to constantly be reminded of the sacrifice made for you. But, there is more. It is the key to a map that leads to a great treasure. You are a smart boy and I trust you can use this key, and the great map your true Father has already given to you, to find it. Now, this will get you to the location of the treasure. Once you find the place, I have given the rest of the information you need to my partner, Duke Charles Chandler of England. Just as I have, he has sent this in the form of a gift to his son. However, the two of you divide the treasure. I trust it shall honor the Lord as it was first meant to.*

*I am so proud of you!*
*Love always and forever,*
*Father*

As he finished reading, Andrew's throat felt constricted. He could hardly imagine being in Preston's place.

"Well?" Cade brought the two out of their thoughts.

Andrew cleared his throat. "*'Once you find the island, I have given the rest of the information you need to my partner, Duke Charles Chandler of England. Just as I have, he has sent this in the form of a gift to his son.'*" Andrew read aloud. "Sir, believe me when I say, I have no idea what he is talking about. I possess no clue to this treasure."

Cade ignored Andrew. "Have ya the map yer adopted father has given yer?"

Preston took the letter back, looking as baffled as Andrew felt. "I shall need time to look over this, sir."

Cade sighed, but had no choice. "Very well. I'll call ya both back on the morrow. In the meantime, get back to yer duties. And find somethin' for Chandler here to do."

# Chapter 15

An Island in the Caribbean

Shivering, Cassidy huddled closer to her tiny, dying fire. Her stomach pinched and rolled, bringing another wave of nausea. The funny fruit had made her sick all night long. She never wanted to eat again. It was her thirst, however, that was worst of all. The significant loss of precious fluid overnight left a far worse feeling then her aching belly. Her mouth was sticky, and her throat dry and scratched.

Cassidy gazed at the waves. *God, do you remember how you stopped the sun for Joshua? I don't suppose you could turn the ocean to fresh water, just for a tiny minute?*

Her second night on the beach was slowly chased away by morning. The stars slowly disappeared as brilliant rays of the sunlight appeared in the east.

She sighed, for not even the sun could clear her foggy mind. Pictures of her family floated by, and Cassidy's heart hurt. She would never see them again, and they would never know what happened to her.

*My dear God…* Cassidy tried to pray, but sobs interrupted her. If she had tears to spill they would have already filled a mug. Her eyes stung terribly, dry and fuzzy. Her body shook and heaved, and Cassidy was forced to empty her stomach again, though little came up. When she left the rest of her insides on the beach, she struggled to her feet weakly, desperately needing to wash herself off.

Stumbling to the ocean, she collapsed into the surf. Her head spun and everything was a fuzzy, spinning world. The cool water moved around her, gently lapping over her legs and cooling her suddenly burning body.

Cassidy closed her eyes. She saw her mother with a cool cloth holding it to her head and neck. The cool dampness seemed to engulf her back and shoulders too, then her arms and face.

With a gasp, Cassidy jerked herself out of the water. She had fallen back into the waves without realizing it.

Dripping, panting, and frightened, Cassidy moved back toward the beach, feeling chilled and disoriented. What would have been a moan came out as a feeble squeak as Cassidy pulled herself away from the water. It took great effort, as she used her arms to pull herself up the beach. When she stopped, her legs and feet rested within reach of the waves, her body quaking in weakness. Utter exhaustion made her muscles seem to spasm and squeeze. She felt like a shriveled leaf, cut off from water and nourishment.

Cassidy knew her brain was shutting down, but she was helpless to stop it. *Lord, help!* She prayed as blackness relieved her from the tipsy world.

"My Lady! My Lady!"

Cassidy's head pounded. She squeezed her eyes shut in hopes that the pain would subside and she could return to that quiet dark place of sleep, or death, whichever came first. She moaned when someone lightly shook her.

"Lady Cassandra, wake up!"

Cassidy forced her eyes open, only to have them stung by the searing Caribbean sun. Quickly, she blinked her eyes closed again.

"Let's take her to the shade." Cassidy felt arms under her, and she was lifted into the air. A shadow passed over her face before she was gently sat down and leaned against a palm tree.

Slowly, she opened her eyes again. Her vision was blurry at best, but she was able to make out several figures. Confused and scared, she tried to push herself away.

"Help," Cassidy croaked, and her voice cracked. The word was probably not audible, nor was she sure she wanted these men to help her.

"Hush now. You are alive and safe, praise the Lord." Tanner Ross had heard her, but he was no less frightened then she. The duchess was not right at all, her skin was red and blistered and her eyelids swollen almost shut. Her face was sunken in and pale where the sun had not reached.

Tanner turned to one of about a dozen of his men who stood around him. "Bring some water, and where on earth is Kit?"

"Here." The middle-aged man hurried over with his bag of first aid. Having a doctor on a ship was a rare, though necessary, blessing. Being of nobility, Andrew was able to both recruit and pay one.

"We need to get some water in her, now," the doctor said, though anyone could have figured that much.

Someone brought over a water jug and Kit held it to her lips. "Not too much at once, my lady," he told her gently, but whether she heard and understood no one knew. When water slid into her mouth and down her throat, she jerked away at the sting of it.

"I know, my lady, but you need it," said the doctor. When the jar was brought to her lips again, she did not refuse. Several long, slow sips later, Cassidy's head lulled back, her emaciated frame lifeless.

Tanner fought panic. "Lady?"

Kit felt for her pulse. Then felt again.

The blood drained from Tanner's face. The duchess of England just died on his watch. He felt faint.

"She's just unconscious."

Tanner slowly let out his breath.

Kit put a hand to her head. "A fever, and a burning one at that. That's why she's rather delirious."

He turned to Tanner. "Let's get her back to the ship. She shouldn't be out in the elements."

Tanner ever-so-gently eased his arms underneath her. When he started to lift her, her lightness caught him off guard and he jerked her accidently. She moaned and recoiled in pain. Tanner glanced at Kit, who frowned.

"She must be injured. Quickly, back to the ship."

Tanner carried her toward the waiting boats as carefully as possible, and they cast off in silence.

On board the *Virtue*, Tanner carried Cassidy toward the captain's cabin, Kit in tow.

"Set course for Virginia in all haste!" Tanner shouted to the men, who gave a round of "Aye, Captain!" before scurrying to work.

In the cabin, Tanner laid her down on Andrew's bed as gently as possible. Her light weight sent chills through his body.

"Let's get some more fluid in her. Then we'll let her rest a while," Kit instructed.

Just as on the beach, Tanner held her in place and Kit poured water at a trickle into her mouth. She swallowed it down instantly. Tanner sighed, comforted that she drank but still haunted by her pale, burned face. What if he lost her? Oh, he could not bear for something to happen to her. Tanner had seen what her kidnapping had done to her brother, and for Andrew, Tanner could not let the duchess die.

Kit put a hand on Tanner's shoulder as they watched the rise and fall of her chest. "Give her time Captain. God designed the body to withstand much more than we can imagine. I believe she'll be alright."

The *Royal Fortune*

"My shift doesn't start for another half hour," Preston told Andrew over his shoulder as the two departed from Cade's cabin and headed down the hall. Preston fought hard to keep his emotions at bay.

*Easy, Preston. Now is not the time for clouded judgment. Focus!* Preston attempted to ease his rolling mind. *Dear Jesus, give me strength. Help me to control myself, and show us what to do. Guide us so that we may not fall into a trap. Give us wisdom, Oh Father, please!*

Preston led the way to his own cabin, which reminded him that he had not been in it since Cassidy used it. Opening the door, he and Andrew entered before Preston closed and locked the door behind them. He did not want to be interrupted.

He sighed and rested his forehead against the door before turning around to face Andrew.

"You alright?" Andrew asked.

Preston's emotions were still in turmoil, and now he was forced to give up the one link he still had to his father. Must they take the legacy that his father left for him? Was not taking his life enough? Preston took in another deep breath and turned around. "What were you saying about Roberts' quartermaster?"

Andrew looked at his new friend, concerned, but said, "Several of the men that were on Roberts' other ship were never found, including the quartermaster. My father assumed he was dragged down with the ship, but later, rumors surfaced that he was alive. Of course, everyone waved it off."

"So?"

"So, I heard my father and some men talking about it once. I distinctly remember one saying 'Even if Ol' Mayson is up to his tricks he hasn't done anything yet that sets him apart from other pirates.' Preston, what if he was referring to Mayson Cade?"

Preston let this sink in. "It makes sense. If Cade was the heir of Roberts' wealth, he would feel it is his very right to go searching for it."

"And, he clearly has resources like Roberts."

"True." Preston laid the two letters on the table, and the two of them sat down. "But wouldn't your father have recognized the name on the ransom note?"

Andrew shook his head. "My father never saw it. The note came straight to me while I was out on business. I left right then."

The two of them were silent a moment.

Preston spoke first. "Okay, we can't prove anything right now. So let's..." He reached for Mr. Cagney's letter. "...focus on deciphering the location of this horrid treasure."

Andrew ignored Preston's grumpiness and picked up the letter from Preston's father to reread it. "Do you know what gift he left for you?" Andrew asked.

Preston nodded slowly. "I think so, but it doesn't make any sense."

"What do you mean?"

Preston reached in his shirt and pulled out the metal cross. Looping it over his head, he gave it to Andrew. "Mr. Cagney gave this to me when I was eleven. He received it from my father before he died."

"That sounds right." Andrew took the object and examined it, frowning when he found the imperfections on the backside. Puzzled, Andrew asked "Anything else he left you?"

"Not that I know of."

Andrew passed the cross back and turned back to the letter in his hand. "'*I trust you can use this key, and the great map your true Father has already given to you, to find it.*' True Father? As in, God?"

Preston shrugged. "Maybe, but what map did God give me?"

"Unless 'you' is a general term. More like, He gave it to all his children." Andrew stood and began to pace the room.

Still regaining his strength, Preston leaned back and watched his friend. "Possibly... the Bible?" Preston glanced at the cross in his hand. "And the cross symbolizing the Crucifixion. Could there be a clue in the story of Christ's death?"

"Maybe. Do you have a Bible in here?"

"On the shelf, right behind you." Andrew turned for it. "Then again, he said very clearly a map. Some Bibles have maps in them, and maybe the cross refers to Jesus' life. Could he have hidden the treasure somewhere Jesus traveled during his life?" Preston felt like that was something. "Then again, I don't think he had time for that. Besides, I remember hearing about it being in the Atlantic."

"Preston."

Preston looked up as Andrew held a book up for him to see. It was not his Bible, but rather one of his books on navigation. On the cover in big letters the title read:

## A Guide to Knowing the Cosmic Map

The two of them stared for a moment, then Preston laughed. "The map in the stars! Yes!"

"You couldn't have thought of that sooner?" Andrew smiled, as he brought the book and Bible to the table.

Preston's smile faded. "So, the map is in the stars, and this is supposed to be the key to the map." Preston held up the cross.

"Is there a constellation of a cross?" Andrew asked as he flipped through the book.

"Not that I'm aware of." The two of them sat in silence. "Do you know what it was that your father gave you?" Preston asked.

Andrew sighed. "Nothing that comes to mind. He has given me plenty of trinkets over the years.

In fact, he used to always bring Cassidy and me something back from his travels."

"Did he bring you back something after catching Roberts?"

Andrew considered this a moment, but only laughed when he remembered. "Yeah, a funny feathered hat. Of course, I don't have it with me." Andrew stood to pace again, talking as he moved about the room. "Didn't your father send it to someone for safekeeping? I'm sure my father agreed to do the same."

"Yes, but if that's so, you may not even have received whatever it is yet."

Andrew groaned. "There is no way of knowing. At least we can get to the spot where the treasure is. I mean, we have the map and its key. Maybe that'll satisfy Cade."

"If we can solve the map, that is."

Just then, the bell rang for shift change. Preston rose stiffly. "Come on. I could use another man at the yards." He paused, realizing he spoke to a duke. "If you don't mind."

Andrew raised an eyebrow at him. "What do I look like? Incompetent? You're the one who just spent a day tied to the main mast."

Preston smiled; he really liked these two Chandlers. He opened the door and headed up to the main deck.

"You are not at all like your sister," Preston commented. Cassidy had shrunk at Cade's overwhelming presence, while Andrew seemed to drink it in. "How much older are you anyway?"

"I'm twenty-one, three years apart from her."

"Oh, that's unfortunate."

"Why?" The corners of Andrew's mouth twitched.

"You're a duke of England, rich, and captain of a fine vessel. You've got the good looks like your sister, *and* you're older than me? How am I supposed to compete with that?"

"*And* a better swordsman." Andrew pointed out, standing a little straighter in attempt to match Preston's height.

Preston snorted. "What makes you think that?"

"Just a probable speculation."

Preston cast his friend a sideways glance as they climbed the last few steps and emerged on the main deck. "From where I'm standing, it's less probable."

# Chapter 16

The *Virtue*

Cassidy awoke with a start, adrenaline coursing through her veins. She looked around, wide-eyed.

*Where am I? What's going on?*

Suddenly, the door opened and a man peered in. Seeing her awake, he ducked back out and a moment later she heard quick footsteps.

Cassidy pushed herself back against the wall. Fear, pain, and hunger lapsed her into an almost animal-like state. She watched the door as the footsteps came closer, her mind flashing pictures of Captain Cade. Even as she watched, she startled when the door opened again. A young man walked in, and right behind him was an older man. The young man's face was withered in worry, but when he saw her awake, the worry converted into a stiff smile.

"Lady Cassandra," Tanner Ross greeted. After a moment of studying, Cassidy finally recognized the man as Andrew's quartermaster and sighed in relief.

"Tanner," she breathed, her voice cracked and coarse.

Tanner's grin widened. "I am glad you're feeling better, my lady. This is Kit Lakeston, the ship's doctor." He motioned to the man beside him.

"Good afternoon, my lady. If you think you could stomach it, I'd like to bring you some bread."

Cassidy nodded. "Please, Doctor," she rasped. The round doctor with a kind, wrinkled face called to the man who had guarded her door to bring in the food.

Tanner helped prop her up, and a light meal was soon brought in and sat on her lap.

"Are you hurt anywhere, Lady Chandler?" Kit asked as he dragged a stool near her bed.

Cassidy considered the question, the past few days slowly coming back to her. Her head throbbed and her ribs still pained her. She felt stiff and her stomach did not feel settled, but she was alive, thank the Lord. "My head hurts, sir."

The man nodded. "I have something for headaches. I'll go fetch it now." Kit glanced at Tanner before leaving the room.

Tanner sat on the stool and sighed. "I'm glad your fever broke. You have been out for over twenty-four hours."

Cassidy's brows rose in surprise. "That long?"

He nodded slowly. "Well, you woke up occasionally..." Cassidy studied him. She knew he tried to carry the world on his shoulders, and he was always more of a serious, reserved person, but Cassidy liked him. He and her brother grew up together, and she knew the two of them were close friends.

Though she and Tanner were never really friends due to their more reserved natures, Cassidy trusted him because Andrew trusted him. She was thankful he was here now.

"And?" she prompted.

"You were not right at all." He shook his head, as though to shake away the images that haunted him. "You were out of it completely."

Cassidy knew enough to know that fever could cause hysteria. She changed the subject.

"How did I get here?"

"We found you on a beach. You were feverish then too. We were able to carry you back here to the *Virtue*."

Cassidy nodded. "Where's Andrew?"

The question hung in the air. Cassidy's stomach felt ill again.

"He stayed behind." Tanner would not meet her gaze.

Cassidy narrowed her eyes on him. His short-cropped brown hair and matching brown eyes made him rather plain, but his strong, masculine jawline reminded her of Preston. With the thought of Preston, tears pushed at her eyes as raw emotion bubbled inside her. She could not help but remember Cade's last words to her. Panic threatened to take hold of her, but she swallowed it down.

"Where?" Cassidy demanded, harsher than she meant, but she disliked the way he gave only the minimal truth.

"Captain Cade demanded Andrew work for him, or he would not disclose your location."

Cassidy cringed and shut her eyes. "I was a diversion and decoy."

Tanner nodded.

"We have to go back for him. Where are we headed now?"

"Virginia." Cassidy gave him a look. He dared not stop there. "Andrew ordered me to take you to your aunt's, but after that I've every intention of going after Cade."

But Cassidy would not take this for an answer. "No, we can't wait! We're talking about my own brother's life!" Cassidy again thought of Preston. If they went back now, maybe they could get him out as well. There was no doubt in her mind that Preston wanted to escape.

"My lady..." Tanner moved his hand as though considering touching her arm but thought better of it. "I want that too. But we have no idea where he is now. It will make no difference if we go after him now or after we deliver you safely to your aunt. Besides, we might be able to ask around. Gather some information even on Cade's possible location."

Cassidy bit her lip. Tanner was right. Perhaps it was just her worry about what Cade wanted with her brother, though Preston was with him and no doubt would help Andrew.

*If Cade hasn't keelhauled Preston by now...*

Cassidy's chest seemed to collapse in on itself at such a thought. *My dear Lord, keep them safe! Bring them out of this unharmed and back home.* Cassidy evoked her last picture of Preston, held captive after trying to protect her. Surely Cade wouldn't kill him. Right? But would he be unharmed by the end of this? What if Cade did decide to kill him? What if Cade just dumped him into the ocean? *Oh dear Jesus!*

"I found it," Kit said from the doorway, snapping Cassidy out of her unwelcome thoughts. He strode across the room and handed her an herbal brew.

"Drink it," he ordered. She gulped it down as Kit turned to Tanner.

"Come, Captain. Let's leave Lady Cassandra to rest." Tanner rose as instructed.

"I'll be back to check on you in a few hours. Please call to Luke if you need anything," Tanner motioned to the door where Luke stood guard.

"Try to sleep," Kit said as he and Tanner exited and closed the door behind them.

The *Royal Fortune*

Preston climbed the main mast with ease, even in the dark. Dawn would not stretch out her bright, shining figures for another half hour.

Relieving the sleepy watchman, Preston sat down in the crow's nest and huddled back against the main mast. His mind pulled him in all direction. Too many things called for his attention.

With a sigh, Preston waited until he could no longer hear the other watchmen before pulling out his cross. He studied it, as he often did on his mornings in the crow's nest. Preston raised his eyes to the stars; thousands of shining specs decorated the sky in stunning beauty. Beauty that Preston failed to notice, as he was unable to think past his own, tiny world and see the huge galaxy that spun in a complete, choreographed pattern. A pattern even his own little world was a part of.

*What did you hide up there, Father?* He and Andrew had talked late into the night about possibilities, coming up empty handed. What is it that is hidden in the heavens? He needed to come up with something for Cade. And he needed it in the next hour.

Tired, his mind strayed from his searching, coming back again to what his father had written.

*Would Father be proud of me now? Even with all my problems? My lack of faith? My irresponsibility with my sister? My running?*

Running. That's what he did all those weeks ago when he signed on to the *Raven*. He was fleeing the life he led before, the one ridden with guilt and worthlessness. Yet here he found himself, the prodigal son. Lost and drowning in a world too big for him. Still stuck in the same guilt and worthlessness he felt before. Preston had wanted to be a man, one that his father would truly be proud of. One that could protect his loved ones and glorify God.

He put his head in his hands and moaned. Why, he couldn't even sing the Lord's praises!

Like a chilly gust of wind, a sudden thought added to his already heavy heart. His lungs constricted at the longing that he had been shoving away for a few days now. How could Preston even think such things when he knew he was not deserving of her? He knew that his imperfect heart could not be valuable enough for her, nor was he a wealthy suitor. One that could give her what she deserved. He was just a broken man with a tugging heart. No, it just could not be.

*Dear Jesus, I am sorry! Could You somehow make me into a real man? A man after Your own heart?* Preston wanted to be better so very badly, but how could he? Only God could help him now. And perhaps, if He did, then maybe... just maybe he could be worthy of her...

Uncomfortable, whether it be in mind or body, Preston moved around to the other side of the mast, leaning against it once more. Clenching the cross in his hands, Preston bowed his head.

"Dear Father, as you once gave to a great king, please give me wisdom. Show me the map in the stars if it is your will to lead us to the treasure. But if not, show me what to do about Cade and turn his mind from wrath." Preston paused and took a deep breath. "And please keep Cassidy safe and out of harm's way."

Preston sat like that for a moment longer clenching the cross tightly. Why did he care for her so?

At first, he had pitied her, and she reminded him of Briana, but something had changed. When, he did not know. But now his heart wondered, just wondered, if something could ever have happened between them. Should circumstances have been different, that is. But now, it was too late.

Finally, he looked up at the night sky. He needed a distraction. Needed to think of something else.

Facing south, away from their heading, he picked out each constellation, counting them off slowly and carefully. He started to the east and ended to the west. It took a while, and he finished more exhausted than when he began.

His tightly clenched hands finally felt sore, and he pulled them apart. He noticed his left hand was marked with the imperfections of the cross. The cross was upside-down in his hand, leaving more marks at the bottom of his palm and a trail of marks leading to the more calloused part of his hand.

Preston stared at it a moment. Its shape was rather different, why, almost familiar.

He licked his lips. Holding up his hand, he compared the marks to each star and constellation in the sky. When the spots on his hand began to disappear, he pressed the cross to his hand again.

A light blue hue threatened of dawn to the east.

*Easy, Preston.*

As quickly as possible, Preston compared the shapes in the sky to the marks on his hand. Nothing matched.

"Maybe a combination of constellations and stars?" he mumbled to himself. Surveying the sky again, Preston's eyes drew a line between the stars

Spica and Arcturus. The star next to Arcturus, making up the constellation Bootes, matched the seemingly random two dots on the left side of the cross's crossbeam.

"That would make the dot on the left side the tail of Virgo..." Preston could barely control his excitement. With the three main points of the arrow found, the rest fell into place quickly.

Standing now, Preston was ready to race down to his cabin and calculate the location, but something stopped him. This would mean the island was in the south Atlantic. Roberts' lair was discovered closer to Greenland. How much time did his father have?

The answer, he did not know.

Two rungs at a time, Preston clambered down from the crow's nest and hurried to his cabin. When he entered, he found Andrew still asleep with his head on the table, but now was no time for sleep.

"Andrew, I found it!"

Andrew turned away.

Leaving Andrew to rouse himself, Preston hurried to his desk and rummaged for paper, pen, and ink.

Preston wasted no time grabbing his sextant and getting back to the deck. As quickly, but efficiently as possible, Preston took his measurements for latitude and longitude based on the length of the stars from the horizon, from the north star, and then the north star to the horizon.

The sun was rising. The stars were fading.

Carefully, Preston double-checked his measurements, then triple-checked. Satisfied, he sat down where he stood and began his calculations. After five minutes of working, dawn chased away the stars and Andrew finally emerged.

"What are you doing?" Andrew asked groggily. Other men also started to appear on deck, all wondering how their navigator did his work during light hours.

Preston did not answer right away, immersed in his work.

"I'm...finding... treasure."

Andrew's eyebrows inched higher, and he knelt down to look over Preston's work. The two huddled there for another fifteen minutes. Few words passed between them.

When all was affirmed, the two men sat back on their heels, staring at the scribblings, then at one another.

"What should we do now?" Andrew spoke rather hushed. Should they take it to Cade? The thought of Cade finding the treasure was not a pleasant thought to either of them. Should they come up with false coordinates? Could they delay until somehow help came?

"You don't go free until the treasure is found, and no treasure is worth bringing harm to you or your sister." Preston's mind was made.

The duke frowned. "I am not leaving this ship without you, Preston."

Surprised at his friend's words, Preston shook his head. "I refuse to let you do that. I could be here for years more. Besides, even if I do get off this ship, I will be marked as a pirate. Permanently." *All the more reason something could never happen between Cassidy and me,* he thought.

Andrew scoffed. "*You* are no pirate. If I must pull strings as a duke of England to protect your name, I shall –" and it was final.

Preston offered him a weak smile of gratitude. If only he could do more.

The two comrades pushed to their feet, gathering the parchments and headed toward Cade's cabin.

Andrew marched up to the door and gave it three sharp raps. *At least he's confident.* Preston's lack of assurance was only too evident.

When permission was granted, Andrew swung open the door and boldly stepped inside.

Pulling himself up to his full height, Preston followed.

Cade stood from behind his desk. "I take it you have our heading? Good." The man's appearance echoed impatience and tension, as though he hadn't slept well. Cade's usually clean and pressed uniform seemed wrinkled and slept-in.

"We have the location. The specifics we will get on our own time." Andrew passed Cade the parchment with Preston's final calculations.

With only an annoyed glance at Andrew, Captain Cade took it and looked it over. When he came to the coordinates, his brows furrowed and his frown deepened. "What is this?"

"The coordinates to the treasure, sir," Preston answered.

"This hardly seems right."

"If my father left a location for me to find, that's it."

Cade scowled, then sighed in resignation. "Set sail for the south Atlantic then."

# Chapter 17

The *Virtue*

After four days of hastened sailing, the *Virtue* prepared to enter the port of Norfolk, Virginia. Cassidy stood at the bow surveying the city. The union jack flew proudly over the fort, daring invaders to threaten the stronghold. Elegant ships of all shapes and sizes were coming and going. At the docks, people scurried around, loading and unloading. Handsomely dressed soldiers in bright red coats turned about the fort. The sweet smell of clean air intermingled with the smell of fish and sweat. Shouts and whistles combined with the gentle lap of the waves, and the screech of the seagulls rang methodically throughout the bustling port.

Cassidy drank it in.

At the helm, Tanner maneuvered the *Virtue* into the port with acquired skill. Within half an hour, the ship was secured, and Tanner left the helm to approach Cassidy.

"I promise, as soon as we have Andrew, we shall come right back here to assure you of his safety."

Cassidy turned to him and nodded.

"Would you do something for me?" Cassidy asked in as sweet a voice as possible.

Tanner tried his best not to show it, but his skepticism shone like the noonday sun. Still, he nodded.

"There is a young man on the *Royal Fortune*, who is there by trickery. He helped me. His name is Preston Williams. I would appreciate it if you would rescue him as well."

"Lord Andrew is our first priority, but I will see what can be done for him," Tanner responded bluntly.

Cassidy stared, blinking at him as though trying to decide what to say. Instead, she gave a simple thank you and turned away toward the gangplank.

"Lady Cassandra!" Tanner called to her. She looked back at him, trying to hide her annoyance. "Please wait and I'll go with you!"

Her weariness of arguing outweighed her weariness of him, so Cassidy nodded and waited while Tanner hurried down the steps to his own cabin. A few moments later, Tanner appeared with his official coat and hat, and the two left the ship. After waving down a carriage, Tanner helped Cassidy in, and the pair settled in for the half hour ride to Bellwood Estate.

Cassidy set her gaze out the window. All was quiet. Finally.

Drained, emotionally and physically, Cassidy was anxious to arrive at Bellwood. She needed to gather her wits. A warm bath and a full night of sleep would do her good. Worry for her brother and Preston still lead her to near panic with worry at times. But it was out of her control, and worrying never helped rescue anyone. Besides, she was too tired to worry now. Or string together a logical conversation for that matter. Oh, how she hoped her aunt would not mind her retiring early!

A half hour later, the carriage stopped in front of a huge iron gate, meticulously molded into a breathtaking pattern. The carriage driver hopped to open the gate then drove his team inside.

So this was Bellwood. The mansion was clothed in stone, giving it an impressive appearance. Flourishing landscaping lined an elegant circular drive on either side. Late summer flowers bloomed in an array of color, vines climbed the three chimneys, trees sheltered the still green grass and house from the afternoon sun, and a fountain stood at the center of it all.

Wide-eyed, Cassidy was accustomed to splendor, but the splendor of such a landscape was unimaginable. *Flowers blooming in September! Who knew?* Nothing like this grew back home. Roses, lilies, jasmine, gardenia, daisies, and forget-me-nots grew in an organized fashion around the house and fountain.

At the front of the mansion, Tanner opened the carriage door and climbed down before turning and offering Cassidy a hand. It was all Cassidy could do to keep from running over and smelling all the flowers like a five-year-old.

"If you would wait a moment and allow me to take her inside I will tip you double for the round trip," Tanner told the driver, whose brows lifted and nodded in reply.

Cassidy was not sure whether she should be glad at his quick departure or annoyed. In the end, however, she decided the sooner Tanner gets back to the ship, the better.

She was suddenly overcome with loneliness. Tanner was going to leave her here. And oh, how long it had been since seeing Aunt Emma! What if she changed? She probably had, at least a little bit. Goodness, her aunt might not even recognize her. After all, it had been nearly a decade.

Tanner led the way up the steps and lifted his hand to knock, then paused. "I shall send a message to your father explaining everything and asking for help. With the royal navy as backup, Cade can't do much."

Cassidy nodded.

"And... uh... I think this should be kept from your uncle."

"What? Why?" Cassidy could hardly imagine turning down help.

"Well, this is a bit of an embarrassment for England. It's an issue of appearance. Things are rather strained with the American colonies right now, and I believe it to be best if the word does not get out of the capture of you and your brother. Being duke and duchess it's—"

"Are you saying my uncle would betray the Queen?"

"Ah... um... no... of course not. I'm just saying that Andrew would not want anyone knowing about this. Trust me, Cassidy, please."

She ran her tongue over her teeth. This would not be an easy secret to keep. "Very well. If you think that's best."

"I do." Tanner turned and knocked on the huge door. "I'll leave as soon as you're settled."

Poor Tanner. His anxiousness was only too evident.

When the door opened, a man in a prim suit greeted them, smiling. The butler, no doubt.

"Welcome to Bellwood, home of Edward and Emma Askew. Please come in." The man had a smooth voice and gracious manner. Though his attempt to hide a scowl at Cassidy's clothing did not slip fast enough.

Cassidy stifled a grin when he led them to a luxurious parlor. His walk was so perched it seemed as though he was a chicken with his tail feathers plucked out. She scolded herself for such a thought. Back in the society of the high and mighty she must act like a lady. No, more than that. She must act like a duchess. She sighed.

The man held back the parlor door for them to enter. "Whom may I tell Mr. and Mrs. Askew they host?" the butler asked, looking down his nose at Cassidy before turning to Tanner for an answer.

Cassidy jumped to answer before Tanner could. She did not like to be treated this way. "Duchess Cassandra Chandler humbly asks if our prior arrangement would still be respected." Cassidy surprised herself at the force and confidence in her own voice. Even Tanner raised an eyebrow at her.

The butler, on the other hand, stood petrified. He struggled to find his tongue. "Of course, my lady." He gave a low bow and fled the room.

Tanner removed his hat and motioned for her to have a seat. After a moment, both realized they were far too restless to sit, though neither said so. Cassidy sent up a quick prayer that they needn't sit long. Her foot itched.

Thankfully, not two minutes later the door burst open.

"Cassandra!" Aunt Emma exclaimed.

No indeed, Aunt Emma had not changed at all.

Elegant as always, Emma Askew swept into the room and encompassed Cassidy in a tight embrace. Her dark French hair was piled high on her head in the latest fashion, and teardrop earrings dangled from her earlobes. A bright blue gown covered in lace looked like something a younger generation would wear, but then, this was Aunt Emma.

On her feet in an instant, Cassidy met the older woman with an embrace of her own. Tanner also wasted no time in scrambling to his feet, ready for a hug should he be forced to endure one.

When Aunt Emma finally released Cassidy, she stepped back to examine her niece with her unfaltering gaze. "Child, you do not look well at all! How thin you are! And your hair!" She turned to Tanner for the first time. "Why on earth have you allowed such things to happen? As her escort I would expect–"

"I am not her escort," Tanner interrupted, his face the color of the roses in the yard.

"Oh, then what are you doing here?" Aunt Emma asked, coming down an octave from her glass-shattering voice.

Tanner fidgeted. "I am Tanner Ross, acting captain of the–"

"He's the captain of the ship I came on." Cassidy quickly interjected, hating herself for the half-truth. "Captain Ross was so kind to see me safely here. He and his men have some very important business to attend to that I am sure he must be getting back too."

"Oh?" said Emma.

"Ah, yes, very important. Yes. Must get back to. I will show myself out if you don't mind." Hat in hand, a flustered Tanner moved toward the exit. "My lady." He nodded to Cassidy, giving her a sincere look, then fled the room much like the butler had.

"My, what an interesting fellow," Aunt Emma commented, staring after him. Cassidy smiled, for no matter how terrible people could be, Aunt Emma never took offense. And as dramatic and overbearing as she was, Cassidy loved her very much.

"Quite," an amused Cassidy replied.

Aunt Emma abruptly turned back with a gasp and grabbed her elbows to lead her to the couch.

"Oh, but you're here! I was getting worried! Two weeks late! How could you do that to me?"

"I do apologize, that wasn't planned."

"Hmm, well I suppose some things can't be helped, but it was a nice voyage?"

"Um, yes, it was." She recalled all the good parts of it. "I made a new friend."

Aunt Emma's eyebrows rose. "Really? Wearing this?"

"Yes... I suppose I was." Cassidy's cheeks were on fire. What did Preston think of her outfit? She hadn't even thought of such a thing.

"Hmm," Emma studied her carefully, her blue eyes searching her for something. "Are you speaking of Captain Ross?"

"No no, I've known Captain Ross for a while."

"I see." The two women were silent a brief moment until a grin broke out on Aunt Emma's face. "Tell me, how handsome is your new friend?"

Was Cassidy so transparent? She desperately hoped not. "Oh, Aunt Emma, please! He is only a friend."

"A better friend than most, I'll say."

Words were rapidly failing her. Cassidy had never been so thankful to see Uncle Edward than in that moment. He entered more calmly than had his wife but looked as eager to see her as she.

"Ah, my niece. How wonderful it is to have you here safe and sound," her uncle assured her kindly.

"It is wonderful to be safe, Uncle," Cassidy replied.

Suddenly, the door burst open and twelve-year-old Eleanor and ten-year-old Dean entered.

"Cousin Cassandra!" the dark-haired girl exclaimed. Eleanor was an exact copy of Aunt Emma. The two children stopped beside their father and gave a bow to her.

"Hello, Eleanor and Dean. How good it is to see you," the duchess greeted her little cousins. Ugh! Children. Why must she be so at a loss with them?

"As it is to see you." Eleanor replied, slipping into a more tight and trained manner.

"Now, go up to your room and clean up, Cassandra. I love you, but I have no wish to dine with you smelling as you do. I'll have a gown brought up to you," Aunt Emma told her niece.

A prim little maid led Cassidy up the stairs and down the hall to a door and into a frilly white room. White curtains, white bedspread, white walls, white carpet, Cassidy felt as though she walked into a room in the clouds. When the door closed, she flopped on the bed and breathed out a long, slow breath. It would be hard to keep this secret. Already it weighed on her.

Back to this life. The life of prim and proper. The life of clean and perfection. Everything was so much simpler at sea. So much more practical. Cassidy sighed. Ah, what useless thinking! Wasn't she here for a purpose? Wasn't she put into this life for a reason? Oh, but how ill-suited she felt!

Cassidy startled at a knock on the door. Hastening to arrange herself in a more ladylike manner, she granted whomever permission to enter. The door opened and servants carried a large metal tub inside. For the next quarter hour, Cassidy sat and watched them run buckets of steaming water up to fill the tub. Their work panged her conscience. But what could she do? She had not asked for a bath, but then, it would be delightful to be clean again. Her hair felt very greasy. No doubt she reeked too.

Once the tub was filled, a young little maid added good-smelling oils and herbs. She must smell terribly foul.

At the leave of the young maid, Cassidy shed her boy's clothes and slipped into the warm water. The pleasant aromas were almost overpowering, but it was probably necessary. Cassidy sat still for a long while, letting the water flow around her and warm her insides. Finally, she picked up the sponge and soap bar to wash.

When the water seemed to have cooled, Cassidy left the tub and donned the underdress the maid left for her. Like clockwork, there was a knock on the door, and the maid entered.

The maid brought with her a pink satin gown with puffy sleeves and a ruffled skirt. Not her style, but Cassidy put it on anyway and allowed the maid to brush her damp hair.

"How would you like your hair done, my lady?" the girl asked in a raspy voice that belonged to someone far older than she.

"Pin it up for me, please. I don't have time to let it dry." Cassidy knew supper would start soon. To Cassidy's surprise, the maid did an excellent job of pinning her hair, and she was confident it would last through the evening. Thank goodness.

The maid applied light cosmetics to Cassidy's sunburned face before Cassidy finally left her room, feeling much revived.

Descending the stairs, she was surprised to see a young man in the foyer talking with her uncle. Cassidy hesitated. Guests? She was not expecting her uncle and aunt to have guests! Was it too late to spend the evening in her room?

Her uncle turned and spotted her, tentative on the stairs.

"Ah, my dear niece! Feeling better now, I hope." Uncle Edward's voice was draftier than earlier.

Oh dear, poor Uncle Edward need not go into details about her previous condition. Not in front of a stranger, especially not a young, male stranger. "Quite. Thank you, Uncle," she replied as she finished descending the stairs.

"My dear, this is Mr. Owen Blackburn, a friend of mine from the office. He does all the bookkeeping for the company, and soon the city." Edward turned to the man. "And this is my lovely niece, Duchess Cassandra Faith Chandler of England."

Faith? Must he bring her dreaded middle name into this?

"It is an honor to meet you, Lady Chandler." He took her hand and kissed it. Dismayed, Cassidy found the familiar look of deep admiration in his eyes. *Terrific.* Perhaps he found her pretty, but must he stare so?

There was nothing interesting about him to Cassidy. Brown hair and a narrow face made up his ordinary appearance. Though no doubt the silly girls back home would have called him dashing.

"As it is to meet you, Mr. Blackburn. Won't you be joining us for supper?"

"Yes, actually. You uncle was very kind to extend me an invitation. The gracious Askews are my home away from home when work can spare me." He was trying to sound fancy. How boring.

"Ah, how delightful." An awkward moment settled. Cassidy's soul groaned. She should have said more to move along the conversation, but did she really want to keep it going?

"Well, shall we continue to the dining room?" Uncle Edward prompted.

"Of course," Mr. Blackburn agreed, obviously relieved. "May I?" The young man extended his elbow toward Cassidy.

Must she be polite?

Guilt swept over her. *I'm sorry, Lord! Kindness, please grant me Your kindness!*

"Thank you." Cassidy smiled at him. Mr. Blackburn walked her in and helped her with her chair. He took a seat next to her.

Soon Aunt Emma and the children joined them at the table, and the meal was served. Cassidy was glad the men did most of the talking because her meal was far too wonderful to be spoiled by conversing. The evening slowly ticked by, and the group withdrew to the parlor where conversation turned to Cassidy.

"How was your trip from England, Lady Chandler?" Mr. Blackburn asked.

Cassidy sat down to her tea. "It could have gone smoother, though it was not altogether unpleasant."

"Hmm, did storms hinder you?" The young man looked generally concerned.

Cassidy's palms felt damp. "No."

The timely interruption of the children's governess came to Cassidy's rescue, as the prim woman called her two charges to bed.

"If you and Uncle Edward don't mind, I shall retire for the evening as well," Cassidy told her aunt, rising from the couch. The three adults rose with her.

"Of course, my dear. I know it has been a long day," Aunt Emma said.

Mr. Blackburn stepped forward. "It has been an honor, Lady Chandler. I do hope to see you in the future."

"And I you." *Liar.*

In her room, Cassidy wiggled out of her stiff dress, without patience to wait for the maid. Donning a nightgown left out for her, Cassidy crawled into bed and promptly fell into a sweet sleep.

# Chapter 18

Norfolk, Virginia

Sunlight spilled through the window and with it the song of mourning doves and blue jays. Leisurely, Cassidy opened her eyes only to shut them again, grimacing. What stunning light! With tightly shut eyes, she laid there several moments more and thanked the Lord.

She was alive! Alive and sleeping full nights again. Cassidy climbed out of bed just as a knock sounded at her door.

Upon Cassidy's permission, the same little maid came in with several frilly dresses to choose from.

"Breakfast is in an hour, my lady. Which of these would you like to wear?" The girl arranged the dresses on the bed.

An hour? Cassidy figured she had missed breakfast, judging by the height of the sun.

"What time is it?"

"Eight o'clock, my lady."

What a late breakfast! Then again, that is how it was at home. My, she had become more accustomed to life at sea than she'd thought.

"I'd like to go out to the garden before breakfast then. Have you anything more... comfortable that I could wear?"

Surprised, the maid hesitated. "Um, I... I could get you one of my dresses, Duchess. Though does time allow for a walk?"

Cassidy gave the girl her best smile. "That would be lovely. And never mind the time. I shall be back to put one of these on for breakfast." She motioned to the fancy dresses the maid had arranged on her bed.

"Yes, my lady." The girl hurried out the door.

A few minutes later the maid returned with what must have been her Sunday dress. Plain, simple, and practical. Perfect.

She slipped into it and Cassidy left the room and made her way to the back door.

Out onto the terrace, the brilliant sun soaked into her bare arms and face. Cassidy tilted her head up. The brisk morning air flowed through her lungs and then out again. *Thank you, Father!*

Stepping off the porch, Cassidy began her leisurely stroll through the gardens, admiring the blossoming flowers all the way. Poppies, jasmine, roses, and her favorite, forget-me-nots decorated in brilliant blue. Brightly colored birds chirped and fluttered through the trees. The path wound around a pond with willows bowing gracefully and reeds concealing the nests of water birds and frogs. The wool dress flowed just short of her ankles, allowing Cassidy to stretch her legs. And stretch she did. Picking up the pace, the cool wind encouraged her with a push from behind, and the doves ahead called to her.

Cassidy laughed, childlikeness taking over and she broke into a run. Her hair flowed behind her like a cape and her arms spread wide. At the outskirts of the garden she came to a field where she stopped. The knee-high grass waved to her. Birds chased in play.

Breathing hard, Cassidy tilted her face up again towards the warmth-giving light. Ah, how free it was here! It seemed all worries would fade with the shadows and all tears dry in the sun. Could anything be more delightful?

But Andrew and Preston were still out there. In pirate clutches. It seemed wrong that she was here, safe, as they fought for their lives.

Reluctantly, Cassidy finally turned and wandered back through the garden, stopping to smell the flowers and listen to the wildlife. The rustling of the trees, the tweet of the birds, the patter of her footsteps, and the plop of the frogs made up the song of the garden. How could she not add her own music? So, she sang her praise songs until her out-of-practice voice grated against her throat.

Not halfway back to the house, she noticed another path. Small as it might be, it was a path worn long ago. Curious, Cassidy stopped to study it. Definitely a path.

She pushed away a few low-hanging branches. The path eventually widened, becoming a clearing hidden to the outside world. In the center of the oasis was a leaning tree that held up a small wooden seat swing. The place was so secluded with its forest canopy that even the birds seemed to have no knowledge of it. First testing the ropes, Cassidy gently sat down and began to swing her legs like she had done as a child.

Ah, if only she could slow time!

Listening to her conscience, Cassidy slowed and waited until her arcs came to a lower circumference. Cassidy hurried to the opening of the little path, casting one last look over her shoulder at the haven. Indeed, she would be back.

Once back on the garden path, Cassidy forced herself into a run. Her aunt and uncle were sure to be waiting on her.

To avoid being seen with windblown hair, muddy feet, and in a dress too short for her, Cassidy went around the house to the back door. As quietly as possible, she opened it and crept in. The cook gasped at her.

Unlike back home, the servants here were apparently not accustomed to young dukes and duchesses creeping through their kitchen doors. Cassidy flashed the cook an apologetic smile, then darted away.

Back in her room, Cassidy leaned against the door. Made it. And according to the clock, none-too-soon. Hastily, she changed into the simplest of the three dresses that lay on her now-made bed. She slid into her desk chair and studied herself in the mirror. She seemed to be sporting that adventurous look of hers. Just what would her aunt think?

After brushing out her dark curls, she twisted her hair back into a bun. Nothing fancy, but it would have to do for now. Cassidy left her room and hurried down to breakfast. Upon entering the dining room, Cassidy found the family just being seated.

"Good morning, Cassandra. Did you sleep well?" Aunt Emma smiled at her but cast an uncertain glance at Cassidy's hair. A shame. Cassidy thought she had done a good job.

"Very well, thank you."

"Good. I'd not like to delay this morning. Mr. and Mrs. Thwart are coming over this afternoon, and we must be back in time to greet them," Aunt Emma bustled.

Cassidy settled into her seat with the help of the wary butler. She received a wave of guilt for her shortness with him yesterday. Poor man now seemed afraid of her. "Are we going somewhere, Aunt Emma?"

"To the market, dearie! Don't you remember? You haven't any clothes but my own to wear!" Emma exclaimed.

Right, shopping. Swell. "Oh yes, of course. I'll be ready."

Aunt Emma shifted her gaze again to Cassidy's hair. "Good, and maybe have Betsy redo your hair."

Cassidy weaved her way to the front of the store with her several purchases. Much to Aunt Emma's dismay, she had picked out three simple, good quality, everyday dresses and one elegant evening gown. Itching to get out of the stiff, frilly dress she was currently in, Cassidy paid the clerk with the money Tanner left her and ducked back into the dressing room to put on one of the simple everyday gowns. Slim at the waist, long sleeved, and a straight skirt made up the dress's practical fit while still showcasing an elegant shade of lilac.

Finished, Cassidy put her aunt's dress with her purchases and hastened off to find Aunt Emma. Near the back of the store, she found her talking with a prim-looking woman that had clearly a lot to complain about.

Great.

Considering the last conversation her aunt had had, Cassidy guessed they would be talking for another half hour. Though more comfortable in her new outfit, her patience had come to a dangerous end. They had been out for hours, and she was more than ready to get home.

Sighing, Cassidy backtracked. At least this time she could avoid taking part in conversation. Outside, she took a deep breath of the clean air. Instantly, her nerves cooled. Much better.

Finding a bench nearby, Cassidy sat down to wait for her aunt. For a while, she watched the crowd and listened to the sounds of American life.

Personally, Cassidy found their accents funny, but then, they probably felt the same about her.

Suddenly, the sack slipped from beneath her arm.

"Hey!" Cassidy swung around to see the thief dart off into a side alley.

If he thought she was some incompetent little snitch then he was badly mistaken. On her feet in an instant, Cassidy charged after the minute man who hastened out of sight. But not fast enough.

Around the corner she caught sight of his coat-tail making the next turn. Turn after turn they made, headed toward the lesser part of town. On and on she followed him, pushing away her conscience's desperate plea.

Finally, near the dock, the man stopped and ducked through the door of a tavern.

Now what? She really should not go in there. Should she turn around? She ought to tell the police. No, by then the man would get away. Not if she could help it! Besides, now he was trapped... if there was no back door.

So, through the door she went. The stench of alcohol and cigar smoke slapped her in the face. She staggered and covered her mouth and nose and pushed on.

When her eyes adjusted to the dimness, Cassidy instantly regretted her decision. Gruff, unrefined men looked up at her from round tables throughout the tavern, large mugs of rum in front of them. They eyed her with an openness that anyone she knew would deem inappropriate. Andrew would have stepped in front of her and beaten any man that came close. What would Preston do? She didn't know.

At the counters, women showing an inappropriate amount of cleavage served rounds of drinks to men who clearly did not need another round. Cassidy grimaced. Perhaps it was a good thing Andrew and Preston were not here after all.

Fighting the redness she knew was coming to her cheeks, Cassidy turned away from them all and caught sight of the thief headed down a side hall, then through one of the many doors that lined the walls. On a mission again, Cassidy stalked after the man. What was she to do when she came to the man? Threaten him? She could tell him her father was related to the king... but that might get her kidnapped again.

At the end of the hall, she was considering which of the doors the tramp had gone through when low voices beckoned to her from a crack in a door. Cassidy stepped quietly past. Best continue on. As she moved by, Cassidy made out one word. *"Cade,"* brought to a sudden halt, she eased back within earshot to listen.

"... surprising, yes? But when he came to me with the job, I knew it was ordained by destiny! You see, how often do easy jobs come along? Low risk, and the pay is like that of rescuing a... a princess, see?" said the first man.

"What'd Cade want with 'im?" said a second, deeper voice, less animated than the first.

"Well, you see…" The man's voice quieted. Cassidy crept closer. "Williams' father was a navy general who helped to capture Bartholomew Roberts."

"Ah, Cade's ol' cap'in."

"Exactly! Apparently, the boy has a clue to where 'is father hid Roberts' treasure."

"Wait. Yer sayin' that Preston Williams, a kid from San Juan, has a clue to the most hunted-for treasure since Constantine, and ya just handed it back to the hands who stole it?" The deep voice harbored clear disgust.

"Well now, that is the rumor, yes? Besides, even if I kept Williams, he was only the first piece of the puzzle. 'Is daddy's partner has the… other clue."

"Well?"

"Well, what?"

"Fer goodness' sake Henry, who's 'is partner?"

Cassidy could almost hear "Henry" smirk. "That is the problem, it would seem, yeah? A duke of England. But you know ol' Mayson. The word is 'e's kidnapped tha Englishmen's daughter… or son… or both perhaps?"

Cassidy moved away from the door and leaned against the wall. She covered her mouth with her hands, and her breath was heavy. *Oh, God! They're after that treasure! Dear, Jesus, what do I do?* The authorities. She had to go to the authorities. Before she could move a muscle, the door opened, and the two men stepped out. One with talismans around his neck and the other a pirate-looking man with broad shoulders and covered in grime.

"Well, well. What have we 'ere, Blake?" The shorter of the two with the animated voice, Henry, grabbed Cassidy's wrists. "A little spy, yes?"

"A pretty little spy." Blake was definitely more pleased by her intrusion than his friend. Cassidy kicked her captor in the shins and jerked away, breaking his hold.

"Oi! Not polite!" Henry exclaimed.

Cassidy tore off to the exit of the hall until a jerk halted her after a few mere steps. She cried out when she was wrenched back into the dark end of the hall, the second man's large hand clamped around her arm.

"Where ya goin,' Missy?" Blake said into her ear. His other caressed her neck. A liberty she had not allowed anyone. His fingers were cold and tough, covered in calluses. Her skin crawled. Oh, Andrew would be livid!

"Take your hands off, idiot! Are you so blind? She's from the wealthy. Her daddy probably has much power, yes? To violate her would mean to unleash all the red coat power on yourself," Henry said, much to Cassidy's surprise. Even more surprised was Blake. Immediately he took his hand off her.

"Well, what'd we do with 'er?" Blake grumbled.

Ignoring his 'friend,' Henry put on his best smile and turned to Cassidy. "What is your name, my dear?" Why did he just switch accents?

Cassidy pushed away the panic threatening to grip and hold her. *No! I shan't be afraid! Not afraid! Oh, Dear Lord, help me!*

Henry's smile faded at her silence. "Fine. At least tell us what you 'eard, Or we can't let you go, yeah?"

Let her go? Would they actually do that?

"Bartholomew Henry?" Cassidy squeaked out.

His smile returned. "Humbly at your service," he bowed. "Glad to hear someone 'as 'eard of me."

"Only from whom you betrayed." This man could be read like a book, and Cassidy was gaining boldness. Was boldness good or bad?

A frown shadowed his eyes, but his smile did not move. "I've betrayed many, yes. But whom do you speak of?"

Should she tell him? "Preston Williams." *Oh dear.*

"Really? You're a friend of 'is? Special friend, perhaps?"

*Why does everyone assume that?*

Lifting her chin, Cassidy tried to redeem herself. "He helped me after I was kidnapped."

New elation lit Henry's eyes. Not good. "Ah, that is interesting. Now what pretty, wealthy young woman would Cade have reason to capture these days?" Henry's eyes now moved past her to Blake.

Blake shifted behind her, but said nothing.

Henry gave a disapproving glance toward him. "The duke's daughter of course!" Henry knelt to

Cassidy's level. "You are the... the duchess from England, yes?"

Any boldness deserted her. As though by her stillness she could hide from his gaze, she stood as motionless as she could, firmly in the hold of the captain's compatriot.

Satisfied, Henry straightened. "Take 'er to the ship!"

Why did this keep happening to her? Except this time, she had no one to blame but herself.

# PART THREE

# *Chapter 19*

The *Raven*

Corey Davis paced the forecastle. He was done with this charade. Captain Henry was all but a counterfeiter, at the moment anyway. It started with Preston, then went down the ranks of the best of the crewmen, whether being sold or traded Corey did not know. He and Mr. Bentley, the old quartermaster, were the only ones left from Corey's original crew. They had acquired all new men since then. Prosperous young sailors, strong and of sound mind, mostly. Of course, they knew nothing of Henry's real work. Clever man. No doubt he made more money off his workers than being a "merchant."

For whatever reason, Corey was still there. He almost wished to be sold to the next pirate. Let it not be mistaken, Henry's efforts were not lacking. The man was always trying to pawn him off. A grand feeling, to be sure.

*I ought to just run.* Corey glanced at his small duffel. Three other times Corey had been in this exact position. Every time he had failed to muster the courage. He was no leader. No hero. But this time, Corey had to do it. He took a deep breath.

*They wouldn't even realize I'm gone until I'm long out of range, and what better place to escape than to America?* It was just a matter of sneaking off the ship. Though really, only Henry and Mr. Bentley would notice or care. Best do it now while at least the captain was gone.

Commotion on the dock alerted Corey of the captain's return.

*Rats.*

Sighing, he shoved his duffle, still packed, to the side.

It was an unusual amount of commotion for Henry's return. Curious, Corey made his way to the main deck and had to push his way through his taller fellow crewmen.

"What's going on?" he demanded. No one bothered to answer him.

When he broke through, Corey's brows lifted. The captain was walking up the gangplank holding a young woman – a beautiful young woman – in his grasp.

*Uh oh.*

"Mr. Lee, take this young woman to our holding cell," Henry ordered, shoving the girl toward an imposing crewman. The girl gasped at the push and nearly fell. Fragile thing.

"Aye, sir," Mr. Lee's gravelly voice responded, though his brows arched in question. Big, broad, and not the smartest, Mr. Lee made a great sailor, but he was also a kind soul, Corey had found.

The poor man looked confused to the point of concern. Why would his captain suddenly bring a girl on board against her will and have her put in a cell? Still, Lee obeyed his commands and led the trembling girl away and down the stairs. Several young men's eyes followed her improperly and Corey scowled at them, though they heeded him not.

"Who is she, Captain?" one asked.

"My royal fortune," Henry muttered under his breath. He then lifted his voice and commanded, "There has been a change of plans! Set sail immediately! We have an appointment to make!"

With excitement in the air, everyone hastened under order. They sailed into open water in a mere half-hour.

When things began to settle, Corey, as he often did, grabbed a pail and brush and got down on his hands and knees to scrub the deck. His mind sailed far faster than the *Raven*.

Henry had never dared to do something so bold before. What had the girl done? Who was she? Should he do something about it?

Corey sighed. Even if he did attempt something, what could he do? Was there any way to help her? A pretty young girl dressed so finely; she probably was to be held for ransom. Kidnapping for ransom happened all the time. No sense in making the situation worse. Yes, Henry probably ran into her and could not help himself.

"Davis!"

Corey spun and looked around to find a frowning Mr. Bentley on the main deck, arms crossed.

Hastening to his quartermaster, Corey straightened respectively. "Sir?"

"Davis, I ain't trustin' any of the men with that girl, so yer gonna tend 'er, got it? Yer can handle that, aye?"

Corey tried not to take offense, not that he wasn't used to it. Bentley and Henry never kept him at a spot long enough for him to learn it. Corey simply was not a fast learner, not like Preston. Bentley and Henry had loved Preston.

"Aye, sir." *Why am I always getting these jobs?*

With another heavy sign, Corey left Bentley and headed down the stairs toward the storage room, having nearly forgotten they had a cell down there. When he entered the room, several men were outside the cell.

"What's yer name, pretty little tha-a-ang?" slurred one.

"Is yer wealthy father gonna come savin' ya?" taunted another.

"'Course 'e will. Who wouldn't come at the call of such a distressed, lovely woman?" a soberer one added.

"Why won't she say somethin'?" the first complained.

"Probably because you all have scared her half to death. Now off with you, or I swear I'll tell the captain you broke into his barrels of rum!" Corey

threatened. It was the only way to get their attention. The men growled, but scampered off.

When they were gone, Corey stepped nearer to
the cell. The girl was huddled at the furthest back
of the cell, trembling. *Poor thing.* Her knees were
pulled up to her chest, though she held her head
up and stared at him. *What beautiful eyes,* he noticed at once.

"I apologize on their behalf. They won't bother
you anymore. Quartermaster has demanded I'm to
be your caretaker, so best get used to me. I'm Corey
Davis. Call me whatever you like." He paused to let
her speak. She didn't, nor did she seem impressed
with his statement. If only he were good with
women!

As the silence stretched on, Corey studied her.
*Well, now what?* "What's your name?" he asked.

She hesitated. "Cassandra Chandler."

"Miss Chandler, while our captain is not the
most, eh, moral of men, he is reasonable and cares
about appearances. As soon as a price is arranged,
he is sure to let you go."

"No, Mr. Davis. That is not the case this time."
The girl looked sad, as though having already seen
too much in her life. He wished to comfort her.
Foolish man he was. He ought to try to make *good*
impressions first.

"How so?"

She shook her head, her dark curls bouncing.
"It's complicated. Pirates and treasure and old
grudges." Her eyes wandered down to her lap.

"Mmm, complicated indeed," he replied dryly. That's how everything was these days.

Cassidy sat at the back of her dark, damp, and depressing cell. Surely, she would not be given her own room this time. What if those horrid men came back?

*You'll just have to grow up!* she reasoned with herself firmly. What a novel idea that was. At eighteen she really ought to be more mature, like Andrew. Oh dear, Andrew would really have scolded her and said she deserved to be kidnapped for such foolish behavior. A young woman chasing after her own thief deserved a scolding.

*What would Preston say?* Probably scold her too, but she liked to think of him being more understanding. Understanding? For goodness sake, how was her behavior understandable?

*Dear Jesus, rescue me, please! I know I deserve this, and I'm sorry!* The tears she had fought the last few hours finally slipped onto her cheek, and the sobs, which had been building for weeks, rose in her chest.

Still arguing with her tears, Cassidy wondered what to do. Had it been just this morning that she was singing her heart out to God? She certainly did not feel that free, blessedness now.

Footsteps approached.

*Oh no, God, please make them go away!* The men were incredibly frightening and Mr. Davis made her uncomfortable. He did not seem to understand social cues at all, and she was not sure how to handle it. Her last caretaker was much better.

*Judging by first impressions, now are we?* Cassidy's conscience pricked. After all, she was terrified of Preston at first. Tall, imposing, with those dark eyes...

Mr. Davis rounded the corner. "Here's your dinner." He opened the door and offered her the plate.

Cassidy had no desire to go near him, or eat, or get up for that matter, but what if he was sneaking her food? It would be horribly rude not to take it.

Slowly, she rose and approached him. "Merci," she murmured, taking the plate before retreating back to her dark corner .

He stood there, watching her, making her feel uncomfortable. Unable to eat under his gaze, Cassidy sat her plate to the side and drew her knees up. She gave him a sharp look. "Have you something else for me, sir?" Her voice squeaked a little, but she hoped he did not pick up on the quivering of her heart.

"No. I apologize." He stepped back and closed the door, locking it again. "I... I'm sorry," Mr. Davis stammered before fleeing the room in a similar fashion to that odd butler.

Cassidy sighed. She just wasn't making friends these days, was she?

## The *Royal Fortune*

Mayson Cade frowned as his ship sailed into the meeting spot. They had arranged to meet here, but the fact that Roy Collin's ship awaited them disturbed him. Collins was tardy, always. *What curse has him on time?*

Cade surveyed the *Royal Fortune*, his pride and glory. The dark, he felt, made it look especially magnificent and mysterious, as it did now. When they snuffed out the kerosene, Cade knew that it was virtually invisible. The crew was also worth his pride. Preston Williams, who stood at the helm, had really shaped the men well. Unfortunate, really, for Cade was hoping he wouldn't like the man.

"Williams! You stay at the helm and be ready to leave at a moment's notice! Prepare yer men!" Cade bellowed up to him.

"Aye, sir!" Williams responded. Amazing, the young man had so much confidence behind the wheel. It made Cade blissful to know the fear he struck in Williams. That man was easily humbled. Truly, he was a perfect quartermaster to have. Maybe Cade could keep him around a little longer.

"Chandler!" The young duke swung around to Cade.

"Yes?" Now this boy was a piece of work.

"Yer shift is done. Go down to the forecastle, and stay there." Chandler eyed him. His brows met above his nose and obstinance lifted his chin.

"Yer heard me! Get lost!"

The young man stared at him a moment, as though trying to think of a retort. Finally, he meandered away.

Cade spat a foul word under his breath.

The *Royal Fortune* slid neatly up beside the waiting ship under Williams' steady hand. The gangplank was quickly lowered, and Roy Collins and his quartermaster came across without missing a beat.

*Odd.*

"Well, well, I didn't know you to be punctual." Cade smirked.

Collins was not amused. "You assured me, Cade, that the girl would be dead before they reached her."

Cade's eyes narrowed. "And?"

"And now, Batholomew Henry is bringing her to you and meddling in our business!" Collins spat out furiously. For goodness' sake, what was he so up-in-arms about?

"Hey, get a hold of yerself! So the girl lived, big deal. Maybe it's for the better. Now we can more easily threaten that brother of 'er's. 'E's been real obstinate. Williams'll follow suit, if we can hold a real price on 'er head."

"Fine, but if this compromises things you *will* pay, Mayson Cade."

Cade lifted his chin. "Fine, but don't you forget that there's a price for yer pretty head."

A muscle jerked in Collins' jaw. The British had been looking for their mole for years, and Collins had become increasingly careful and clever to compensate his double allegence. Even Collins himself had been sent looking for the "Ghost Conspirator," who seemed to disappear without a trace.

Painfully, Cade had to admit, Collins had made a name for himself, literally. Yet ironically, because of Collins' hard work as the Ghost Conspirator, the navy would no doubt choose him over Cade. All Cade would need to do was drop a few hints...

Collins looked around for a change of subject, becoming weary of their banter. "Where's Chandler? And Williams?"

"I sent Chandler to the forecastle. Wasn't sure if you wanted to be seen. Williams' at the wheel."

"Good." He looked toward the helm. "I want to meet him."

"Williams?"

"Yeah."

Cade frowned. "'E's good behind the wheel and a natural seaman, but 'e's nothin' special."

Collins was already headed toward the helm. Cursing under his breath, Cade followed.

Before Collins could say something to humiliate either of them, Cade bellowed up to Williams. "Mr. Williams! I have someone I want ya to meet!"

After leaving the wheel in capable hands, Williams cautiously made his way to meet them. For being as capable of a leader as he was, his meekness was surprising. Maybe Cade was too hard on the lad.

Not one to be patient, Collins introduced himself... well, his alias anyways. "I'm Oliver O'Toole. I've 'eard lots 'bout ya, Mr. Williams."

Cade rolled his eyes. Slipping into a slobbish pirate accent was overdoing it, Cade thought.

"A pleasure, Captain O'Toole." Williams politely shook Collins' hand.

"Are yer the quartermaster?"

"Oh no. Second mate, sir."

Collins slid a look at Cade before averting his eyes back to Williams. "I 'ear yer have a clue to Roberts's lost treasure. A little goodbye present from yer daddy, aye?"

Williams' eyes narrowed, and even in the darkness Cade could see his sturdy jaw clench in warning. Cade sighed inwardly. *Way to go, Collins.*

"That is none of your busness, Captain."

Collins laughed. "Like ya know anything."

Cade could see Williams' chest quiver in fury. "Enough, Captain," Cade spat.

"I'm sorry, is me welcome worn, Mayson?" The question hung with such a threat that Cade considered socking the smirk off Collins' face.

Collins was met only by silence.

"Fine, I hope ya find what yer looking for, *Captain*." Collins shouldered past him and back to his own ship.

Cade did not turn around. This young snoop would not take all of his dignity. Williams watched him go, then cast Cade a questioning glance.

"Continue on course!" Cade bellowed for all to hear before storming off to his cabin.

# Chapter 20

The *Royal Fortune*

Preston watched Cade out of the corner of his eye as the man descended the stairs to his cabin. Meandering back to the helm, Preston saw Andrew coming toward him with a look on his face that reflected what Preston felt: wary mistrust.

"What on earth was that about?" Andrew was obviously still fuming at Cade for quarantining him.

"I have no idea, but I don't like it." Preston's grimness did nothing to hide his still-boiling blood. Fine. Let it simmer.

"What happened?" Andrew crossed his arms.

"A man came over from the other ship. He and Cade talked. They came over to me, and he introduced himself. Captain Oliver O'Toole. Have you ever heard of him?"

Andrew thought only a moment before shaking his head. "Never. And he introduced himself because...?"

"I don't know."

"Then what?"

"He stuck his nose into our business, Cade told him 'enough,' and he left."

"So, some pirate came to introduce himself to you but didn't want anything to do with me, a duke?" Andrew gave an offended pout.

"Maybe he's particularly peeved at the nobility, and let's be honest, who could blame him?" Preston dodged a playful punch from Andrew. "Hey! No smacking the helmsman!"

"Ha! I'd like to do just that!" Andrew finally landed a fist on Preston's bicep.

"Ow! Okay, okay!"

Andrew stood tall, grinning, proud of his triumph. "Told you I could beat you."

"That hardly counts. I had one hand on the wheel. Besides, we were talking about swords."

"Ah, so you're admitting I'm better with a sword!"

"What? Nonsense!"

The duke smirked.

Wrinkling his nose at his friend, Preston turned away and put both hands on the ship's wheel. He squinted into the darkness at the main sails. "Now go check the nine-yards! It looks like they've come untied again."

Even from the corner of his eye he caught Andrew's eye roll. "Yes, your majesty."

Like a cat swishing his tail, Cade sat in his desk chair, grating his fingernails against the desk. *So the girl lived. So Henry is bringin' 'er to me. It ain't nothin' I can't handle.* Another kink in his plan, that was all. But the risk of being caught was mounting, and with it, the stress. He could not let Henry and the duchess just wander the seas for days with the navy on their heels.

But Henry was smart enough to fill in the gaps. And though Cade would never admit it, he simply could not let Henry be captured. Henry had been on the seas since Cade signed on to Robert's ship at least. No, Cade felt some responsibility for the old coot. Like it or not. It was Cade's way of taking care of the elderly. Even though Henry annoyed the life out of him.

Mayson sighed and felt his temples. *It had been going so well!* As planned, he'd acquired the Williams boy from Henry. He had then captured the duchess with ease. Next, he had put her on a deserted island, sent the royal navy searching, and struck a bargain for the duke's life. The duchess should have died, sending the Queen's ships all the way back to England with her body for a proper burial. In that time, Mayson Cade finally would have what he needed to find his beloved captain's treasure, which was rightfully his. The sons of Bartholomew Roberts's assassins were in his grasp.

Williams turned out to be just as smart as his daddy, finding the treasure's location in impressive timing. It irked Mayson, just a little, that the boy could find it so quickly after Cade's own years of pondering the location. Then there was Chandler. *If that brat don't dig somethin' up soon...* In Mayson's opinion, the young duke had not inherited his father's intelligence.

All that was needed now was to avoid getting captured before finding the treasure, by whatever means necessary. *Perhaps having the duchess would not be so terrible after all...* She had made nice leverage on the obviously smitten Williams. He would have to rekindle that fire.

Mayson chuckled to himself. *A pirate playing matchmaker, who would have thought?*

As the days rolled by, Captain Cade became increasingly anxious. He worked his men hard and wanted every stitch of sail catching wind.

Preston seemed to receive the brunt of his agitation. Not to mention the way Cade hounded Preston and Andrew for more details of the treasure. Details they continuously looked for, but to no avail.

"Sail ho!" The lookout called.

At the wheel, Preston yelled for a man to take his place and hurried to the railing with his spyglass. Sure enough, a vessel sailed directly toward them.

As he studied the ship, the spyglass was snatched from his hand.

Cade brought the glass to his eye and cursed.

Preston winced.

"Henry," the captain muttered in fresh irritation.

*Henry? Bartholomew Henry?* A second look at the ship, and indeed Preston recognized it. *Oh, when I get my hands on him...*

Cade turned to glare at Preston. "How dare ya leave yer post! Back to the wheel! And stop this ship!" He spun on his heels, leaving Preston to wipe the spit from his face and smooth his own ruffled feathers, not that either of those things where foreign to him.

He had been meek enough through this whole charade. How dare Cade treat him so! He was neither animal nor servant! *Well, not an animal, at least.* This thought lit him up again. *No! I'm not a servant! Never ever!*

'*Really?*' A still, small voice inquired.

Preston recognized it. *Well, not to man, I mean.*

'*Is that so?*'

He swallowed. *Your will be done, O'Lord.*

'*Show Me.*'

*Ugh!* Preston knew exactly what He meant. *I need to do Your will, Lord, not mine. But Father, how do I know what that is?*

Silence.

"All right there?" Andrew came up beside him.

"Mm-hmm."

Andrew raised an eyebrow.

"That's the ship I worked on before coming here." Preston jerked his head toward the oncoming ship.

Now both brows lifted. "Hey, didn't you say you had a friend on board?" Andrew asked.

Preston's heart leapt. "Corey! We have to get a message to him," he said, a plan already formulating in his mind.

The *Raven* looked small and insignificant next to the dark, imposing *Royal Fortune*. The graceful curves and elegant lines of the *Fortune* made her truly a piece of art. If Cade would just get some new sails, scrub off the salt and sand, and scrape off the barnacles, she really could be breathtaking.

Motioning for a deck hand, Preston left the wheel to greet his former captain and crew. He hoped Cade would focus on Henry and not notice he had left his post. Again. But his plan was too important now.

When a gangplank was stretched across, Captain Cade waited in all his glory, frowning, for the other captain to come to him. Bartholomew Henry, flanked by Mr. Bentley and a few others, strode across the gangplank jangling all the way.

Preston could almost sense the grating effect the sound had on his captain's nerves.

At the rail, Preston eyed the crew on the other side. Not one did he recognize. Disappointed, he moved back with the other men. Where was Corey? Had his friend been traded like he was? Preston prayed he had not been.

"Captain Mayson Cade!" Henry gave a sweeping, jingling, bow. Cade winced. "I come out of friendship!" He winked. "As always."

"Cut it, Henry!" Cade snapped. "I've business to attend to. Give me what ya came for, then be on yer merry way."

"I seemed to have stumbled upon a lovely jewel you lost, and I am here to return her."

*Her?* Preston's pulse quickened. *Henry, what have you done?*

"May I present her ladyship!" He made a sweeping gesture to the stairs of his own ship.

Preston watched in horror.

Gagged, with her hands behind her back, Lady Cassandra Chandler was pushed from behind into the light. Andrew's gasp could be heard from across the ship.

Furthering Preston's distress, Corey stood behind her, tightlipped and solemn.

*Oh, Jesus, no, please no!* Preston's heart beat at his chest like a newly-caged animal. How could Corey do this? Were they not friends? Was this man really the man he was about to ask for help?

Preston felt as though everything was collapsing. Not only was Cassidy back in harm's way, but their plan would likely fail. Preston took a resigned breath.

*Too late now.*

Cade stood silent. His reaction unreadable.

Corey pushed Cassidy across the plank and onto the dark ship. Her jade eyes were wide and wild with fear as she stepped from one prison to the other. Preston's chest hurt. With a glance at Andrew, Preston found him ghostly white.

"Williams!"

Preston startled. "Yes, Captain?" He stepped forward to face Cade.

"Resume yer duties with the lady. And Chandler, take 'is place at the helm." Cade did not even look at him; his glare was locked on Henry.

"Yes, Captain." Preston's jaw was tight and his gaze fierce. He approached them and Cassidy gave him a pitiful look that affected the rate of his heart.

*Alive, she's alive!* Looking at her now gave Preston a lifting peace. How terrible it would have been for her to die.

"Mr. Davis," Preston acknowledged with a curt nod. He kept his eyes locked on Corey, who seemed to shrink from him in shame. Preston did not care.

Offering his hand, Preston received a surprised look from Corey, who warily extended his own hand. Preston held Corey firm. Perplexed, Corey's brows knit together as he glanced from their locked hands to Preston's face. Preston nodded slowly and pulled away.

He next turned to Cassidy. Preston faced a question. Should he take her arm and lead her? Or walk ahead for her to follow? He made a quick decision and gently took her elbow.

*Forgive me, Andrew.* At least this way it would be less tempting for the other men to reach out to her.

"Come, my lady," he whispered into her ear. She shuddered visually. Was he too close? He hadn't thought so. A quiver ran through his own muscles, disturbing him, so he pulled away.

As soon as they were out of sight, Preston stopped her and spoke softly. "Let me get this off of you." He untied her gag and pulled it away from her. "Are you alright?"

"Yes. They did not harm me." Her voice was melodic, her accent thicker than even Andrew's. Preston realized how much he had missed it.

He let out his breath. *Thank you, Lord!* "Let me get the ropes off." After fumbling with the bonds a few minutes, he felt her getting anxious. "I'm going to cut it. Be still, my lady."

Cassidy barely breathed until Preston sheathed the dagger.

"That was a good test of trust." He grinned at her.

The edges of her lips curled upwards. "I suppose so."

He loved her smile, her dimples. He didn't know she had dimples.

"Are you going to lock me away?" Cassidy prompted, watching him.

"Of course. I mean, no. Well, you know what I mean. This way," Preston hurried forward, hoping to hide the heat in his face.

He held the door back for her, and she entered. "I'm going back to the helm, I'll be back, and I'm sure Cade will release your brother soon. Here's the key."

Cassidy took it. "Thank you."

With a nod, he turned to leave.

"Preston, they were going to punish you when I... you know... did they..."

Preston turned back to see the concern etched on her face. A sudden yearning to go to her and pull her close pulsed through his blood. Disturbed, he shoved it away.

"...did they hurt you?" she finished quietly.

"Some hours at the main mast and the taste of a cat 'o nine," he offered a smile. "Nothing I didn't bargain for."

Her blank expression told him she had no idea what he meant, as he wished.

"I'm sorry you went through that for me."

"I'm not." He gazed down into her wide, wonder filled eyes. Her chest fluttered visibly. *Easy Preston, best not do anything stupid.*

"I'll take my leave." He started out before she could reply. Best to leave it that way. Unsaid. Why did he do this? Why taunt himself so? Why taunt *her* so? He could not have her; he knew that. Yet this ache in his chest was becoming unbearable. Indeed, he was falling for Cassandra Chandler, and falling hard.

"Cassidy!" Andrew rushed into the room, almost colliding with Preston. "Thank the Lord!" He drew her into a tight embrace. "Are you alright?"

Cassidy nodded against her brother's shoulder. "Yes. Are you?"

"How could I not be? You're alive and well and here with us!" Andrew drew back.

"Us?" Cassidy glanced back and forth the two boys. "I knew you two would be friends!"

"Well, two people fighting for the same goal have at least one thing in common." Andrew shrugged toward Preston before focusing again on his sister. "So, what happened to you?"

Cassidy was in turmoil. What on earth had happened? Something. She was sure of it. The question is: what? Good? Bad? Was she disturbed or exuberant? She had not expected anything from him. But yet, either her heart or her mind told her something passed between Preston and her earlier that day. The way he looked at her. The gentleness of his fingers on her arm. It was as though he thought she was the most treasured person on the whole earth.

Cassidy groaned. What if he was just like all those other boys? Shallow, attracted to beauty or money or standing. She would make a wife with benefits. But benefits did not make a marriage. Could he love her? Her, for who she really was?

Nothing had happened. Besides, she barely knew him. There may not be anything there. Maybe she imagined the whole thing.

But what if she hadn't?

It was hard to grasp someone choosing her. *Her.* Cassidy could hardly imagine someone truly loving her. Only God, so big and powerful, seemed to be big enough to love her. Surely no once here on earth could love her for her. Could Preston..?

No.

She would not let herself hope. She would not fall.

But the thoughts, oh, they were somewhere between torture and paradise. Uncertain, Cassidy sat in deep thought for a long while.

Finally, she rose from her thoughts to tidy up. She dusted and straightened and organized the little room as best she could. Before long, she sang a pleasant tune as she lost herself in work.

When would his heart slow down? Preston's restlessness finally forced him to let someone else take the wheel. On all fours, Preston scrubbed the deck, channeling all his anger, unrest, and burning energy into the scrubbing brush in his hand.

What did he even have to offer her, her father? Nothing. He was just an orphan from a Spanish settlement. Adopted by a shipbuilder. Signed to the crew of a scoundrel. Traded to do the work of a pirate. And hopelessly smitten with a member of the most revered, powerful royal family in the world.

At least he dreamt big.

"If you scrub any harder, Preston Williams, I swear you'll break the board."

Preston looked up into Andrew's face. "That's a good idea. Maybe if I break enough of them I'll get kicked off this ship."

"Unlikely."

Preston shrugged. "Well?"

"Well what?"

"Are you going to help me or not?"

Andrew waved a hand at him. "Hey, not all of us need to burn off energy like you do."

"Who said it's energy I'm burning?"

The duke just looked at him for a moment. "Fair enough." He dropped down and grabbed the other brush.

"So, what are you burning?" Andrew questioned, with a sidelong glance at his friend.

Sitting back on his heels, Preston wiped the sweat from his lip. "I guess I'm upset that Corey was involved in all this. I thought he was on our side."

"Maybe he is."

"He should have at least tried to stop it."

"Just like you stopped the pirates from dumping my sister into the ocean?"

Preston's cheeks grew hot. "At least I tried."

"Well at least Corey had the good sense to know what would happen and not get flogged for trying to change the outcome."

Annoyed, Preston went back to scrubbing. "Why are you defending him? I thought you would be more mad than I am."

"I want to figure out what happened before I get too upset." Andrew's face was set in a deep frown. "Knowing Cassandra, she may have waved a flag in front of Henry's face to get back to us."

"To you."

"What?"

"To get back to you. She would never leave you behind."

Andrew cocked his head. *Just like Cassidy does in thought…* "Well anyway, I'm simply saying she may be more to blame than Henry and your friend. Besides, it's harder to be mad at her."

"True."

Silence followed as the two scrubbed and pondered.

"I hope the *Virtue* is alright." Andrew looked out toward the ocean.

Preston counted in his head. "If your crew made no stops, then Henry assumingly must have taken her after they dropped her off. And… let's see… if Henry made no stops that would put the two of them meeting up no more than a few days after her arrival to Virginia."

Andrew's brows inched higher. "You did all that in your head? Just now?"

"Would you be impressed if I did?"

"Mmm, maybe."

"Not completely. I did the distance estimations earlier while I was at the helm. I enjoy doing random calculations when I'm bored."

Shaking his head, Andrew let out a low whistle. "Why anyone would want to do math is beyond me."

Preston laughed until a gentle sound met his ears. He stilled, listening.

"What is it?" Andrew stopped as well.

"Listen." The noise grew stronger. Singing, it was someone singing! A lovely, sweet melody, though it was too quiet to make out the words.

"Do you hear that?" Preston asked Andrew, mystified.

"What? Cassidy singing?"

*Of course, it's Cassidy!*

"It's beautiful."

Andrew laughed. "Just wait, she's still warming up."

# Chapter 21

The *Royal Fortune*

Preston moved food to his mouth with his left hand and scribbled numbers onto a page with his right. Immersed in thought, he sat at his little table with the young duke and duchess. So immersed was he that he missed Cassidy's glance at her brother, who just shrugged in Preston's direction and continued eating. Straight-backed, Cassidy gave up the silent conversation with her brother and sat quietly watching Preston work.

As they were finishing their meal, Preston sat down his pencil and leaned back in his chair. "We'll be at our destination by nightfall tomorrow, if this wind keeps up."

"The sooner we get this over with the better," Andrew said.

"If we can even find the treasure," Preston reminded him.

"Time is getting us nowhere. I have no clue from my father. Our best chance is to simply start looking."

Preston stretched and yawned. "You think Cade will settle for that?"

"Does he have a choice?"

Preston shrugged. "Cade strikes me as one that makes his own options." He glanced at Cassidy.

Andrew scowled and lifted his chin. "Maybe. But he can't get what doesn't exist."

Preston quickly finished the last few bites of his dinner. "Well, I would like to sleep a little before the next shift." Rising, he bowed his head to Cassidy. "Goodnight, Cassidy. See you in six hours, Andrew."

Andrew grunted his reply while Cassidy gave a lady-like nod and shy smile.

As Preston walked out the door, Cassidy's eyes trailed him in thoughtless curiosity.

"Well, well, little sister, what have we here?" Andrew was watching her across the table with a smirk.

Color rose to her cheeks. "You were awfully rude. Snorting like that. And to think you were raised a royal."

He relaxed back into his chair. "The snort? Why, I'm practically a pirate for a few weeks. Might as well make the most of it." He gave her a brotherly glance. "Besides, Preston's not a class act either, and you clearly think well of him."

"Uh!" Cassidy stood, heat rushing through her body. "Do stop, Andrew! It's nothing, so just leave be!"

Andrew stood as well. "I'm not saying I don't approve. Rather, he's the only one I've met that just might be worthy of you."

Cassidy was taken aback. Her brother had never liked anyone coming around to court her. Then again, she did not like them either. It didn't really matter anyway. Preston was probably not interested in her.

She winced. The truth hurt. Throughout the entire dinner he gave her nothing. Not one long look, or interested smile, or even a word.

As though reading her thoughts, Andrew went on. "You should have seen him earlier today. He was thoroughly upset that you ended up here again. Then the look on his face when he heard you sing." At the horror on her face, he laughed. "Oh yes, we could all hear you, little sister. Everyone stopped to listen. Only a voice like yours could get away with it. Though I think Preston was the most impressed."

Cassidy sat down in the reading chair, embarrassed and flustered. He liked her voice? Did he really?

Andrew yawned. "Well, I'm going to try to sleep." He started for the door.

"Wait, Andrew, I've been meaning to ask you."

Andew turned to her, brows arched.

"What is a cat o'nine?"

Her brother frowned. "Where did you hear about a cat o' nine?"

"Preston mentioned it." Cautious, Cassidy frowned. "Why?"

He thought for a moment, then shook his head. "No reason. It's just a whip. Don't worry about it." Andrew turned back to the door. "Sleep well."

Cassidy's color drained from her face. "Goodnight," she squeaked.

Standing at the bow with Andrew to his left and Cade to his right, Preston scanned the ocean with his spyglass. "It should be right here." How many times had he done these calculations? Countless. How could he be mistaken?

"Find it, boy, or the duchess pays," Cade threatened, turning on his heels and heading to his cabin.

*So, already threatening to use Cassidy as a bargaining tool are we?*

With a deep sigh, Preston left the helm and went to the cabin to work on his calculations. When Cassidy let him in, he gathered all his papers at the table and checked and rechecked his work. Could he have done his measurements wrong?

"I simply don't understand. What happened?" Preston said. He put his head in his hands.

"Is the decimal in the right place?" Andrew asked dryly.

Cassidy slipped to Preston's side and studied his notes. "What about round off error?"

Preston lifted his head. "I took the measurements to four decimal places, but two is accurate enough to find it. Plus, it's easier."

"What if the island is so small it needs to be more accurate?" Cassidy asked.

"It would have to be awfully small, but at this point it's probably a good idea to be as accurate as possible." Preston pulled out a clean sheet and started working.

Cassidy watched him over his shoulder, which he did not mind. But it was hard to keep his mind on the work when she accidently brushed his shoulder, leaving behind an imprint of warmth.

A quarter-hour later, Preston had a pair of numbers to the fifth decimal place ready and waiting.

"Well, about another mile west and we should be on top of it," Preston said as he stacked his papers.

"Forget the parchments, Preston! Let's go find this place!" Andrew was already at the door.

Leaving the stack at the table, Preston turned to Cassidy. "I'll be back soon to clean this up and let you know what happens."

She gave him her best smile.

"Land ho!"

Preston saw it too. A small, jutting island that could barely be seen over the waves. Maneuvering the ship within a quarter mile, he saw it was not as small as he would have thought. Other than the right half, it was very flat with a short ribbon of vegetation stretching out about half a mile. Beaches snaked around the island's circumference.

He hollered for the anchor to be lowered, and a landing party readied. As he supervised the crew, Preston scanned the horizon.

*How long will it take to find the treasure?* He did not want to be here longer than necessary, but if he needed to stall, he would.

"Well, Lord Chandler," came a taunting voice from behind them. Preston turned to find Cade striding toward them, pushing Cassidy ahead. "I trust yer have all the pieces needed to find this here treasure."

Blood came dangerously close to boiling in Preston's mind. He fought the desire of every muscle in his body to push Cade away from her. He did not like the hold Cade had on her arm, nor how close he held her. *How dare he!*

Back rigid, Andrew faced Cade head on. His dark hair fell into his eyes, and his answer was tight-lipped. "Enough pieces."

Cade snorted but said nothing.

The two boys were silent as Cassidy and Cade got into one of the two boats and were lowered to the water. The rest of the men divided themselves between the boats and swung down.

Preston and Andrew were the last to board. Taking the ropes in both hands, Preston realized there was one spot left in the boat in which Cassidy and Cade sat.

*It's not your place, give it to Andrew. He protects her, not you.* With a final nod to himself, Preston turned back to his friend.

"You should go with Cassidy."

Andrew nodded. "See you on shore."

Shore was not much of a shore. In fact, it consisted more of rock than sand. On one side the rocks rose to make a sharp cliff, while the other was flat and thickly shrubbed.

"What is this place?" Andrew approached Preston with a frown on his face.

"Hot, for one."

"You don't say."

"So, Chandler, where is it?" Cade demanded.

Never lacking in audacity, Andrew ignored him. "Alright everyone, split up and start looking! And no skipping corners, unless you want to spend all day out here!"

Cade scowled. "That's yer plan?

"If the heat is too much for you, Captain, you can always go back to the ship," Preston remarked, rewarded with a smirk from Andrew. Preston grinned, though he had made the suggestion in hopes of getting Cassidy out of the sun. Her fair skin would roast.

"Ha!" Cade grunted. "Fine. We'll do this yer way."

As they split up, Preston started off down the shoreline to the right. For hours he wandered around looking for, well, treasure. The further he went, the steeper the ground became.

Preston walked to the edge of a cliff that dropped a dozen feet into the sea. He peered over the edge cautiously. Rocks jutted up from the water.

*What a terrible misfortune it would be to fall here.*

For hours more Preston searched the shoreline and into the dense underbrush. Finally, he gave up his tedious hunt and headed back. Maybe they'd already found it.

Back where he started, Preston found the beach empty, until he spotted Andrew further down.

"Find anything?" Andrew yelled.

"Yes, but not pirate treasure." Preston and Andrew met in the middle. "I take it you didn't either then."

"Not even a single coin. I just sent everyone out to look again. Though I'm quite sure the entire island has already been searched."

Preston nodded. He had searched a good portion of it himself. "Where are Cade and Cassidy?"

"They went back to the ship hours ago." Andrew stared at the sand, still thinking about the treasure. "We need to figure out where we haven't seached." He picked up a stick and started drawing in the sand.

"Is that a frog?" Preston frowned at the funny shape on the ground.

Andrew swung his head around and gave Preston an unimpressed look. "Yes, it is. His name is Froggy Went a'Courtin'." He rolled his eyes. "This is the island." He pointed to it with the stick.

Preston sent him a sidelong glance. "Really? Froggy Went a'Coutin'? That's what you named it?"

"What? He doesn't look like a Mr. Croak."

Grabbing the stick from the duke, Preston erased one part of the frog-shaped island.

"Hey!" Andrew protested.

Preston drew a line again, carefully accounting for all the bulges and dents in the shore line as best as he could remember.

"That's exactly what I had!" Andrew said.

Preston threw the stick at him. "Sometimes I wonder what world you're from."

"Ow! Not the same one as you, apparently."

"Well aren't you the tough one, your lordship."

Andrew wrinkled his nose. "You threw that hard, Mr. Congenial."

Preston rolled his eyes and knelt to study their map. "This is north." He pointed to the top of the drawing. "So I think we need to cover the north-west area again. It's more rocky but maybe..."

"No, not at all. North is here." Andrew pointed more toward the right of the drawing.

"What? No way! I did the calculations earlier, remember? North is definitely that way."

"I can settle this." Andrew reached into his leather waistcoat pocket and opened his hand to reveal a gold compass.

Preston's eyebrows arched.

Andrew glanced at him and held up a hand. "I know what you're thinking. Don't say it."

Preston opened his mouth to assure his friend but closed it quickly. He was charged and guilty.

"A friend gave this to my father. My father already had a gold compass, so he passed it down to me." Andrew explained, running his thumb over its smooth lid.

Preston stared at it. He had never seen anything like it. Something so, gold. When Andrew noticed Preston's fasination he held it out.

"Take a look."

Preston tried to hide his awe, and thus his penniless life. He had no desire for Andrew to know just how poor he was. Of course, not as poor as many in San Juan, but compared to the lowest of Andrew's friends, he was in poverty. Never had the two young men's difference in class been so evident.

Flipping open the lid, Preston found on the lid's interior a striking design of a compass pointing northeast. On the body of the device, a decorated backdrop showcased the elegant red arrow. North was actually between Preston's and Andrew's designated north.

"Neither of us were right." Preston remarked with a chuckle.

Andrew looked over Preston's shoulder. "I guess so."

Standing, Preston followed the little arrow in a circle till he faced north. His eyes narrowed, studying the compass intently. Keeping his hand positioned where the compass could still point north, he shifted his body to face the arrow on the lid. Preston glanced up in that direction.

"What is it?" Andrew asked from behind him.

Jerking his head around to look at Andrew, Preston locked his dark gaze on him. "Which friend?"

Andrew's brows came together. "What?"

"Which friend gave this to your father?" Preston demanded.

"I... I don't know. Father never said."

With an exasperated snort, Preston took off at a brisk walk toward the east part of the island.

"Where are you going?" Andrew called from a few steps behind him.

"Come on, dimwit!" With the compass in hand, Preston charged through the brush with an annoyed Andrew lagging behind.

When he began to recognize his surroundings, Preston slowed and emerged into the light. Andrew came crashing behind him and smacked into Preston's back.

"Ah!" Preston had to grab onto Andrew in order to keep from going over the edge of the cliff.

"Whoa," Andrew glanced over the edge. "You almost died."

Prseton glared at him. Another name was on the tip of his tongue, though his conscious pinged. *I called the duke of England a dimwit. You've done it now, Preston Williams.*

"So, where's the treasure?"

Preston looked around, then at the compass. "This is the furthest northeast point on the island." He glanced over the edge. "Wait…"

"What?" Andrew looked into the surf again.

Glancing around, Preston spotted a rocky way down. "Come on."

Andrew groaned but followed.

The two carefully made their way down. When they ran out of rocks, Preston stopped only a couple feet from sea level, peering at the cliff. Taking off his boots, he slid down the rest of the way and into the water. He sank only to his waist. Both relieved and surprised, he stepped lightly closer to the cliff.

A faithful splash from behind him told Preston that Andrew did no more than hesitate. It made him smile.

"Come look!" The closer he got to the rock wall, the lower the water was.

"Preston, the tide is going out!" Andrew called.

But Preston wasn't listening. He noticed an opening barely visible above the rising and falling of the waves. "Look!"

Andrew came up beside him and put his head down to look into the hole. A wave came up and soaked his lowered head.

"Ah!" Andrew sputtered. Laughing, Preston patted him on the back until he stopped coughing.

Preston retrieved a shell from the ocean bottom and lowered his head to listen, but not close enough for a lick from the waves. Tossing the shell inside the cave, he heard it hit rock and bounce off. An echo followed not far behind before the shell splashed into the water. Judging by the echo, it was no small space.

"We found it," Preston whispered.

"How big do you think this hole is?" Andrew asked.

Preston felt along the edge with his hands and feet. His arms easily spanned the width of the opening and felt along the bottom. It seemed to go down to the sandy floor. "Big enough. Come on, let's go make a torch. By the time we get back the tide will be low enough."

"Are we going inside?"

"Why not?"

Andrew grabbed Preston's arm. "What if there are traps?"

Raising an eyebrow, Preston surveyed his friend. "First, our fathers left this for *us* to find. Second, I'd rather us find it than Cade pushing Cassidy in front of him."

Andrew nodded slowly, studying him.

Discomforted, Preston turned away. He did not want Andrew knowing about his unwanted feelings.

Not much later, the men slipped back into the water, Andrew carrying a lit torch. The water had lowered enough only to fill half the opening. The two easily entered by ducking their heads.

The torch's light hurried off to explore all corners of the room, revealing not a cavern, but a tunnel. With water at their knees, the two tramped further into the unknown.

"Are you sure about this, Preston?" Andrew walked ahead of Preston with the torch.

"Not at all. That's why you're in the lead."

Andrew shot Preston a spiteful glare.

For long, haunting minutes, they trudged deeper and deeper until the tunnel opened into a large room. Preston's jaw dropped. Close to twenty chests were stacked neatly against the back wall.

"It's real. It's really real!"

"Yeah," Preston breathed. This was his father's legacy. His last great act of heroism. It suddenly occurred to Preston that he could not allow this to fall into pirate hands. Not after his father died to end Roberts' rule.

"This chamber fills up at least halfway with water." Andrew observed the water line. Barnicles covered the wall and most of the chests.

"Which means there's an air escape back in the tunnel. Once the water seals it off, it will stop rising in here." Andrew looked at him. "What?"

"Stop being so smart."

Grinning, Preston picked his way over to the chests.

"Let's open one." Andrew came up behind him.

"The locks will need to be broken. Unless you have a hammer, we'll have to wait," Preston fingered the lock.

"Why, I have one right here in my boot." Andrew reached down and tossed water up at Preston.

"Hey!" Preston splashed Andrew back. "Let's get back to the ship. No sense in leaving Cassidy by herself with those pirates longer than necessary."

Andrew stopped. "You're right. We found it. Now she's out of danger."

Preston grabbed Andrew's arm to stop him. "We can't tell Cade about this."

"How much longer do we need to stall?"

"It'll take at least two days to get all this out with the tide. Plenty of time. But that's not what I mean."

"What do you mean?"

"I'll not let this fall back into pirate hands." Preston paused to gather himself. "Not after my father died to stop it."

Andrew was silent for a moment. "I understand, Preston, but if our plan backfires, I will hand over this treasure to secure my sister's safety." He paused, facing Preston squarely. "And I thought you would too."

Preston grimaced. That was not what he he'd meant at all. Of course Cassidy's safety was of upmost importance. But his father...

"If this were to fall into the wrong hands..." Preston motioned to the chests, "It could do a lot of damage."

Andrew offered a weak smile. "What makes you think we'll let him have it forever? I, for one, shall not let him get away with kidnapping. He shall receive justice. And Preston," he put his hand on Preston's shoulder and shook him lightly. "your father's legacy shan't be lost."

Preston nodded, but his heart hurt. He felt confused and conflicted. He did not want Andrew to think he was willing to sacrifice Cassidy for his father's legacy. But how could he protect both?

"I'm sorry, Andrew. I don't want you to think...Of course, Cassidy's safety is..." Preston's chest constricted, choking his lungs. He cared for Cassidy more than he'd comprehended.

"Hey," Andrew said, bringing Preston's eyes back to him. "I would have said the same. Now let's get out of here before we're missed."

With Preston a few slow steps behind, Andrew led the way.

# *Chapter 22*

## An Island in the Atlantic

Cassidy sat on the beach. Her hands were tied behind her back, adding to her growing discomfort. She watched Cade pace back and forth.

*Where are they?*

Andrew and Preston had not been seen by anyone for hours, according to the crewmen, as Cassidy and Cade had just returned from the ship. The crew discovered that their absence left her unguarded. A few wandered close enough to study her. Ironically, her captor's presence kept them at bay, thank goodness.

She sat quietly and prayed. What on earth could have happened to them? Though she was hardly surprised; together those two were bound for misfortune. Cassidy could not help but picture the two on a grand adventure, only to stumble upon pirate treasure.

Just then, movement in her peripheral swiveled her head. Andrew and Preston bounded out of the brush like two school boys late to class. They stopped short when they spotted them all on the beach, but Cade's bellow brought them the rest of the distance.

Only then did Cassidy notice that they were dripping wet. While Andrew wore a waistcoat, Preston's white sailor shirt clung to his toned body, and his hair, darkened with water, fell in front of his eyes.

Cassidy's heart broke into a gallop and hot blood pulsed through her body. She turned away.

"'Bout time! Where the 'ell have you two been?" Cade glowered at them.

The two glanced at each other uncertainly. Cassidy groaned inwardly. She knew Andrew was a terrible liar, and Preston was obviously not much better. Right away she knew that they'd found it.

Struggling not to weep, Cassidy implored them with her eyes. Andrew looked at her indecisively. Preston's deep eyes stared at her with a resigned fate. It sorrowed her soul and shredded her heart to see him in such a hopeless state. She knew Preston had been through a lot in his life, but to see it in his eyes was agonizing.

"Exploring the shoreline," Andrew spoke up. His sister hung her head.

"Really?" Cade grabbed Cassidy from behind and pressed a knife to her smooth neck. "Still exploring the shoreline?"

Eyeing the knife, Andrew swallowed. "If you kill her, you shan't have anything to hold over our heads."

"I didn't say I would kill her." Cade slid the knife across her throat. Cassidy gasped when it's sharp edge cut her tender skin.

"Enough, Cade!" bellowed Preston. "It's hidden in a cliff on that side of the island." He pointed.

Cade smirked. "Come on." He motioned for the crew behind him to follow. They tramped off into the thicket, not looking back.

Cassidy saw Andrew give Preston a nod. "He won't win."

Preston sighed, "I know."

The two strode over, and Preston knelt down to untie her as Andrew examined her neck.

"It's just a scratch, Andrew," said she, fingering it gently. Andrew ignored her. He batted away her hand and studied the wound until Preston pushed him away to take a look.

"Oh, so you're a doctor now, Preston." Andrew's brows arched mockingly.

Preston studied her neck. "I've stitched a few things in my life."

"People or fabric?" Andrew prodded.

"Both." Preston stood and offered her his hand. "It's not deep enough for stitches, I think." She took his hand and rose.

Cassidy rubbed her wrists. "So you two found it?"

"We did," said Preston. "If you walk straight that way you would walk off a cliff into the sea. But when the tide's low it reveals the entrance to a small cave. We won't be able to get the treasure out very easily this time of year. It will take time."

"Chipper. Let them play around with it for a while." She dusted off her dress.

Preston smiled down at her. "Indeed, Lady."

"I don't think they are headed the correct way," Andrew commented. He jogged over to a large boulder and scrambled to the top. He looked out in the direction the pirates took.

Cassidy turned back to Preston, catching his gaze. Locked in, Cassidy half-heartedly fought for a way to escape those charming, chocolate eyes, but she stilled when something stirred in him.

It was as though he allowed an opening to her, timid though it was. He looked at her beseechingly, and her heart melted till she was sure it would evaporate. She saw his wounds, still healing. She saw his struggle, the struggle against guilt and worthlessness. She saw his need, the need to be understood by someone. She saw his hesitancy to trust, so willing yet so fearful. Most of all she saw a hope, a hope so young and barely kindled. So childlike. So unaffected by the world.

So pure.

Pure. It struck her like nothing had ever struck her before. After all he had been through and seen, he was pure.

"... should we go after them...?" Cassidy was drawn back by her brother's words. "They won't be able to find it and Cade will be all the more more impatient," Andrew called down.

"Probably." Preston blinked and took a step back, looking as unsettled as she felt.

Cassidy lowered her eyes.

Preston walked over to Andrew. "But I'm in no hurry. Let them search, and while they do that, I am going to get some wood. We'll probably be sleeping here." He strode off into the brush toward the higher part of the island.

Alone to wonder, Preston spent nearly an hour gathering wood as his mind considered the incident on the beach. He was spooked by the entire thing. It was going to end badly, he was sure. But alas! He wanted it so! What to do?

Preston saw that Cassidy cared about him. But did she love him? Preston rebuked himself. She had no reason to.

He would probably be making a fool of himself. After all, he could not have her. Any sensible father would not allow it.

Preston sighed. He was back to square one. Working his way back to the beach, he carried all the wood he could and tried to clear his mind. He needed to talk this out with someone. Uncle John would be preferable. There was Andrew, of course, but it *was* his sister. *Awkward.* Preston smiled to himself. Andrew had become a good friend.

Emerging onto the beach, Preston found the two siblings sitting on the rocks facing the water. He smiled at the likeness. Both had such dark hair. Andrew's would probably be curly like Cassidy's, if he let it get that long.

Preston ambled into the open and dropped the wood down where he could build a fire without interrupting them. As he worked, he watched them mingle and wondered if he and Briana would have been friends like the Chandler siblings.

Sensing movement, Cassidy looked back and saw him. She offered him a smile. Preston was immediately drawn out of his depressing thoughts. He smiled back. Cassidy turned back to her brother, who continued talking, unaware of their exchange.

Preston sighed to himself. He knew she had seen through him, and yet she still thought of him as a friend.

Deep in thought, he pushed his flaxen hair out of his eyes and worked to start a fire. Did he have a chance with her? A real chance? What if he did? Could he be a worthy husband?

*Worthy.* The word churned in Preston's mind. *But I'm not worthy.* He looked out to where Cassidy sat.

*'Are you worthy of Me?'*

Preston startled at the words in his head. "No, my Lord. Not at all."

*'Have you accepted my gift?'*

"Yes, though I am not worthy."

*'That is why it is called a gift, child. Is not every good and perfect gift from above?'*

"Yes, Lord."

*'So why do you not accept all the gifts I give you?'*

Preston paused. Did God give him gifts that he pushed away? What a haunting thought. "Forgive me, my Lord, that I am so blind to your blessings."

A breeze blew on his hot face, and fresh ocean air entered his lungs.

Preston smiled. "Praise Your glorious Name," he whispered. Happily, he went back to work clearing a spot and began arranging the wood for the fire. When gentle footsteps came up to him, he sat back on his heels and looked up at her.

"Get tired of his company, did you?" Preston grinned.

Cassidy laughed lightly. Her dirty, wrinkled lavender dress danced around her feet as she came up beside him. "Andrew could not bore me if he wanted to."

"Oh? Surely you were not the boring one."

"I dearly hope not. Andrew wanted to wash off. Whether prompted by our conversation, I am not sure."

Preston chuckled. "I don't think you have anything to fear. He thinks the world of you." Preston motioned to the ground a few feet from him. "Please, sit." He shifted to a more comfortable cross-legged position.

She sank down gingerly, her feet off to one side and leaning on her outstretched arm. Her cheeks had a healthy pink hue to them, and her dress no longer swallowed her tiny frame.

Preston forced his gaze away.

"Andrew has always been my protector. You and he are a lot alike."

A smile formed on his lips and he met her gaze gladly. It surprised him to see a sudden blush to her cheeks. Though Preston knew he should look away and spare her further embarrassment, his will won out and he teased her instead. "I thought I scared you."

Cassidy met his eyes with her own, surprising him yet again. "Very much so. You still do, sometimes."

Delighted at the mirth in her face, Preston tilted his head back and laughed. "Tell me, little duchess, what is it I do that intimidates you, so I can be sure to avoid it in the future?"

Smiling, she shook her head. Her dark, tangled hair swished around her face. "I have no desire to tell. Though I do believe it is more me than you."

Preston's brows came together as he watched her. "Do explain."

"Why Preston, there are some things that ladies don't tell. Especially to men."

Preston studied her. She was both open and secretive. Puzzling, yet delightful. "Oh?"

A moment of quiet hung in the damp air, and Preston watched as Cassidy observed the hem of her skirt.

*Don't let her retreat,* Preston told himself. "Where did you learn to sing?" As soon as the words deserted his tongue he regretted them. Singing was the last thing he wanted to talk about.

She glanced at him shyly through her lashes. "My mother is a natural singer. She was always singing as I grew up. It just seemed right when I started to sing. Though I was so terrible at first that my father hired a teacher for me."

"Best money ever spent," Andrew added as he ambled up from the ocean, dripping wet.

"One swim wasn't enough for you today?" Preston eyed his drenched friend.

"It was. I just couldn't stop thinking about that spider web I walked through on the way back." Andrew shivered.

"Afraid of bugs, are we?" Preston winked at Cassidy. She tucked her hair behind her ear and looked away. The corners of her lips lifted in a toothless smile.

"Not bugs, Preston, spiders." Andrew plopped down on the sand between Cassidy and Preston to put on his boots.

"Oh well, you don't need to worry about that. I already swiped it off of you."

Andrew froze, his foot half way into the boot. "What?!"

"It was just a garden spider. She was on your back, but they don't sting." Preston lifted his hand to show Andrew. "I didn't get stung."

Andrew jumped up as though Preston had just thrown the spider at him. "You said it was a leaf!"

"Well... there was a leaf too."

Andrew just stared at him, horrified. Unable to stifle it any longer, Cassidy giggled. Preston laughed. Finally, Andrew joined in.

"I don't know what ya have found to be funny, but I'm less amused," Cade thundered, stomping out of the underbrush.

Cassidy startled. Preston took his time rising to his feet. *What now?* By the look on Cade's face, the search had not gone well.

"Well, sir, if you can be otherwise, you are welcome to join us," Andrew retorted.

In a mere second, Cade grabbed his pistol from his belt, cocked it, and aimed it at Cassidy's head. The trio froze, all staring at the gun.

*Oh Jesus!* Preston fought panic. *Lord please, please...*

"The next time you mock me, Chandler, you shall lose. And you have a lot to lose," Cade threatened through bared teeth.

Andrew was tight-lipped and silent.

*Lord, don't let him do anything else stupid!* Preston prayed silently.

"Good. Lead the way, Williams." The captain walked closer to Cassidy with the gun. Cassidy swallowed, her eyes wide as she stared down the pistol's barrel.

"Sir, I might be more prompted if the gun were on my own head," Preston spoke up, unable to tear his eyes from her frightened face. "She doesn't know where the treasure is, so she is nothing but leverage. In order for you to still have your leverage, you cannot kill her. We both know that. So there is no incentive for us to lead you to the treasure. Thus, we would be untrustworthy."

Preston stepped slowly toward Cade as he talked. "It would seem that threatening her does not benefit your mission. If you kill her, we won't cooperate, but if you threaten her we are not trustworthy. So really, she is not useful at all. But if you threaten either of us," Preston moved his pointer finger back and forth between Andrew and himself, "then we must lead you to the right location. Because if you kill one of us, you still have the other to lead you to the treasure. So really, you just need me, him, and your gun." Preston stopped when Cade's pistol rested on his chest. "Understand?" His eyes rested on Cade's.

Cade studied him. Preston had to shove away a tempting grin. Captain Cade looked genuinely perplexed.

*Keep him thinking,* Preston told himself. "Now, it will take many trips to get all of the treasure on board, and we will need to move the ship around to the northeast side of the island. As close as we can get it." Pushing the barrel of the gun against his chest, he stepped around Cade to have the pirate pivot slowly away from Cassidy. When his back was to the forest, Preston took a step back. "This way to the treasure." Preston turned and started off briskly, heartened to hear footsteps behind him.

"Unless you want him to die, you two better come along!" Cade bellowed to Andrew and Cassidy.

*Drat. There's nothing I can do about that no,.* Preston thought as he trudged through the underbrush.

Shaken, Cassidy's heart pounded in her chest, as she rushed after Preston and Cade, Andrew at her heels. Her mind was fuzzy. Cassidy tried to decide whether Preston was an idiot or a genius.

When the foursome stopped, they found themselves standing on a cliff with a straight drop to the sea. She scooted back from the edge.

"The treasure is down there." Preston fearlessly stood at the edge and pointed down. "The high tide is covering the small entrance to a tunnel which leads to a room where the treasure is. You will only have access to it a few minutes each day, but if we work efficiently, we should be able to get it out within two days."

Cade looked into the sea, suspicion written across his face. "If it's as ya say, we can get the treasure out now. We would have to duck under the entrance with the chests."

"Yes, except that judging by the water marks on the wall, there is an air escape inside. The tunnel completely fills up, sir."

Cade glanced at Preston with a resentful threat in his eyes. "If yer lyin' to me Williams, I swear–"

"I'm not." Preston met Cade's glare with startling ferociousness. "And you're welcome to go look for yourself, sir."

"This would explain why they were all wet when they returned, sir," Cassidy squeaked, feeling the need to defend Preston's honesty.

"I forgot you could speak," Cade snapped at her. He turned back to Preston. "Fine. We'll retrieve the treasure tomorrow. *All* of it! And you will make sure of it! Prepare the men! I want every man workin' tomorrow!"

Cassidy saw a flash of animosity cross Preston's face. Cade saw it too. A mirthless grin spread the length of Cade's face. "Yer a smart man, Mr. Williams. But you were wrong about one thing. I do still need my leverage. She shall be the last thing removed from the cave, so you better work quickly, or you'll be the one responsible for 'er death!"

# Chapter 23

## An Island in the Atlantic

As the tide began to retreat the next day, they stood ready. The crew had their instructions. They would work in pairs, bringing out one chest at a time in a single file line. Several men would be ready to help the chest under the door. They would repeat the procedure until everything, and everyone, was out safely.

*Safely. Lord, let us get through this safely!* Preston shifted his weight as he watched for the receding water to reveal the top of the cave's entrance. His heart beat wilder with every wave that lapped at the rock.

He, Andrew, Cade, and Cassidy stood in the water up to their waists. Preston bit away the temper threatening to burst inside of him at the hold Cade had on Cassidy's tied wrists. Cade was awfully close to her, and why bind her hands? Preston worked constantly to retain control of himself. He *must* not let his temper make this worse. Could he even handle worse?

When the top of the entrance finally showed, he signaled to the men. Andrew dove in first. Cade pushed Cassidy along ahead of him. Preston winced. Before Cade could push her through, Cassidy dove under

*Brave little duchess,* Preston thought with a smile.

Cade was next, and Preston last. Diving under the surf, Preston kicked himself forward blindly. Groping at the dark, he startled when a hand gripped his arm and pulled him to the surface. When Preston's head broke through the surface, he gasped for breath and opened his eyes to find only darkness.

"Alright?" Andrew asked as he steadied his friend.

Slowly, Preston's eyes adjusted to the dimness. But he could barely make out the faces of the others. "Yes." He spat salt water.

"Take them down to see it. I'll help the men," Andrew whispered into Preston's ear.

"As you say." Preston turned to Cade and spoke louder. "It's this way, Captain." He trudged further into the cave through waist-deep water.

The further they went, the shallower the water became, and the darker it got. Unfortunately, they would have to work in the dark until the tide was low enough to bring a lantern through. Preston had to run his fingertips along the wall as a guide.

Finally, the space opened. "This is it."

"Where's the treasure?" Cade growled.

Preston tramped to the other end of the room until his hand hit wood and the water was only ankle-depth. "The chests are here."

The pirate came up behind him with his captor and ran his hand over the chests. Preston could hear when Cade's fingers found a lock. A delighted, deep chortle filled the room. "I must admit, Williams, I underestimated you."

Preston's brows rose. Surely that was no compliment. "No harsh feelings," he replied sarcastically.

Preston could hear Cade moving to the corner of the room with Cassidy in tow. A yelp from Cassidy and a splash nearly stopped Preston's heart. "Cassidy!" Preston fought panic. He groped in the dark in their direction. What had Cade done?

"Relax, hero, I did 'er no harm," Cade growled.

Ignoring Cade, Preston stumbled forward, searching for her. "Cassidy, are you alright?"

In a quiet, timid voice Cassidy spoke. "I'm alright. Apparently he wanted me to sit down."

Cade snorted in disgust. "Touching. Yer'll stay there, little duchess, until every chest has been removed. And in case you haven't noticed, I have no need for any of you any more! So accept that as leverage!" Cade spun and stomped back the way they came. Or so he thought.

An "omph" shook the room, and Preston bit back a chuckle. He could hear Cade slide his hands along the wall until he found the tunnel.

"Cassidy, where are you?"

"I'm here."

Preston carefully followed the voice. "Are you hurt?"

"No. He could have just asked me to sit," Cassidy said.

Kneeling next to her, Preston could not help himself and reached out to touch her. He felt her recoil, then relax. He finally found her hands and felt the rope. "Stupid. I should have brought my knife."

"It's okay, it doesn't hurt. Let's just get these horrid chests out of here so we can go home." Her voice was so gentle, yet so full and unwavering.

*Home.* Preston had hardly thought of home. A thought hit him like an avalanche. After this, if they survived, Cassidy would be going home. He may never see her again.

The splashing of approaching men echoed throughout the cavern, interrupting his musing. They were going to do this.

"Wait here. I will be back for you." Preston let his fingers slide across her silky hand as he pulled away.

"Don't worry about me," she whispered, no tremor to her voice.

"You're so brave," he whispered back.

"Not at all. I trust my God."

"I wish I had your faith." His faith seemed like a fish on solid ground. Jumping up and down, useless, helpless, and dying.

Preston felt her hand brush against him. "Oh Preston, I…"

"Preston! Cassidy! Where are you?" Andrew shouted.

His heart grieved and thirsted for the words she had yet to speak. Preston had to bite his tongue to rein in the irritated response to Andrew's summons.

Time. Such an unusual, intangible anomaly that always repeats itself but remains terribly unpredictable. For the men, it raced ahead as though it's life were on the line. For Cassidy, it stood over her leisurely, taunting her with every footstep of the men at work. She tried to count how many chests went by. Preston had said there were about twenty. Surely they were getting close. A light appeared down the tunnel and bobbed its way toward the main cavern. Several men cheered. When the lantern-bearer entered, Cassidy got her first look at the room and nearly gasped at the large chests against the wall.

Her first reaction was awe. So mysterious was the dark wood and lavish designs. They were certainly impressive, even foreboding. Heavy iron locks sealed them shut. *How do they plan to open them?*

Cassidy watched as two men pulled down another chest and grunted under its weight. "Hey!" one exclaimed, staring into the place where the chest had sat. "There's another row!"

*Oh, dear God, no!*

Preston sloshed through the water to look. His grim expression made her want to cry. He looked over at her with those distressed dark eyes. She tried to give him an affirming nod. Locking his jaw, Preston turned back to the men. "Double-time it, or you'll be left in here with the rest!"

Already the water had begun to rise and swirl over her lap.

Preston hoisted the chest above his head. Every muscle in his body screamed at him, but adrenaline pushed him on. Departing from the main room, he and another man walked the much-too-heavy chest down into the tunnel, the water at their waists.

"Hurry!" he yelled, letting it echo throughout the cave. He had long ago lost count of the chests he had hauled, nor did he care.

An eternity later, they reached the end of the tunnel, and Preston let the chest pull him under. The water was strong and shoved him back ferociously, but he struggled on. When he, the chest, and the other sailor emerged on the other side, Preston fought for his remaining strength and dragged what seemed like all three of them to shore.

"How's it goin', Williams?" Cade taunted from above him.

Breathing hard, Preston looked up at him, uncontainable fury boiling in his blood. "It can't be done," he hissed.

"Poo. She was such a pretty girl."

"Heartless man!" Rage surged through him, and he dove under the water back toward the tunnel for more.

Perhaps Cade was heartless, but he knew how to get a man moving.

Trip after trip he made, only aware of his mission. As he prepared to dive under for the countless time, he almost swam into Andrew, who came up with another chest.

"Preston!" he sputtered. "This is the last one! We had to tread water to keep our heads above water."

Preston prepared to dive after Cassidy. *Was the water over her head yet?*

Andrew grabbed his arm. "Let me go, Preston! The current is too strong. There is a water escape somewhere down there! There's no chance of survival!"

Preston stared at his friend. They had lost to time and to the rate of the incoming tide. Where had it gone? How had it come to this?

Preston understood. One of them had to try to save Cassidy, but neither he nor she would survive.

"I shall not have your parents suffer both of your deaths!" With that, Preston dove under the surf, the current sweeping him away.

Beneath the swirling water, Preston fought hopeless dread. If he could just save Cassidy, he did not care what happened to him. After all, he was no one. No parents. No possessions. No fortune. No future.

If only he could save her... if only he could have saved *her*. Sweet Briana.

Yet now, his strength was fading. He was weak, just as he was all those years ago. For his childlike mind could never have known the danger.

It suddenly dawned on him. He could not save Cassidy, weak as he is. Just as he could never have saved Briana, weak as he was.

Would he ever be strong enough to save the ones he loved?

There are some moments in life when one asks a question only to receive the answer thrown into their face. Like an angry wave crashing into the beach which it had traveled far to find.

This was one such moment.

*Lord, I am not strong enough. But you are. Jesus, I surrender this responsibility to you. I am your servant.*

He gathered the last of his strength and surged on. When he came to the opening, no light of the lantern greeted him, but rather the rushing sound of water.

"Cassidy!" He waited. One heartbeat. Two heartbeats. Three…

"Preston…"

He charged toward the weak sound. "I can't see you! Keep talking!"

"I… I can't tread much longer. It's too… too strong."

Preston reached out and touched fabric. "Keep going! I'm here! I'm here! Give me your hands!" Preston felt Cassidy's tied hands bump him, and he grabbed hold of them. He dove under the water, drawing her arms over his head and through one of his arms. "Fight for me!"

Her arms tightened around him, and he positioned her on his back. Now he had a choice to make. Should they stay and try to wait out the water? Based on the water mark, it never completely submerged the room, which made sense now. It wasn't the air that escaped in the cave, it was the water.

*Stupid of me.* How could he not have noticed where the water would drain? But he would never last another six hours, especially fighting the current with Cassidy clinging to his back. If even one chest had remained they might have been able to stand on it...

Option two, they could go back through the tunnel, which was bound to be completely sealed off by now. That meant they would need to hold their breath the entire way. Preston's strength was fading fast. Fear rose and brimmed in his chest, threatening to drown him before the water had a chance. The thought of going back through the tunnel was almost too much to bear.

Cassidy's head rested weightily against his back. The tunnel it was.

Kicking them forward, Preston felt his way to the entrance. "Cassidy, hold your breath for as long as you can." He felt her lift her head.

"Okay."

Preston thought about saying more, but words failed him. Instead he breathed deeply for several seconds before taking in as much air as his lungs could hold. Even if Cassidy blacked out, he had to keep going.

*You are my strength, God Almighty! I am weak, but you are strong!*

Under the water, Preston swam like he never had before. Unable to see, he kept his eyes closed tight and stayed close to the tunnel wall. He felt Cassidy kicking behind him.

Seconds passed. He dared not count them. A minute. Maybe two minutes. His body was stinging for air. His lungs were on fire and felt as though they would collapse. Preston could feel Cassidy's effort slow until she went limp behind him.

*Keep swimming. Keep swimming. Keep swimming.*

He did not think about her being dead. He couldn't.

Opening his eyes, Preston hunted for the end, hoping it was just ahead. He was met with blackness so thick it nearly consumed him. It snaked its way into his mind, until he lost all sense of time, space, and his surroundings. He drifted into the current.

# Chapter 24

## An Island in the Atlantic

Water and sand bits rose in his throat. He rolled over, seizing mercilessly. He coughed water and blood up onto the rocks. Pain clawed at him in his chest. His lungs stung like liquor poured over a whipped back. He tried to push himself away from his own vomit, but instead his head lulled to the side, resting on the rocky surface. Why was his body not working?

Without another choice, Preston rested, slowly becoming aware of water tugging at his legs. Sounds met his ear. Men. Running water. Panting.

Memory returned in a gust. Preston moved his arms underneath him and pushed himself up as fast as his tired brain allowed. Looking around, he found a cluster of men a few yards from him, all leaning over or kneeling around something.

*Cassidy? No, no, please God.*

Pulling himself the rest of the way, Preston crawled over to them. Not the picture of dignity after almost dying, but no one seemed to care anyway. When he pushed through, he found

Andrew bent over Cassidy's limp form, his head near hers.

Preston swayed. Someone grabbed him and prevented him from toppling. As blackness threatened his mind, a gasp of breath pierced through the darkness and Preston opened his eyes. Cassidy sputtered and coughed up water.

*She's alive!* And he lapsed from consciousness.

Cassidy had never been in such horrific pain. Even her sickness on that dreadful island could not compare.

"You're okay." Andrew helped her sit up after she emptied her stomach onto the rocks. He was breathing hard.

She leaned into him. Her body shook uncontrollably and her eyelids fluttered. Then Preston's lifeless body came into focus. One of the men eased him onto the rocks only feet from her.

"Guess we can't keep both of 'em," said the burly man, void of emotion.

Cassidy's heart seemed to fall from her chest. She rasped his name unintelligently and was rewarded by searing pain that flooded her chest. Pushing away from Andrew, she crawled up to Preston. She reached out to him and moved a wet lock of hair out of his handsome face, not caring who watched. *Preston, Preston, no! Please, no! Dear God, no!*

"He's not dead," Andrew announced. He leaned over and put his hand above Preston's nostrils. "Mm-hmm, breathing."

Cassidy nearly collapsed with relief. *Praise you, Mighty One! Surely you are the only God! Thank you! Thank you, my God!*

"The two of you, carry him and follow me to the top of the cliff. And be *gentle*, please!" As Andrew spoke, he slid his arms beneath his sister and lifted her into the air.

"Are... are you sure... he's al-alright?" Cassidy barely managed to whisper and hoped her brother understood.

"He came to, but then fainted at the sight of you. He's just weak."

Cassidy mulled this over. "He sw-swam the both of us o-out."

Andrew attempted a smile that failed, exhibiting to Cassidy just how afraid he was. "Now now, let's not give him all the credit. I went in after you two and nearly collided with Preston, limp as a rag doll. A few more seconds of breath and Preston would have found the exit." He shook his head, now solemn. "That was too close. Let's keep this part of the adventure from our parents."

Cassidy nodded, too scared and weak to argue. Andrew sat her down on the grassy cliff, and the men lowered Preston a few feet away.

"Go help your captain," Andrew told them. They quickly trotted off, eager to see the treasure.

"Where is he?" Cassidy whispered.

"Cade? Went to get the ship, I believe. Here it comes now." Cassidy straightened her head to see until Andrew gently pulled her down. "Rest, and regain your strength. We will be undisturbed here for a while."

The duchess allowed herself to lie on her side, positioned to watch both Preston and the sea.

For the first time in weeks, things were peaceful. She watched the waves rise and fall and listened to the rustle of the trees. The breeze began to dry her hair and garments. Her heartrate slowed, her muscles relaxed. Sleep did not pull at her, nor did she will it. She just rested, and prayed. A prayer of thanksgiving and praise.

For a long time, the three rested.

What must have been an hour later, Cassidy saw Preston stir. She slowly sat up to strech, though well aware of her sleeping brother behind her. Preston's fingers twitched and his eyelids quivered. When his eyes opened fully, he coughed and started to roll over.

Cassidy caught his shoulder to keep him from face planting in the dirt. "Hush now."

He looked up at her with those soul deep eyes.

She offered him a smile. Her voice a whisper. "You're okay. I'm okay. Our God is good."

He started to speak, but winced and allowed himself to fall onto his back. He closed his eyes.

"Thank you." Tears pushed to her eyes as she looked at him.

Preston opened his eyes again and turned his head to gaze at her. He swallowed. "An-anything."

*Anything?* But he almost died. Was she worth that much to him? Cassidy turned to stare out into the ocean. Tears slid down her cheeks.

Preston reached up and brushed the wetness from her face. She dared not turn to him, for she was sure she would break down. But then his fingers came to her jaw and gently pulled her head to look at him. She complied and felt her heart would agree to anything he asked. What a dangerous thing for a man to possess! Yet Cassidy had never been so sure that it was not misplaced.

"It's okay to cry," he murmered. She realized that tears brimmed in his eyes too.

Cassidy buried her head in her hands and wept.

With meager amounts of strength, the threesome met Cade's long boats that were returning to the beach for the last of the chests. Preston could almost see the *Fortune's* lowness in the water from where they stood.

"Help us load the chests!" Cade ordered them curtly.

"Preston is too weak. Unless you want him dropping them and spilling the contents, I suggest you leave him out of this," Andrew retorted.

"Fine. Good for nothing..." Cade's harsh tone wandered off. Preston wished he had the strength to sock the man.

When the boats were loaded, Preston offered Cassidy his hand and lead her to the boats. The cocking of a gun brought them to a halt. Preston clenched his jaw, done with this entire charade. He turned slowly to face Cade's gun, again.

"Cade?" Preston rasped. His heart pounded in his chest. Adrinaline made his muscles twitch with fight. Was this the end? Had they come all this way to die by bullet?

Cade raised his eyebrows at Preston's voice, or lack thereof. "I know enough to know that the duke and duchess are being hunted on every ship, boat, and floating piece of wood throughout the sea. No one knows I've had them, there's no proof. Or there won't be, anyway."

"So you plan to kill us?" said Andrew.

"Yer too much of a risk, Chandler. You and yer sister. I was gonna take Williams along, but he can't lift a finger, and he's not worth enough to nurture back to health."

Preston felt both his friends stiffen.

"You could still get a hefty ransom for us. Or better yet, a reward," Andrew said.

"Too much risk, and in case you haven't noticed, wealth is no longer an issue."

"That's the funny thing about wealth, it–"

"Shut that mouth of yers for once! Before I cut out yer tongue and eat it! Nevermind, I'll just kill you now!" Cade grabbed Andrew and turned him to face Preston and Cassidy.

Preston stepped in front of Cassidy, knowing what was about to happen. Cade growled into Andrew's ear, "Nighty-night, your grace!"

A boom deafened their ears, and an explosion threw them all to the ground. *What on earth?* Preston mustered his strength and staggered to his feet. Before he regained his balance, another boom and explosion sent him down. Preston looked around frantically. His eyes widened.

Four ships were fast approaching, two sailing toward the magnificent *Fortune* and two coming near the shoreline. Cannon balls flew through the air and splashed into the water to either side of the lonely pirate ship. Warning shots.

Preston stared, trying to gather his wits.

"The treasure! Quick! To the ship!" Cade screamed and went running toward the boats with men at his tail. They jumped in and ferociously paddled to the *Fortune*.

*Fool.* For the first time, Preston truly questioned Cade's intelligence. His wits came back in a rush and Preston spun around. "Cassidy, are you alright?" He helped her to her feet.

She nodded, a stricken look on her face.

"I'm alright too, thanks." Andrew shook sand from his boots a few yards away. "I'm the one that almost died, after all."

"Well, you nearly gave your sister a heart attack. So well done," Preston rasped. A boom thundered, then a splash and water soared into the air just offshore, near Cade's boats. It rocked the island, and the three wrestled with their footing.

"He came though, Preston!" Andrew shouted with a huge grin. "You were right!"

Preston shook his head. "He did. I can't believe it."

"Who?" Cassidy's new look of curiosity was a welcome change to her worried face.

"Preston's friend... your captor... my hero!" Andrew jumped and danced around them.

"Praise the Lord. You know He did this!" Preston smiled as he watched Andrew. The words grated on his throat, and he winced.

"Yes! Praise Him!"

"Wait, what?" Cassidy stared at them.

"And with impeccable timing!" Andrew continued. "And the entrance! Exquisite!" Andrew stopped suddenly. "Hey! That's the *Virtue!*"

Preston studied the ships as Andrew raced down to the water. Three of them he recognized as belonging to the Spanish navy. *Unusual.* The closest to them was a lovely barque with a proud British flag wafting in the ocean wind. The *Virtue.*

They watched as the ships worked together, cutting off Cade from his ship. When the ships were upon them and Cade could do nothing more, he seemed to be exchanging with the *Virtue.*

"I want to get out there!" Andrew paced at the water's edge.

"It looks like your quartermaster has it handled," Preston said. Cassidy smiled at his side. He longed to put his arm around her waist and pull her closer.

The largest of the Spanish ships came up behind Cade. The three powers seemed to be in discussion. As time dragged on, Preston felt Andrew's longing to be part of it. After all, this was mostly about them, no doubt.

Suddenly, the *Virtue* slid through the water toward the island. Cannon fire came down upon Cade's tiny boats. The *Royal Fortune* lowered her sails and doused her black and red flags.

Preston clenched his jaw.

The swift *Virtue* stopped as close to the island as possible before sending out the longboats. When they neared, Andrew splashed into the water to help them in.

Cassidy shook her head. "My parents would rather him try to keep his dignity." She walked with Preston toward their rescuers.

"Then I suppose it's a good thing I haven't dignity to lose." Preston grinned weakly.

Preston continued to stare forward when Cassidy looked up at him. He knew his teasing tone did not reach his eyes. She was silent.

Another man leapt out of the boat and threw his arms around Andrew. "Shame on you, Captain. I thought you were dead," the man huffed.

"I am not dead, thanks to you! Come, come, Tanner, I would like you to meet…" Andrew quickly led the way to Preston and Cassidy. "My friend, Preston Williams, another of Cade's victims. Preston, this is my quartermaster, Tanner Ross."

Tanner bowed to Cassidy then turned to Preston. "Ah, you are the one they tied to the main mast and whipped bloody."

Cassidy gasped. Preston cringed. "I'm afraid I don't remember you, but it is a pleasure nonetheless. Any crewmember of this hooligan must be a saint." Preston swept his hand toward Andrew, attempting to brighten the topic.

Tanner looked stricken, then laughed. "Sir, you just called a Duke of England a 'hooligan' I would be offended if it were not a true statement."

*I've called him worse,* Preston thought ruefully.

"Hey, Preston, help me out, won't you? If this guy quits, I'm done for!" Andrew said.

"Pish posh, come, Lord and Lady, Mr. Williams. We've business to discuss. And you each need to clean up, eat, and rest. Our doctor, Kit, is on board as well to examine any injuries." Tanner eyed Preston as they climbed into one of the boats. "He can take a look over your back."

"It's healed, I assure you," Preston tried.

"Nevertheless, it should be examined."

Preston indeed got an examination. The scabs on his back were so covered in sand that the kind, stubborn doctor insisted it be cleaned with alcohol. Both Cassidy and Andrew seemed to have escaped with less excruciating experiences.

When Preston emerged from the cabin, feeling worse than when he'd walked in, he caught sight of a man walking up and down the deck. Corey. Preston slid over to the rail further down without being seen. He leaned against the railing and watched Corey's nervous walk. Up and down, up and down the deck he walked.

"Something on your mind?" Preston asked nonchalantly when Corey came close.

The young man swung around. "Preston! I uh… got your message."

Preston smiled and went to embrace him. "Thank the Lord you did."

"What message?" A feminine voice came from behind. Cassidy and Andrew walked from the doctor's cabin.

Corey smiled and bowed humbly. "My lord, my lady." He cast a sheepish look at Cassidy. "I do apologize for the, um, previous conditions of our meeting. Please don't judge me for that behavior. I wish I could amend my rudeness. Perhaps I–"

"All is forgiven." She rewarded him with a breathtaking smile. Preston's heart lunged out of his chest. "Now, what have you all neglected to tell me?" She waved her hand toward the captured *Royal Fortune* and the three spanish ships.

Preston recovered his wits. "When Andrew and I saw the *Raven* approaching, I wrote a note to give to Corey."

"And we had just recently discovered the location of the treasure," Andrew said.

Preston cast him an annoyed glance. "Right. While it was quite unfortunate that you were captured again, Cassidy, it did allow me to get the note to Corey."

"You gave it to him when you came and got me?" Cassidy looked between Preston and Corey.

Corey nodded. "When we shook hands, he pressed it into my palm." Corey pulled a small piece of paper from his pocket. "See?" He handed it to Cassidy.

Sure enough, written on the torn, wrinkled piece of parchment were the island's coordinates and the words: *GET HELP*

"Ideally, we just had to stall as long as possible on the island and Corey and his, well, fleet would show up," Preston continued.

"Which reminds me." Andrew turned to Corey. "You have impeccable timing, sir!" Corey shook Andrew's outstretched hand in cautious silence.

"So where did you find the Spanish armada?" Preston asked. "And the *Virtue*, for that matter."

"The first stop the *Raven* made after we left you was Puerto Rico. I left Henry and convinced the Spanish captain to help me. He was not interested until I told him I had the location of Robert's treasure, once hid by Captain Jonathan Williams, and that he would capture Mayson Cade in the process."

"And how could I refuse such an enticing offer?" A deep, accented voice joined their group, along with Tanner and two other men. With tan skin, black hair, and deep-set eyes, the captain stood tall and imposing. "My name is Commodore Alejandro Gaspar, Captain of the *Sea Bird* and general of the Spanish navy. This is Captain Jaménez and his ship, the *Ceasar* and Captain Reyes with the *Tirano.*" Captain Gaspar motioned to the men on either side of him. "Captain Williams was a dear friend of mine, and a good seaman. And you are undoubtedly his son." The man looked at Preston.

"Preston Williams, sir." Preston stepped forward with as much bravado as he could summon.

"Good. Come, everyone. We have much to discuss and limited time."

The party filed into the dining hall and filled the seats. Preston sat between Cassidy and Corey. To Cassidy's left sat Andrew, and next to him sat Tanner. The other men sat across from them.

The youngest of the Spanish captains, Captain Reyes, turned to his commodore and spoke in clear Spanish, easy for Preston to follow.

"Why do you bother with these men? We are the victors! We should sail home with the pirate and his ship as rewards. These people are rewarded enough with their freedom."

Commodore Gaspar replied sharply in Spanish. "Those two are duke and duchess of England. Good relations with Britain is more valuable a reward than a ship and the hanging of a deserving man."

"And you shall all be fully rewarded in gold for the duke and duchess' safe return. Do not fear a loss." Preston addressed the younger man in Spanish. Both men looked at him, startled. Preston returned to English. "And since English is the common language on this ship, I think it polite to our host to regard tradition."

The young man nodded. The commodore grinned. "I should not be surprised. Your father knew five languages. Collected them like art, I recall. You are much like him."

Preston smiled, doing his best to mask his delighted surprise. His father liked learning languages, too?

"Now," the commodore regained the group's attention. "I believe the gold should be distributed back to its original owners. Any objections, Duke of England?"

Andrew straightened to fill his impressive title. "None, Commodore. England needs not the wealth."

"Indeed. I would, however, like to take Cade to my own country as a prize. Fear not, as you Brits like, his execution shall be swift and painless."

"Please do. I think we have had our fair share of him." Andrew grinned. "Though I would be a terrible leader if I did no negotiating. Allow us the *Fortune* as our prize, and the men are yours. Make no mistake, you and your fleet will be rewarded in gold for our rescue. Plenty to build your own ship of dark wood."

"We have no need for her. The ship is yours," Gaspar said. "The treasure in our country would only make the rich richer. But your reward will be appreciated by my men and me, Lord Chandler."

Preston listened as the two powers discussed details. His elbow itched. How could Cassidy sit so still for so long? She seemed to be a statue beside him. Maybe it was an inherited trait for one born into power. Preston sighed inwardly. Another reminder he did not belong here.

Finally, the group adjourned and dispersed to their own ships, but before Commodore Gaspar left, he turned to Preston.

"I do not believe in the god your father worshiped. A god that offers life for nothing? To gain nothing? It makes no sense to me, but your father loved his God. And his God never failed him. I used to think that, if there was a god, it was the God of your father. Then he died and I thought, 'then there is no god!' After all, why would a god let his most faithful follower die? Now I realize, it was not just about your father. It was in accordance with His plan." He eyed Preston. "I can see His plan moving. Continuing His work in you."

"In me?" The words stumbled and fell out of Preston's tight throat.

"Well, you did seem to pick up where Jonathan left off." Gaspar smiled and looked around. "And may God bless you for it!"

# Chapter 25

The *Virtue*

Cassidy stood behind Preston as the commodore walked away. She could feel his waves of emotional turmoil. The longing to comfort him was almost unbearable. *He's so hard on himself. Jesus, please encourage him through the commodore's words!* Cassidy racked her brain for something to say. Instead, she stepped up beside him, not daring to touch him.

Preston brought his eyes down to her. She smiled, filling her eyes with the compassion and pride she felt for him. His dark eyes softened and his lips turned up.

"We seem to have a problem," Andrew mused as he walked up to them.

"And what is that, dear brother?" Cassidy asked.

"Well, dear sister, England hasn't any need for another ship. Not to mention the *Fortune* just isn't her majesty's style. I mean, she would require a lot of work, and I doubt anyone would buy her with that dark wood. What to do with the ship then?" Andrew rubbed his chin in thought.

Cassidy recognized where her brother was going. "That is a problem, Andrew."

"Perhaps you could sell her and send the money to the families of those lost on the *Queen's Merit,*" Preston suggested.

*Preston!* An uncomfortable itch spread through Cassidy's body. She felt sorry she had forgotten about the sad fate of the *Queen's Merit* and those on board with her who were lost. Count on Preston to suffer from the memory of their fate.

Andrew clearly had forgotten as well. "She would not sell for enough to help them, but I'm sure Father will help them generously." Andrew cleared his throat. "But just as deserving, Preston, you have asked for nothing for yourself, even though you have nothing. Not even a job."

Preston frowned. Cassidy winced.

Andrew visibly scrambled for words. "I mean, I... we... would like to give you the *Royal Fortune.*" Andrew stomped his foot in finality.

Preston's brows rose, but he shook his head. "I cannot take her. I do not deserve—"

Cassidy had had enough. "Preston Williams, you *do* deserve this! You deserve a ship of your own more than anyone. You saved my life at least three times. You stopped one of the most ruthless pirates on the sea. You found one of the greatest lost treasures that has ever existed. You helped uphold good relations with Spain. And..." Cassidy quieted. "You lost your father to this mission. Besides, whether you deserve it or not, it is a gift, and a gift is not given to us based on our own actions. Just as you have accepted Jesus' gift of eternal life, accept this gift from us."

Preston bowed his head to her, not averting his eyes from her determined face. "As you say, my lady."

Cassidy nodded.

"Great," Andrew enthused from the side lines. "We'll sail with you to your home, since you need some of my crewmen. If you wish to keep and captain the *Fortune,* I am happy to help you find a crew. Now, where is your home?"

"Captain?" Preston stared out at the empty *Royal Fortune.*

"Tell the men to set sail for San Juan," Cassidy told her brother with a smile. San Juan, where this whole mess had started. Both happiness and fear washed over her. They were nearing the end of this dreadful, horrid, wonderful adventure. What if they never saw Preston Williams again?

Standing at the helm, Preston looked out across the ship. His ship. The *Royal Fortune.* Dirty as she was, she was his. That fact was still sinking in.

As they sliced through the water, the *Virtue* not far behind, Preston made a checklist. *New sails, repairs on the deck, scraping off the barnacles, new ropes. It will take lots of muscle…*

If there was any money left over after that, he might buy some teak oil to rub on the railing, the wheel, and the lady carved on the front of the ship. Thank goodness the carver was decent enough to fully clothe the wooden woman, or Preston would have had to hire a carpenter, which would have required more funds.

As he surveyed the borrowed sailors, Preston spotted Corey pulling on the ropes. Ah yes, they needed to talk.

"Mr. Davis!" Preston called down to him. Corey waved for a man to take his place and then hurried to the helm.

"Yes, sir?"

"Are you working for the duke now?" Preston's tone was crisp.

"If he should accept me as part of his crew, yes. But for now, I work for you, sir."

Preston nodded and outwardly contemplated this. Finally he shook his head vigorously. "I don't recommend it, not at all. A bad idea, I'd say."

Corey blinked. "Truly? His men say he is one of the best captains–"

"Well I'm a better swordsmen, and taller. And I have, um, less experience, so I would not be as harsh. And I have the bigger ship. And I am in need of a quartermaster." Preston smiled. "And I think we would work well together."

Corey eyes widened. "You're asking me to be your quartermaster?"

"As truly as I stand here."

Corey smiled and extended his hand. "Offer accepted, Captain."

Preston strode down to his captain's cabin feeling confident with Corey's hands on the wheel. Corey, shy and awkward as he was, had a good head on his shoulders.

When he opened the door, Preston realized he would need to completely rearrange the room. It reminded him too much of troubled times. The imposing desk would be moved to the back of the room and the bed shifted to the side. Perhaps the table should be more centralized. Best to get it done now before the two royal siblings joined him for supper. He would get their opinion on the design of the room. Cassidy planned to measure the windows for the curtains she promised to make him once they got to San Juan.

For the next half-hour, Preston moved furniture around and sorted through Cade's belongings. When he went to the bed, he heard faint scuffling noises coming from the mattress. Sickened, Preston tied back his hair, adjusted his sleeves, and hoisted the mattress up. He whisked it out of the room and onto the deck. Marching across the main deck, Preston drew several pairs of eyes as he carried the mattress to the railing and tossed it over the side.

He shook himself out like a dog.

"Everything alright, Captain?" Corey hailed down to him.

"Quite alright, just bed bugs," Preston shouted back, immediately regretting it as the men looked around at each other in dread. Already they scratched imaginary bites. "Whoever wants to sleep on the floor like myself is welcome!"

The perfect San Juan sun welcomed Cassidy from her comfortable bed in John and Marcy Cagney's house. *Sweet people.* Cassidy especially liked Mrs. Cagney, whom she had spent the previous day with. After they arrived at port that morning, the young captains took Mr. Cagney to the docks to admire the *Fortune,* where they spent the rest of the day cleaning. At first, Cassidy had been frustrated that they'd left her with a stranger, but she quickly found that Preston had left her in good hands. The two women got along well. Together, they cleaned and cooked, talking all the while.

Later that afternoon, Mrs. Cagney had taken Cassidy to the market, since Cassidy only had the dress she wore. While managing to keep track of her loveable, forgetful companion, Cassidy was also able to buy fabric for Preston's curtains.

"Green," Preston had requested. Cassidy had asked what shade: mint, emerald, hunter. "Have Aunt Marcy hold the fabric up to your eyes. Only get the one that matches them perfectly."

Rolling out of bed, Cassidy brushed smooth her bedraggled curls and changed into a sophisticated gown for the Sunday church service. She fought her dark hair into a bun on the back of her head and tied in a green ribbon, courtesy of the flirtatious shopkeeper.

Her ensemble complete, she stepped from her room and made her way to the kitchen, drawn in by the morning aromas.

"Lady Cassandra," Mrs. Cagney greeted her. "We're a bit informal here. Everyone has eaten, and the boys already went out back before readying for church. John ran to the shipyard but shan't be long. Now hurry and sit down to eat, dearie."

Cassidy slid into her seat. "I apologize for oversleeping, Mrs. Cagney. I hope I didn't inconvenience you."

"You did nothing of the sort, dearie. Once you're finished, would you tell the boys to get ready for church, please?"

"Of course." Cassidy finished her food in her own record time.

When she opened the back door, the clashing of metal resounded off the walls. Were they sword fighting?

*Oh dear, Andrew's done it now.* She was fairly certain her brother would not be victorious in a fight with Preston.

Following her ear, Cassidy sought out the duel. With every step, the fight became faster and the meeting of metal rang out in danger and doom. Cassidy picked up speed.

Rounding the corner, Cassidy found them. Their shirts soaked through in sweat, the two had their arms raised as they came at each other. Cassidy's breath fluttered in her chest. Any sound died on her lips.

Preston grinned. Andrew scowled and charged again, furious and at lightning speed. Quick as ever, Preston jumped back and batted away his opponent's sword. This time Preston attacked, and Andrew was forced to retreat. On and on they went.

"Give up, Pres," Andrew said, gasping for breath. "We're an equal match."

Preston smirked, also chasing his breath. "I'm sorry, *my lord*, I didn't know you were ready for the match to end."

Cassidy's brows rose. She had never seen this cunning, sardonic side of Preston.

With those words, Preston tossed his sword to his left hand. In another attack, he swung his weapon with surprising ease and accuracy. Within seconds, Andrew's sword was flung to the ground. "I guess you don't train with your weaker hand at your luxurious academy."

Andrew gave him an unimpressed look. "Oh please, I'm not such a dimwit to not know you're left-handed." He picked up his sword with his left. "What you didn't know is that all of us Chandlers are ambidextrous." Andrew lead a ferocious series of attacks, which Preston managed to block. "So maybe you're the dimwit now."

"You're both terribly dimwitted," Cassidy chimed in. She knew her mother would be very displeased. Both boys looked at her in surprise.

"For what?" Andrew asked scowling. "We've been perfectly behaved."

"Well, you and your skirmish shall make us all late for church if you don't get cleaned up right now."

"Yikes, she's right. Let's go!" Andrew started off to the house.

"Ocean's that way!" Preston called to Andrew, who promptly changed directions. Before following, Preston walked up to Cassidy. "He was awfully quick to abandon our fight. Clearly he knows I'm the better fighter. After all, we still have fifteen minutes before we have to leave."

"Ah, so you are aware of the time."

Preston waved his hand. "Of course. Maybe I'm not such a dimwit."

"Maybe not." Cassidy glanced down, trying hard not to be so playful, though Preston was not helping. "Still, you should go wash off, Captain."

"Indeed, my lady," Preston replied quietly. He lingered a second longer before bounding off to join Andrew.

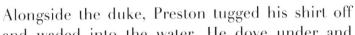

Alongside the duke, Preston tugged his shirt off and waded into the water. He dove under and allowed the salty ocean current to push him about. When he finished, Preston and Andrew walked back to the inn where they were staying. Though Preston had a room in the Cagney's house, he would stay at the inn until Cassidy left for home. Not that Preston rushed them.

"I think we startled your sister," Preston commented.

"You mean with the duel? Nah. She's seen plenty of it. My father and I used to practice all the time together." Andrew slid a glance at Preston. "What did you say to her when I walked away? Come on, I know you talked."

"Nothing really. Just small talk. I told her you gave up the fight rather quickly."

The boys stopped to face each other.

"Preston, you told me once that your intentions were as simple as caring for my sister's basic needs. Is that still true?"

Preston's stomach did a somersault. How should he respond? A million thoughts raced through his mind. *The truth. Tell the truth. To Andrew and yourself.*

He could not marry her.

"It's still true. I'm sorry I have caused you to question it." Preston turned away.

Andrew kept pace. They walked on in silence. "I wrote to my father, I told him to send his instructions to my aunt's house in Virginia. Cassidy and I must leave very soon in order to be there when they are received. Will you do one thing for me before we go?"

Preston nodded, his heart hammering in his chest.

"Talk with Cassidy. She cares for you. For both of your sakes, bring about some level of peace."

Forcing words through his shrinking throat, Preston said, "I will." *Today.* His heart already ached from what he knew was inevitable.

Preston led the Cagneys and the Chandlers to a pew in the old church building. He managed to acquire the seat next to Cassidy. His heart tore in two as she smiled at him. Half of him danced in delight, and the other half blared warnings. For the first time in his life, he ignored the warnings. If being around her for a time was God's gift, then he would not spoil it. He grinned down at her, but when his eyes left her lovely face they collided with her brother's gaze. Andrew looked sad, as though pitying them both.

When the worship started, the congregation stood and sang, all except Preston. He listened, mostly to Cassidy. Her voice stole his breath.

Somewhere from the depth of his mind came a pure, young voice. The voice of his little sister sang a slow, old story, a waltz taught to her by one of the elderly village women. Briana had been sitting at the window when he had walked in, her curls loose around her shoulders. The song was sad, but when Briana turned her head to him, she had smiled. A smile that lit her whole face as though he was the most special person in the world.

Breath rushed into his lungs with a gasp. Music filled his ears, and with Briana's smile at the forefront of his mind, he willed a note.

At a growing whisper, Preston sung along. As the song progressed, Preston concentrated on singing the right words at the right notes. Frustration grew and Briana's face faded behind his eyes. He just was not getting the song right. Where did his terrible voice fit into all this loveliness? Only then did he notice Cassidy was no longer singing.

Preston looked down at her, catching her watching him. *Drat. Now what?*

Cassidy looked at him with such tenderness that he wrestled with himself. "Don't stop," she whispered.

Preston shook his head. "I don't know how to sing."

"I'll help you." Cassidy turned back to her hymnal and started the song again, this time on a higher note than before. She nodded to him.

Preston gathered his tattered courage and sang. His voice found an easy spot an octave lower than the duchess beside him. *How did she do that?* Perhaps this *was* where he belonged.

*Dear Jesus, show me what to do!*

Cassidy smiled when Preston was attacked by little boys. They came at him as soon as he walked out of church.

"Mr. Williams! Mr. Williams! Play ball with us!"

"Look, look, Mr. Williams! I got a new tooth!"

"You're back! Come on, come on!"

Preston laughed and gave them each individual attention. "Of course I'll play! Now off you go to find the balls, quickly now." The herd scampered off.

Someone tugged at Cassidy's dress. She looked down to find a tiny, dark-haired girl sucking her thumb.

"That's Honey." Preston smiled at them. Cassidy sent him a what-do-I-do look. "Just be honest and smile. Treat them as an equal."

An equal? Cassidy considered refusing. But Preston had sung today at her prompting, so she should try this. Cassidy knelt down. "Hello, Honey." That was boring. If this were a girl her age, what would she say? "I like your dress. It's very pretty."

Honey stared at her. "You talk funny." She replied by taking her thumb from her mouth for only a second before burying it again.

Unsure, Cassidy glanced at Preston. He nodded for her to go on. *Okay. What would she say if...* "That's because I'm from London. Have you ever met someone from London?"

The girl shook her head.

*Now what?*

Preston knelt. "Hey Honey, it looks like your mama is serving biscuits. Would you like a biscuit?"

Honey looked toward her mother to confirm the truth and trotted away.

Cassidy breathed out a sigh of relief.

"Not bad." Preston smiled at her. "You'll be comfortable with kids soon enough."

"Did Andrew tell you I struggle with children?" Cassidy asked.

"No, but you looked like you needed help."

"Well, thank you for rescuing me... again."

Preston's smile faded. Now was the time. "Would you walk with me? Just to the garden and back?"

A look of surprise and curiosity came over her face. Cassidy nodded.

Preston led the way and nodded to Andrew, who was stuck in conversation with Captain Anderson as they passed. Andrew glanced at Cassidy and nodded back before returning to his conversation with the captain.

"So I hear," Preston heard Andrew say. He would have to rescue the duke after this.

As they walked, Preston lamented. If only he could somehow figure out a way he could pursue her without disgracing her or her family. *But I'm not royal or of high standing. I have no fortune.*

*'You are My royal, and I am your Fortune.'*

Preston's breath caught. *My God, my God!*

"Are you alright?" Cassidy asked as they entered the garden.

Preston smiled. "More so than I've been in a long time." They continued walking in peaceful silence. "I've been considering something."

She looked up at him with wide, patient eyes. "Have you?"

"When I earn enough money, I'd like to apply to Oxford." He studied her reaction.

A huge smile appeared on her face. "That is a wonderful idea! I've no doubt you will be accepted."

"Thank you, I appreciate that."

"Though I must ask," she paused, while he waited. "What will you do with your degree? Sailing is wonderful of course, but–"

"Not quite requiring a college degree?" Preston interjected, unable to keep the smile from his face.

"Precisely."

"Well, I have always dreamt of being an astronomy teacher."

Cassidy's brows rose. "At the university?"

"If I'm good enough for that, yes, I'm not sure–"

"Preston." She turned him to face her. "You are."

Never had he wanted more to kiss her. "Whatever you say, my lady." His gaze rested on a patch of blue flowers. "What kind of flowers are these?"

Cassidy glanced at them briefly before looking back to him. "Forget-me-nots, I believe."

Leaning down, he plucked a lovely blue bud. He tucked the delicate flower behind her ear, her hair tickling his hand. He let his hand brush her cheek as he pulled away. "Forget me not, my lady."

# Epilogue

Preston sat on the baker's flat roof. The same roof on which he had done so much stargazing and figuring. But today, the sun had just made its usual, dramatic entrance to welcome the day. At dawn, the *Virtue* had departed from the docks of San Juan with the duke and duchess of England.

He sighed.

Weeks ago, if you had asked Preston how he would feel in this moment, he would have said "sad," perhaps "lonely," or maybe he would have confessed to a sense of "loss." But none of that burdened his heart now.

Preston knew, with all certainty, that it was God's will that ordained every aspect of his adventure. That if it was God's will that Cassidy and his paths crossed again, then it would be so.

*Lord, let your will be done.*

As Preston surrendered Cassidy, his future, and his past to God, it was as though whatever was broken inside of him was mended. After all, no matter how hard he tried himself, he clearly could not fix it. He supposed that only God could fix broken hearts, if only we give Him the chance to do so.

He took his new, empty notebook out of his sack, and plopped down on his belly, and began to write.

*The log of the Royal Fortune, kept by Captain Preston W. Williams...*

Cassidy was quite ready to be home, this whole ordeal put behind them. She had heartily decided that sea life was not for her and that one pirate adventure was enough. Nasty business was pirate business.

Then again, Cassidy would not have traded those last few months for anything. Anyone could guess why.

She was at peace. If it was God's will that she ever saw Preston again, then let it be. Or if it was not, Cassidy was alright with that as well. Preston Williams would become like a dream. An incredible, indescribable dream. Precious and beautiful as it was, this duchess of England would remember it forever.

Cassidy leaned over her desk, opening her Bible to Psalms. She reached for her quill and began to write notes to go with a song King David had written hundreds of years ago.

Andrew leaned back and put his hands behind his head. Sweaty and tired, he looked over the dimly lit hull of his ship. Stacks of chests were neatly arranged. All of the locks were broken, he knew, for he and his quartermaster Tanner had just gone through the contents of all of them.

"Hmm..." Tanner rubbed his chin as he studied the log in his hand. "It's impossible to know who all Cade and Roberts stole from. But we do know 40,000 moidores and jewelry belong to Portugal. Oh, and that cross with the diamonds is the King of Portugal's. That was when Roberts raided the *Sagrada Família* in the Tados os Santos' Bay. Then there was also—"

"Let's organize all that later, why don't we?"

"You just don't want to do this at all." Tanner crossed his arms.

"Of course, I don't. But I will... later. I'm too tired now. Besides, my father will know more about all this."

Tanner flipped the little book closed with a snap. "Fine. Later then." He looked over the treasure. "This is quite the collection. Is this all of it?"

The duke closed his eyes and shifted back to get comfortable. "No."

"Where's the rest?"

"Three I sent with the Spanish as reward for our rescue. One I left on the *Fortune*. But no one knows that." The duke smiled, his eyes still closed, clearly proud of himself for his own cleverness. "And then... there are a few unaccounted for."

"What do you mean?"

Andrew opened one eye. "Well, God forgive me, I told a little lie. We never did get all of the chests out of that cave."

The quartermaster raised his eyebrows. "There are more? How many?"

Shrugging, Andrew said, "Dunno. At least one. But one more minute and my sister would have drowned." He shifted. "You know what's odd, though? The last one was small. Very small. Big enough to hold a few pounds, but no more."

"What do you reckon was in it? More treasure?"

"Your guess is as good as mine. One day, I'm going back for it. Preston and I are. After all, Corey has, or had, the only written copy of the coordinates of the island. No doubt that paper is gone with the wind. Only Preston can ever find it again."

"In the eye of the storm
You remain in control
In the middle of the war
You guard my soul
You alone are the anchor
When my sails are torn
Your Love surrounds me
In the eye of the storm"


*Eye of the Storm, by Ryan Stevenson*

# Author's Note

During the Golden Age of Piracy, Bartholomew Roberts was among the most successful pirates despite the shortness of his "reign," which lasted between 1719-1722. In fact, the *Royal Fortune* was his ship. While he did own a fleet, including *Ranger* and the *Little Ranger*, the *Fortune* was Roberts' prized ship. Roberts' real *Royal Fortune*, the first of several ships he named the *Royal Fortune*, was a French ship chosen by Roberts from a fleet of 26 he had captured. The rest of the ships he burned.

The treasure mentioned by Tanner in the Epilogue was also real and was captured by Roberts off of the *Sagrada Familia*. However, in reality, Roberts spent it almost immediately after stealing it from the Portuguese. Pirates weren't known for their money management, after all.

Although the circumstances of his death are not as portrayed in this novel, Roberts was indeed a real pirate, having captured over 400 vessels in his three reigning years.

Everything else in this book is purely fictional, based on what could have happened to the bravura *Royal Fortune*.

# *Chapter 1*

The *Adventure Prize*, October of 1737

A massive ship crawled along the ocean's surface. Her huge hull sat so low in the water that it was a wonder that she continued to float. She groaned and strained to pull along her old bones, faithful as always. It was not the first time the *Adventure Prize* had sustained storm damage; however, this particular hurricane reminded her captain that she was not as young as she once was.

At the helm, Captain Damien Lee searched the horizon though his spyglass. "Keep going, Love. Not much further, I think." He and his beloved ship had been through a lot together. Working for the East Indies, the birth of his daughter, the death of his wife, the dismissal from the company, and turning to piracy. Not that Damien set out for any of those things, but they all seemed to just happen.

"See anything, Annie?" Damien shouted up to the crow's nest to his daughter.

No answer

"Annie!" Damien could not see her. "Rex, take the wheel, will ya." The giant of a man did not respond, but simply waddled over and did as he was told, his dark skin glistening with sweat.

The captain made his way up the main mast rigging. "I'm getting too old for this," he mumbled under his breath.

"Annie?" Still, no answer. He pulled himself into the crow's nest and looked around. No Annie. *Where is that wild girl?*

"Land hooooo!" a girl's voice called from... above him?

Damien looked up and, to his horror, found Annie perched comfortably atop the skysail. "Annie Lee, get down from there this instant!"

Annie looked down at him, her red hair flowing behind her. She scowled but slowly dismounted the skysail and climbed down the mast like a squirrel on a pecan tree.

"How could you do something so stupid, Annie? One slip from that height and you would be dead! That was reckless, going all the way up there like that when you could see just as well from here! Do you know that?"

Annie folded her arms. "Actually, there is a much better view from up there. And why can't I risk my life? It's my life and I'll do as I please with it."

"No, you won't. I am your father and for as long as you are under my care, I will protect you, even if you don't like it."

"Well that won't be very long, now will it? Since you refuse to let me be an official member of the crew. I might as well stay on that island I found for you. For which you are welcome."

"And you're welcome for bringing you into this world and feeding you and clothing you for the last seventeen years!" Damien's face was hot, as was his daughter's. His little copy.

Annie snorted. "You did not bring me into this world. Mother did."

Silence.

Annie knew she'd crossed a line. She knew the instant the words abandoned her tongue. She would have liked to say they came out on their own accord. Sure, Annie had a temper, but she didn't lie. Father prided himself on his honesty. That and the temper seemed to be a package deal in the genes that came to her.

Pain clouded her father's red face, so much so that Annie had to fight away remorse. He turned and started down the rigging. An apologetic call to him tickled the base of her throat.

*Oh Annie. You've done it now. He will never look at you again.* Silence on deck told Annie that the crew heard the entire squabble. Not that it would be the first time.

Her father broke the silence to give orders, commanding and calm as always. "Make for that island. We make repairs there. Gather the tools and the extra boards into the longboats." He paused. "And we'll look for food while we're there, too."

As the men got to work, the sound of Captain Lee's footsteps moved across the deck to his cabin.

Tears brimmed her hazel eyes. She ferociously swiped at them. Unchained anger burned inside her, seeming only to mount as the seconds passed. Not with her father. With herself.

*If he weren't such a controlling man...* Her thoughts died. Annie plopped down on the deck of the crow's nest and hung her feet over the edge. The wind in her face felt good. If only it could cool off her heart.

The *Adventure Prize* coasted toward the rocky island. When she finally entered the bay, the crew let down the anchor and prepared a landing party. They would sleep on shore tonight while repairs were made to the ship.

After a while, Annie heard someone coming up the ratlines. She ignored them, knowing they came for her.

"Miss Annie?"

It was Tubs. The man was like a grandfather to her. He would sit and listen to her, never giving advice. Just listening. Annie liked him. Somehow, she could never be angry or rude to him.

Annie swallowed back the knot in her throat. "Yes, Tubs?" she squeaked.

Tubs' bones creaked as he sat down beside her. "Just checkin' on ye, little lady."

The two listened to the waves and the wind for a moment.

"Did Father send you up here?"

"Nah. But 'e would like yer to come ashore at some point. Help the men find food. They ain't as smart as ye."

Annie smiled. She was the best at sniffing out seagull nests or distinguishing between plants. Rex nearly ate poison ivy once. "Will you come to shore?"

"Later. I've gotta help repair the ship. Make sure Smiley don't break 'er." Tubs patted the mast. Smiley was Tubs' son, and also the quartermaster.

"I suppose I could try to have somethin' cookin' for you when you finish here."

Tubs cast an approving glance at her. "Yer mother used to do that for us animals."

"You're not animals. You're pirates." She let the comment about her mother slide. Annie barely remembered her.

"Animal, pirate. Most don't see the difference. Then again, an animal treats every other animal lesser than himself. That's what makes 'em an animal. So anyone that treats anyone lesser than their ol' self is an animal."

Annie glanced at him, not entirely sure about his logic. She followed his gaze to the helm. The exslave her father freed, Rex still stood faithfully at the wheel. They had all seen the whip scars along the man's back and shoulders.

"That is very deep, Tubs. Especially for a pirate," Annie said.

Tubs grinned with a mouth half-full of teeth. "That's the deep thought for the day." He started to stand and Annie hurried up to assist him. "I'm getting too old fer this. I ain't got a hankering fer why yer papa keeps feedin' me."

"We can't live without you, Tubs."

He patted her on the head. "Well, one day ye'll have to. But I only pray ye'll be all grown up and know how to cool yerself down without me straining me ancient bones to come checkin' on ye. Maybe yer pa could even marry yer off."

Annie's cheeks flushed. "I'm sorry I got angry."

"I know. Do me a favor, though, and don't go get angry so often. I wanna die in peace."

"Please, let's not talk about dying," Annie begged.

"Only for you, Miss Annie."

Annie climbed out of the longboat with some of the crew and helped them pull it onto rocky shore. The island was probably the top of a dormant volcano, she decided. Her father and some men were already setting up camp not far away.

"I'm goin' to look for food!" she yelled towards her father.

"Take Swade with you!" Damien shouted back.

Annie bit her lip, refusing rights to her rising frustration. "Swade! Let's go!"

Always eager to assist her, the lanky fifteen-year-old trotted after her. Annie ignored him as she set out, weaving among the rocks looking for bird nests or mushrooms or pools of clams.

After thirty minutes of Swade's constant chatter, Annie ran out of patience. Face flushed, she spun to face him. "You're supposed to be helping me! Go over that way and search for seagull nests! We will work our way that way," she pointed away from camp. "And together we'll cover all this area. Got it?"

Swade nodded vigorously. "Yes, yes." He bounded off.

Annie sighed and continued her search along the ocean's edge. *He's so, clingy!* Her conscience panged. She was awfully short with him. *Must I always be so bad-tempered? Swade didn't completely deserve that. He's just so... so annoying!* Annie climbed up onto a rock and looked out over the rocky shoreline, her sharp eyes picking out the island's hidden details.

*Wait, what's that?*

Annie jumped down and hurried along the beach. As she came close, she found it was a gathering of birds. *A nest!* As she neared, the birds quickly took to the air. *What in the name of...*

Annie gasped and sprinted the rest of the distance. "Swade!" She slid to a stop, suddenly frightened.

A body lay before her. A man, belly down with his head cocked to the side. Blood soaked his ripped shirt.

Bumps covered her arms, and the fine hairs stood on end at the thought of what had torn the shirt. A cat o' nine.

The man's hair was still wet, as though the waves carried him there only minutes ago. Annie tentatively stepped closer. She sniffed the air. Either he recently died, or...

Annie knelt down and watched his back. Swade rushed up behind her and gasped. "Swade! Go get help!"

"Is... is he alive?"

"Barely, and not for much longer. Now go!" The boy was off. Thank goodness her father had sent her with the fastest crewmember as an escort.

Rolling him over, Annie covered her mouth with her hand. A wide gash stretched across the man's forehead.

"What happened to you?" Annie muttered. She ripped off the forearm of her sleeve and dabbed at the blood on his face. His right eye was swollen and purple, and his lips were bloody and cracked. When she touched his gash, the man made a gurgling noise in his throat, almost like a weak moan.

"Easy," she murmured to him. The piece of her sleeve was quickly soaked through, but it did enough to make his face more visible. The man was younger than she first thought, perhaps early twenties, with flaxen hair and a prominent jaw. He was probably quite handsome without a black eye and an open forehead, Annie decided.

*Who is he?*

## London, England

The London channel was hushed. Barely a breeze warning of winter blew. The moon, full with light hung heavy in the sky and the stars sat in their place in the heavens. A galleon sailed into port, regal and proud in new white sails and shinning dark wood. Yet there was an anxious, wary air about her. Her crew worked wearily to secure her in place before the captain stepped from her deck. Or, acting captain, as it turned out.

"Get some rest," was all Cory Davis could say to the crew. He headed for the livery stable and convinced the sleepy stableman to lend him a horse and directions. For a half hour, Corey rode through the streets and into the countryside. Finally, he came to a gated mansion.

*This must be it.*

Corey dismounted and led the horse to the guard house.

"What is your business here?" A uniformed guard asked, well awake.

"I come in search of an audience with Lord Andrew Chandler. Is this where he resides?"

The guard eyed him. "Yes, though he is not currently home."

Corey's heart sank. He knew the young duke traveled a lot, but he had hoped...

"The young Lord Chandler and his family are out at a formal gathering and due to be home tonight. You will be welcomed back tomorrow."

"What time is he expected tonight? With your permission I shall wait for him here. It is a most urgent matter."

The guard hesitated, then came out of the tiny building. "Allow me to search you for weapons."

Corey pulled out his pistol and a knife then let the guard pat him down. When the man was satisfied, he opened the gate and led Corey and his horse through.

"I will bed down your horse in the stable. Tell the butler that Phil sent you in to wait for Lord Andrew."

Corey nodded, not about to refuse an opportunity to get out of the chilly night air. "Thank you." He did as instructed and was led into spacious parlor. The whole house was impressive with marble floors and thick curtains. There was white crown molding and chandeliers in each room. Corey stared.

A maid brought him tea and some sort of small pastry. He settled in to wait, feeling very English as he sipped the bitter tea and devoured the sweets.

Only a half hour later, Corey heard a carriage come up the circle drive and stop in front of the manor. Unable to help himself, he rose and peaked out the window. Corey was not surprised when Andrew jumped from the carriage without waiting for the hurrying driver. The young duke turned to help his lovely sister out. Indeed, she was lovely.

Unsure of what to do, Corey decided to greet them. Striding out of the parlor, he was a step ahead of the elderly butler. He opened the door wide as the young Chandlers came up the steps, their parents a few passes behind. "Good evening, your Graces." Corey's voice was low but ended with a smile.

The family stopped. "Uh, Corey?" Andrew stared at him, as though not fully recognizing him.

"I am relieved you are here. Come in." He motioned to them.

"This is where we live, you know that right?" Andrew said.

*Ah, Andrew was always the smarty.* "Certainly."

"Where is Preston?" A small, feminine voice came from behind Corey.

Corey paused mid step, but then continued into the entryway. "My Lord Andrew, I have to speak with you. Shall we step into the parlor?"

Andrew nodded slowly. He glanced at his sister as he followed Corey.

In the parlor, Corey shut the French doors. Andrew leaded against a plush loveseat. "Alright, as to my sister's question. Where's Preston?"

"Last month, we were delivering a shipment of cargo to Iceland."

"We meaning...?"

Corey eyed Andrew. "We, as in the *Royal Fortune*. Me, Preston, Liam, Conrad –"

"I get it."

"So, a few clicks from our destination we were attacked. By Otto Schenck and the *Northeastern*."

Andrew's eyes widened. He took a heavy, dreading breath.

Corey swallowed. "Schenck took all the valuables. All the cargo. All the provisions. And, like all his other victims, the captain."

Made in the USA
Middletown, DE
07 May 2020